The Collected Supernatural and Weird Fiction of H. H. Munro

The Collected Supernatural and Weird Fiction of H. H. Munro

Thirty-Four Short Stories of the Strange and Unusual Including 'Laura', 'The Open Window', 'The Wolves of Cerogratz', 'The Blind Spot' and 'The Lumber Room'

H. H. Munro

(Saki)

LEONAUR

The Collected
Supernatural and Weird
Fiction of
H. H. Munro
Thirty-Four Short Stories of the Strange and Unusual Including 'Laura', 'The Open
Window', 'The Wolves of Cerogratz', 'The Blind Spot' and 'The Lumber Room'
by H. H. Munro
(Saki)

FIRST EDITION

Leonaur is an imprint of Oakpast Ltd

ISBN: 978-1-915234-40-7 (hardcover)
ISBN: 978-1-915234-41-4 (softcover)

http://www.leonaur.com

Contents

"Ministers of Grace"

Although he was scarcely yet out of his teens, the Duke of Scaw was already marked out as a personality widely differing from others of his caste and period. Not in externals; therein he conformed correctly to type. His hair was faintly reminiscent of Houbigant, and at the other end of him his shoes exhaled the right *soupçon* of harness-room; his socks compelled one's attention without losing one's respect; and his attitude in repose had just that suggestion of Whistler's mother, so becoming in the really young. It was within that the trouble lay, if trouble it could be accounted, which marked him apart from his fellows.

The duke was religious. Not in any of the ordinary senses of the word; he took small heed of High Church or Evangelical standpoints, he stood outside of all the movements and missions and cults and crusades of the day, uncaring and uninterested. Yet in a mystical-practical way of his own, which had served him unscathed and unshaken through the fickle years of boyhood, he was intensely and intensively religious. His family were naturally, though unobtrusively, distressed about it. "I am so afraid it may affect his bridge," said his mother.

The duke sat in a pennyworth of chair in St. James's Park, listening to the pessimisms of Belturbet, who reviewed the existing political situation from the gloomiest of standpoints.

"Where I think you political spade-workers are so silly," said the duke, "is in the misdirection of your efforts. You spend thousands of pounds of money, and Heaven knows how much dynamic force of brain power and personal energy, in trying to elect or displace this or that man, whereas you could gain your ends so much more simply by making use of the men as you find them. If they don't suit your purpose as they are, transform them into something more satisfactory."

"Do you refer to hypnotic suggestion?" asked Belturbet, with the air of one who is being trifled with.

"Nothing of the sort. Do you understand what I mean by the verb to *koepenick?* That is to say, to replace an authority by a spurious imitation that would carry just as much weight for the moment as the displaced original; the advantage, of course, being that the *koepenick* replica would do what you wanted, whereas the original does what seems best in its own eyes."

"I suppose every public man has a double, if not two or three," said Belturbet; "but it would be a pretty hard task to *koepenick* a whole bunch of them and keep the originals out of the way."

"There have been instances in European history of highly successful *koepenickery*," said the duke dreamily.

"Oh, of course, there have been False Dimitris and Perkin Warbecks, who imposed on the world for a time," assented Belturbet, "but they personated people who were dead or safely out of the way. That was a comparatively simple matter. It would be far easier to pass oneself off as dead Hannibal than as living Haldane, for instance."

"I was thinking," said the duke, "of the most famous case of all, the angel who *koepenicked* King Robert of Sicily with such brilliant results. Just imagine what an advantage it would be to have angels deputizing, to use a horrible but convenient word, for Quinston and Lord Hugo Sizzle, for example. How much smoother the Parliamentary machine would work than at present!"

"Now you're talking nonsense," said Belturbet; "angels don't exist nowadays, at least, not in that way, so what is the use of dragging them into a serious discussion? It's merely silly."

"If you talk to me like that, I shall just do it," said the duke.

"Do what?" asked Belturbet. There were times when his young friend's uncanny remarks rather frightened him.

"I shall summon angelic forces to take over some of the more troublesome personalities of our public life, and I shall send the ousted originals into temporary retirement in suitable animal organisms. It's not everyone who would have the knowledge or the power necessary to bring such a thing off—"

"Oh, stop that inane rubbish," said Belturbet angrily; "it's getting wearisome. Here's Quinston coming," he added, as there approached along the almost deserted path the well-known figure of a young Cabinet Minister, whose personality evoked a curious mixture of public interest and unpopularity.

"Hurry along, my dear man," said the young duke to the minister, who had given him a condescending nod; "your time is running short," he continued in a provocative strain; "the whole inept crowd of you will shortly be swept away into the world's wastepaper basket."

"You poor little strawberry-leafed nonentity," said the minister, checking himself for a moment in his stride and rolling out his words spasmodically; "who is going to sweep us away, I should like to know? The voting masses are on our side, and all the ability and administrative talent is on our side too. No power of earth or Heaven is going to move us from our place till we choose to quit it. No power of earth or—"

Belturbet saw, with bulging eyes, a sudden void where a moment earlier had been a Cabinet Minister; a void emphasized rather than relieved by the presence of a puffed-out bewildered-looking sparrow, which hopped about for a moment in a dazed fashion and then fell to a violent cheeping and scolding.

"If we could understand sparrow-language," said the duke serenely, "I fancy we should hear something infinitely worse than 'strawberry-leafed nonentity.'"

"But good Heavens, Eugene," said Belturbet hoarsely, "what has become of—Why, there he is! How on earth did he get there?" And he pointed with a shaking finger towards a semblance of the vanished minister, which approached once more along the unfrequented path.

The duke laughed.

"It is Quinston to all outward appearance," he said composedly, "but I fancy you will find, on closer investigation, that it is an angel under-study of the real article."

The Angel-Quinston greeted them with a friendly smile.

"How beastly happy you two look sitting there!" he said wistfully.

"I don't suppose you'd care to change places with poor little us," replied the duke chaffingly.

"How about poor little me?" said the angel modestly. "I've got to run about behind the wheels of popularity, like a spotted dog behind a carriage, getting all the dust and trying to look as if I was an important part of the machine. I must seem a perfect fool to you onlookers sometimes."

"I think you are a perfect angel." said the duke.

The angel-that-had-been-Quinston smiled and passed on his way, pursued across the breadth of the Horse Guards Parade by a tiresome little sparrow that cheeped incessantly and furiously at him.

"That's only the beginning," said the duke complacently; "I've made it operative with all of them, irrespective of parties."

Belturbet made no coherent reply; he was engaged in feeling his pulse. The duke fixed his attention with some interest on a black swan that was swimming with haughty, stiff-necked aloofness amid the crowd of lesser water-fowl that dotted the ornamental water. For all its pride of bearing, something was evidently ruffling and enraging it; in its way it seemed as angry and amazed as the sparrow had been.

At the same moment a human figure came along the pathway. Belturbet looked up apprehensively.

"Kedzon," he whispered briefly.

"An Angel-Kedzon, if I am not mistaken," said the duke. "Look, he is talking affably to a human being. That settles it."

A shabbily dressed lounger had accosted the man who had been viceroy in the splendid East, and who still reflected in his mien some of the cold dignity of the Himalayan snow-peaks.

"Could you tell me, sir, if them white birds is storks or halbatrosses? I had an argyment—"

The cold dignity thawed at once into genial friendliness.

"Those are pelicans, my dear sir. Are you interested in birds? If you would join me in a bun and a glass of milk at the stall yonder, I could tell you some interesting things about Indian birds. Right oh! Now the hill-mynah, for instance—"

The two men disappeared in the direction of the bun stall, chatting volubly as they went, and shadowed from the other side of the railed enclosure by a black swan, whose temper seemed to have reached the limit of inarticulate rage.

Belturbet gazed in an open-mouthed wonder after the retreating couple, then transferred his attention to the infuriated swan, and finally turned with a look of scared comprehension at his young friend lolling unconcernedly in his chair. There was no longer any room to doubt what was happening. The "silly talk" had been translated into terrifying action.

"I think a prairie oyster on the top of a stiffish brandy-and-soda might save my reason," said Belturbet weakly, as he limped towards his club.

It was late in the day before he could steady his nerves sufficiently to glance at the evening papers. The Parliamentary report proved significant reading, and confirmed the fears that he had been trying to shake off. Mr. Ap Dave, the chancellor, whose lively controversial style endeared him to his supporters and embittered him, politically speaking, to his opponents, had risen in his place to make an unprovoked apology for having alluded in a recent speech to certain protesting taxpayers as "skulkers." He had realised on reflection that they were in all probability perfectly honest in their inability to understand certain legal technicalities of the new finance laws.

The House had scarcely recovered from this sensation when Lord Hugo Sizzle caused a further flutter of astonishment by going out of his way to indulge in an outspoken appreciation of the fairness, loyalty, and straightforwardness not only of the chancellor, but of all the members of the Cabinet. A wit had gravely suggested moving the adjournment of the House in view of the unexpected circumstances that had arisen.

Belturbet anxiously skimmed over a further item of news printed immediately below the Parliamentary report:

"Wild cat found in an exhausted condition in palace yard."

"Now I wonder which of them—" he mused, and then an appalling idea came to him. "Supposing he's put them both into the same beast!" He hurriedly ordered another prairie oyster.

Belturbet was known in his club as a strictly moderate drinker; his consumption of alcoholic stimulants that day gave rise to considerable comment.

The events of the next few days were piquantly bewildering to the world at large; to Belturbet, who knew dimly what was happening, the situation was fraught with recurring alarms. The old saying that in politics it's the unexpected that always happens received a justification that it had hitherto somewhat lacked, and the epidemic of startling personal changes of front was not wholly confined to the realm of actual politics.

The eminent chocolate magnate, Sadbury, whose antipathy to the Turf and everything connected with it was a matter of general knowledge, had evidently been replaced by an Angel-Sadbury, who proceeded to electrify the public by blossoming forth as an owner of race-horses, giving as a reason his matured conviction that the sport was, after all, one which gave healthy open-air recreation to large numbers of people drawn from all classes of the community, and incidentally stimulated the important industry of horse-breeding.

His colours, chocolate and cream hoops spangled with pink stars, promised to become as popular as any on the Turf. At the same time, in order to give effect to his condemnation of the evils resulting from the spread of the gambling habit among wage-earning classes, who lived for the most part from hand to mouth, he suppressed all betting news and tipsters' forecasts in the popular evening paper that was under his control. His action received instant recognition and support from the Angel-proprietor of the *Evening Views*, the principal rival evening halfpenny paper, who forthwith issued an ukase decreeing a similar ban on betting news, and in a short while the regular evening Press was purged of all mention of starting prices and probable winners.

A considerable drop in the circulation of all these papers was the immediate result, accompanied, of course, by a falling-off in advertisement value, while a crop of special betting broadsheets sprang up to supply the newly created want. Under their influence the betting habit became if anything rather more widely diffused than before. The duke had possibly overlooked the futility of *koepenicking* the leaders of the nation with excellently intentioned angel under-studies, while leaving the mass of the people in its original condition.

Further sensation and dislocation was caused in the Press world by the sudden and dramatic *rapprochement* which took place between the Angel-Editor of the *Scrutator* and the Angel-Editor of the *Anglian Review*, who not only ceased to criticize and disparage the tone and tendencies of each other's publication, but agreed to exchange editorships for alternating periods. Here again public support was not on the side of the angels; constant readers of the *Scrutator* complained bitterly of the strong meat which was thrust upon them at fitful intervals in place of the almost vegetarian diet to which they had become confidently accustomed; even those who were not mentally averse to strong meat as a separate course were pardonably annoyed at being supplied with it in the pages of the *Scrutator*.

To be suddenly confronted with a pungent herring salad when one had attuned oneself to tea and toast, or to discover a richly truffled segment of *pate de foie* dissembled in a bowl of bread and milk, would be an experience that might upset the equanimity of the most placidly disposed mortal. An equally vehement outcry arose from the regular subscribers of the *Anglian Review*, who protested against being served from time to time with literary fare which no young person of sixteen could possibly want to devour in secret. To take infinite precautions, they complained, against the juvenile perusal of such eminently innocuous literature was like reading the Riot Act on an uninhabited island. Both reviews suffered a serious falling-off in circulation and influence. Peace hath its devastations as well as war.

The wives of noted public men formed another element of discomfiture which the young duke had almost entirely left out of his calculations. It is sufficiently embarrassing to keep abreast of the possible wobblings and veerings-round of a human husband, who, from the strength or weakness of his personal character, may leap over or slip through the barriers which divide the parties; for this reason, a merciful politician usually marries late in life, when he has definitely made up his mind on which side, he wishes his wife to be socially valuable.

But these trials were as nothing compared to the bewilderment caused by the Angel-husbands who seemed in some cases to have revolutionised their outlook on life in the interval between breakfast and dinner, without premonition or preparation of any kind, and apparently without realising the least need for subsequent explanation. The temporary peace which brooded over the Parliamentary situation was by no means reproduced in the home circles of the leading statesmen and politicians. It had been frequently and extensively remarked of Mrs. Exe that she would try the patience of an angel; now the tables were reversed, and she unwittingly had an opportunity for discovering that the capacity for exasperating behaviour was not all on one side.

And then, with the introduction of the Navy Estimates, Parliamentary peace suddenly dissolved. It was the old quarrel between ministers and the Opposition as to the adequacy or the reverse of the government's naval programme. The Angel-Quinston and the Angel-Hugo-Sizzle contrived to keep the debates free from personalities and pinpricks, but an enormous sensation was created when the elegant lackadaisical Halfan Halfour threatened to bring up fifty thousand stalwarts to wreck the House if the Estimates were not forthwith revised on a Two-Power basis. It was a memorable scene when he rose in his place, in response to the scandalized shouts of his opponents, and thundered forth, "Gentlemen, I glory in the name of Apache."

Belturbet, who had made several fruitless attempts to ring up his young friend since the fateful morning in St. James's Park, ran him to earth one afternoon at his club, smooth and spruce and unruffled as ever.

"Tell me, what on earth have you turned Cocksley Coxon into?" Belturbet asked anxiously, mentioning the name of one of the pillars of unorthodoxy in the Anglican Church. "I don't fancy he *believes* in angels, and if he finds an angel preaching orthodox sermons from his pulpit while he's been turned into a fox-terrier, he'll develop rabies in less than no time."

"I rather think it was a fox-terrier," said the duke lazily.

Belturbet groaned heavily, and sank into a chair.

"Look here, Eugene," he whispered hoarsely, having first looked well round to see that no one was within hearing range, "you've got to stop it. Consols are jumping up and down like bronchos, and that speech of Halfour's in the House last night has simply startled everybody out of their wits. And then on the top if it, Thistlebery—"

"What has he been saying?" asked the duke quickly.

"Nothing. That's just what's so disturbing. Everyone thought it was simply inevitable that he should come out with a great epoch-making speech at this juncture, and I've just seen on the tape that he has refused to address any meetings at present, giving as a reason his opinion that something more than mere speech-making was wanted."

The young duke said nothing, but his eyes shone with quiet exultation.

"It's so unlike Thistlebery," continued Belturbet; "at least," he said suspiciously, "it's unlike the *real* Thistlebery—"

"The real Thistlebery is flying about somewhere as a vocally industrious lapwing," said the duke calmly; "I expect great things of the Angel-Thistlebery," he added.

At this moment there was a magnetic stampede of members towards the lobby, where the tape-machines were ticking out some news of more than ordinary import.

"*Coup d'etat* in the North. Thistlebery seizes Edinburgh Castle. Threatens civil war unless government expands naval programme."

In the babel which ensued Belturbet lost sight of his young friend. For the best part of the afternoon, he searched one likely haunt after another, spurred on by the sensational posters which the evening papers were displaying broadcast over the West End.

General Baden-Baden mobilises boy-scouts. Another *coup d'etat* feared. Is Windsor Castle safe?

This was one of the earlier posters, and was followed by one of even more sinister purport: "Will the Test-match have to be postponed?" It was this disquietening question which brought home the real seriousness of the situation to the London public, and made people wonder whether one might not pay too high a price for the advantages of party government.

Belturbet, questing round in the hope of finding the originator of the trouble, with a vague idea of being able to induce him to restore matters to their normal human footing, came across an elderly club acquaintance who dabbled extensively in some of the more sensitive market securities. He was pale with indignation, and his pallor deepened as a breathless newsboy dashed past with a poster inscribed:

Premier's constituency harried by moss-troopers. Halfour sends encouraging telegram to rioters. Letchworth Garden City threatens reprisals. Foreigners taking refuge in Embassies and National Liberal Club.

"This is devils' work!" he said angrily.

Belturbet knew otherwise.

At the bottom of St. James's Street, a newspaper motor-cart, which had just come rapidly along Pall Mall, was surrounded by a knot of eagerly talking people, and for the first time that afternoon Belturbet heard expressions of relief and congratulation.

It displayed a placard with the welcome announcement:

Crisis ended. Government gives way. Important expansion of naval programme.

There seemed to be no immediate necessity for pursuing the quest of the errant duke, and Belturbet turned to make his way homeward through St. James's Park. His mind, attuned to the alarums and excursions of the afternoon, became dimly aware that some excitement of a detached nature was going on around him. In spite of the political ferment which reigned in the streets, quite a large crowd had gathered to watch the unfolding of a tragedy that had taken place on the shore of the ornamental water.

A large black swan, which had recently shown signs of a savage and dangerous disposition, had suddenly attacked a young gentleman who was walking by the water's edge, dragged him down under the surface, and drowned him before anyone could come to his assistance. At the moment when Belturbet arrived on the spot several park-keepers were engaged in lifting the corpse into a punt. Belturbet stooped to pick up a hat that lay near the scene of the struggle. It was a smart soft felt hat, faintly reminiscent of Houbigant.

More than a month elapsed before Belturbet had sufficiently recovered from his attack of nervous prostration to take an interest once more in what was going on in the world of politics. The Parliamentary Session was still in full swing, and a General Election was looming in the near future. He called for a batch of morning papers and skimmed rapidly through the speeches of the Chancellor, Quinston, and other Ministerial leaders, as well as those of the principal Opposition champions, and then sank back in his chair with a sigh of relief. Evidently the spell had ceased to act after the tragedy which had overtaken its invoker. There was no trace of angel anywhere.

Esmé

"All hunting stories are the same," said Clovis; "just as all Turf stories are the same, and all—"

"My hunting story isn't a bit like any you've ever heard," said the Baroness. "It happened quite a while ago, when I was about twenty-three. I wasn't living apart from my husband then; you see, neither of us could afford to make the other a separate allowance. In spite of everything that proverbs may say, poverty keeps together more homes than it breaks up. But we always hunted with different packs. All this has nothing to do with the story."

"We haven't arrived at the meet yet. I suppose there was a meet," said Clovis.

"Of course, there was a meet," said the Baroness; "all the usual crowd were there, especially Constance Broddle. Constance is one of those strapping florid girls that go so well with autumn scenery or Christmas decorations in church. 'I feel a presentiment that something dreadful is going to happen,' she said to me; 'am I looking pale?'

"She was looking about as pale as a beetroot that has suddenly heard bad news.

"'You're looking nicer than usual,' I said, 'but that's so easy for you.' Before she had got the right bearings of this remark we had settled down to business; hounds had found a fox lying out in some gorse-bushes."

"I knew it," said Clovis; "in every fox-hunting story that I've ever heard there's been a fox and some gorse-bushes."

"Constance and I were well mounted," continued the Baroness serenely, "and we had no difficulty in keeping ourselves in the first flight, though it was a fairly stiff run. Towards the finish, however, we must have held rather too independent a line, for we lost the hounds, and found ourselves plodding aimlessly along miles away from anywhere.

It was fairly exasperating, and my temper was beginning to let itself go by inches, when on pushing our way through an accommodating hedge we were gladdened by the sight of hounds in full cry in a hollow just beneath us.

"'There they go,' cried Constance, and then added in a gasp, 'In Heaven's name, what are they hunting?'

"It was certainly no mortal fox. It stood more than twice as high, had a short, ugly head, and an enormous thick neck.

"'It's a hyaena,' I cried, 'it must have escaped from Lord Pabham's Park.'

"At that moment the hunted beast turned and faced its pursuers, and the hounds (there were only about six couple of them) stood round in a half-circle and looked foolish. Evidently, they had broken away from the rest of the pack on the trail of this alien scent, and were not quite sure how to treat their quarry now they had got him.

"The hyaena hailed our approach with unmistakable relief and demonstrations of friendliness. It had probably been accustomed to uniform kindness from humans, while its first experience of a pack of hounds had left a bad impression. The hounds looked more than ever embarrassed as their quarry paraded its sudden intimacy with us, and the faint toot of a horn in the distance was seized on as a welcome signal for unobtrusive departure. Constance and I and the hyaena were left alone in the gathering twilight.

"'What are we to do?' asked Constance.

"'What a person you are for questions,' I said.

"'Well, we can't stay here all night with a hyaena,' she retorted.

"'I don't know what your ideas of comfort are,' I said; 'but I shouldn't think of staying here all night even without a hyaena. My home may be an unhappy one, but at least it has hot and cold water laid on, and domestic service, and other conveniences which we shouldn't find here. We had better make for that ridge of trees to the right; I imagine the Crowley road is just beyond.'

"We trotted off slowly along a faintly marked cart-track, with the beast following cheerfully at our heels.

"'What on earth are we to do with the hyaena?' came the inevitable question.

"'What does one generally do with hyaenas?' I asked crossly.

"'I've never had anything to do with one before,' said Constance.

"'Well, neither have I. If we even knew its sex, we might give it a name. Perhaps we might call it Esmé. That would do in either case.'

18

"There was still sufficient daylight for us to distinguish wayside objects, and our listless spirits gave an upward perk as we came upon a small half-naked gipsy child picking blackberries from a low-growing bush. The sudden apparition of two horsewomen and a hyaena set it off crying, and in any case, we should scarcely have gleaned any useful geographical information from that source; but there was a probability that we might strike a gipsy encampment somewhere along our route. We rode on hopefully but uneventfully for another mile or so.

"'I wonder what that child was doing there,' said Constance presently.

"'Picking blackberries. Obviously.'

"'I don't like the way it cried,' pursued Constance; 'somehow its wail keeps ringing in my ears.'

"I did not chide Constance for her morbid fancies; as a matter of fact the same sensation, of being pursued by a persistent fretful wail, had been forcing itself on my rather overtired nerves. For company's sake I hulloed to Esmé, who had lagged somewhat behind. With a few springy bounds he drew up level, and then shot past us.

"The wailing accompaniment was explained. The gipsy child was firmly, and I expect painfully, held in his jaws.

"'Merciful Heaven!' screened Constance, 'what on earth shall we do? What are we to do?'

"I am perfectly certain that at the Last judgment Constance will ask more questions than any of the examining *Seraphs*.

"'Can't we do something?' she persisted tearfully, as Esmé cantered easily along in front of our tired horses.

"Personally, I was doing everything that occurred to me at the moment. I stormed and scolded and coaxed in English and French and gamekeeper language; I made absurd, ineffectual cuts in the air with my thongless hunting-crop; I hurled my sandwich case at the brute; in fact, I really don't know what more I could have done. And still we lumbered on through the deepening dusk, with that dark uncouth shape lumbering ahead of us, and a drone of lugubrious music floating in our ears. Suddenly Esmé bounded aside into some thick bushes, where we could not follow; the wail rose to a shriek and then stopped altogether. This part of the story I always hurry over, because it is really rather horrible. When the beast joined us again, after an absence of a few minutes, there was an air of patient understanding about him, as though he knew that he had done something of which we disapproved, but which he felt to be thoroughly justifiable.

19

"'How can you let that ravening beast trot by your side?' asked Constance. She was looking more than ever like an albino beetroot.

"'In the first place, I can't prevent it,' I said; 'and in the second place, whatever else he may be, I doubt if he's ravening at the present moment.'

"Constance shuddered. 'Do you think the poor little thing suffered much?' came another of her futile questions.

"'The indications were all that way,' I said; 'on the other hand, of course, it may have been crying from sheer temper. Children sometimes do.'

"It was nearly pitch-dark when we emerged suddenly into the high road. A flash of lights and the whir of a motor went past us at the same moment at uncomfortably close quarters. A thud and a sharp screeching yell followed a second later. The car drew up, and when I had ridden back to the spot, I found a young man bending over a dark motionless mass lying by the roadside.

"'You have killed my Esmé,' I exclaimed bitterly.

"'I'm so awfully sorry,' said the young man; 'I keep dogs myself, so I know what you must feel about it. I'll do anything I can in reparation.'

"'Please bury him at once,' I said, 'that much I think I may ask of you.'

"'Bring the spade, William,' he called to the chauffeur. Evidently hasty roadside internments were contingencies that had been provided against.

"The digging of a sufficiently large grave took some little time. 'I say, what a magnificent fellow,' said the motorist as the corpse was rolled over into the trench. 'I'm afraid he must have been rather a valuable animal.'

"'He took second in the puppy class at Birmingham last year,' I said resolutely.

"Constance snorted loudly.

"'Don't cry, dear,' I said brokenly; 'it was all-over in a moment. He couldn't have suffered much.'

"'Look here,' said the young fellow desperately, 'you simply must let me do something by way of reparation.'

"I refused sweetly, but as he persisted, I let him have my address.

"Of course, we kept our own counsel as to the earlier episodes of the evening. Lord Pabham never advertised the loss of his hyaena; when a strictly fruit-eating animal strayed from his park a year or two previously he was called upon to give compensation in eleven cases of sheep-worrying and practically to restock his neighbours' poultry-yards, and an escaped hyaena would have mounted up to something on the scale of a Government grant. The gipsies were equally unobtrusive over their missing offspring; I don't suppose in large encampments they really know to a child or two how many they've got."

The Baroness paused reflectively, and then continued:

"There was a sequel to the adventure, though. I got through the post a charming little diamond brooch, with the name Esmé set in a sprig of rosemary. Incidentally, too, I lost the friendship of Constance Broddle. You see, when I sold the brooch, I quite properly refused to give her any share of the proceeds. I pointed out that the Esmé part of the affair was my own invention, and the hyaena part of it belonged to Lord Pabham, if it really was his hyaena, of which, of course, I've no proof."

Gabriel-Ernest

"There is a wild beast in your woods," said the artist Cunningham, as he was being driven to the station. It was the only remark he had made during the drive, but as Van Cheele had talked incessantly his companion's silence had not been noticeable.

"A stray fox or two and some resident weasels. Nothing more formidable," said Van Cheele. The artist said nothing.

"What did you mean about a wild beast?" said Van Cheele later, when they were on the platform.

"Nothing. My imagination. Here is the train," said Cunningham.

That afternoon Van Cheele went for one of his frequent rambles through his woodland property. He had a stuffed bittern in his study, and knew the names of quite a number of wild flowers, so his aunt had possibly some justification in describing him as a great naturalist. At any rate, he was a great walker. It was his custom to take mental notes of everything he saw during his walks, not so much for the purpose of assisting contemporary science as to provide topics for conversation afterwards. When the bluebells began to show themselves in flower, he made a point of informing everyone of the fact; the season of the year might have warned his hearers of the likelihood of such an occurrence, but at least they felt that he was being absolutely frank with them.

What Van Cheele saw on this particular afternoon was, however, something far removed from his ordinary range of experience. On a shelf of smooth stone overhanging a deep pool in the hollow of an oak coppice a boy of about sixteen lay asprawl, drying his wet brown limbs luxuriously in the sun. His wet hair, parted by a recent dive, lay close to his head, and his light-brown eyes, so light that there was an almost tigerish gleam in them, were turned towards Van Cheele with a certain lazy watchfulness. It was an unexpected apparition, and Van

Cheele found himself engaged in the novel process of thinking before he spoke. Where on earth could this wild-looking boy hail from? The miller's wife had lost a child some two months ago, supposed to have been swept away by the mill-race, but that had been a mere baby, not a half-grown lad.

"What are you doing there?" he demanded.

"Obviously, sunning myself," replied the boy.

"Where do you live?"

"Here, in these woods."

"You can't live in the woods," said Van Cheele.

"They are very nice woods," said the boy, with a touch of patronage in his voice.

"But where do you sleep at night?"

"I don't sleep at night; that's my busiest time."

Van Cheele began to have an irritated feeling that he was grappling with a problem that was eluding him.

"What do you feed on?" he asked.

"Flesh," said the boy, and he pronounced the word with slow relish, as though he were tasting it.

"Flesh! What Flesh?"

"Since it interests you, rabbits, wild-fowl, hares, poultry, lambs in their season, children when I can get any; they're usually too well locked in at night, when I do most of my hunting. It's quite two months since I tasted child-flesh."

Ignoring the chaffing nature of the last remark Van Cheele tried to draw the boy on the subject of possible poaching operations.

"You're talking rather through your hat when you speak of feeding on hares." (Considering the nature of the boy's toilet the simile was hardly an apt one.) "Our hillside hares aren't easily caught."

"At night I hunt on four feet," was the somewhat cryptic response.

"I suppose you mean that you hunt with a dog?" hazarded Van Cheele.

The boy rolled slowly over on to his back, and laughed a weird low laugh, that was pleasantly like a chuckle and disagreeably like a snarl.

"I don't fancy any dog would be very anxious for my company, especially at night."

Van Cheele began to feel that there was something positively uncanny about the strange-eyed, strange-tongued youngster.

"I can't have you staying in these woods," he declared authoritatively.

24

"I fancy you'd rather have me here than in your house," said the boy.

The prospect of this wild, nude animal in Van Cheele's primly ordered house was certainly an alarming one.

"If you don't go. I shall have to make you," said Van Cheele.

The boy turned like a flash, plunged into the pool, and in a moment had flung his wet and glistening body half-way up the bank where Van Cheele was standing. In an otter the movement would not have been remarkable; in a boy Van Cheele found it sufficiently startling. His foot slipped as he made an involuntarily backward movement, and he found himself almost prostrate on the slippery weed-grown bank, with those tigerish yellow eyes not very far from his own. Almost instinctively he half raised his hand to his throat. The boy laughed again, a laugh in which the snarl had nearly driven out the chuckle, and then, with another of his astonishing lightning movements, plunged out of view into a yielding tangle of weed and fern.

"What an extraordinary wild animal!" said Van Cheele as he picked himself up. And then he recalled Cunningham's remark "There is a wild beast in your woods."

Walking slowly homeward, Van Cheele began to turn over in his mind various local occurrences which might be traceable to the existence of this astonishing young savage.

Something had been thinning the game in the woods lately, poultry had been missing from the farms, hares were growing unaccountably scarcer, and complaints had reached him of lambs being carried off bodily from the hills. Was it possible that this wild boy was really hunting the countryside in company with some clever poacher dogs? He had spoken of hunting "four-footed" by night, but then, again, he had hinted strangely at no dog caring to come near him, "especially at night." It was certainly puzzling.

And then, as Van Cheele ran his mind over the various depredations that had been committed during the last month or two, he came suddenly to a dead stop, alike in his walk and his speculations. The child missing from the mill two months ago--the accepted theory was that it had tumbled into the mill-race and been swept away; but the mother had always declared she had heard a shriek on the hill side of the house, in the opposite direction from the water. It was unthinkable, of course, but he wished that the boy had not made that uncanny remark about child-flesh eaten two months ago. Such dreadful things should not be said even in fun.

Van Cheele, contrary to his usual wont, did not feel disposed to be communicative about his discovery in the wood. His position as a parish councillor and justice of the peace seemed somehow compromised by the fact that he was harbouring a personality of such doubtful repute on his property; there was even a possibility that a heavy bill of damages for raided lambs and poultry might be laid at his door. At dinner that night he was quite unusually silent.

"Where's your voice gone to?" said his aunt. "One would think you had seen a wolf."

Van Cheele, who was not familiar with the old saying, thought the remark rather foolish; if he *had* seen a wolf on his property his tongue would have been extraordinarily busy with the subject.

At breakfast next morning Van Cheele was conscious that his feeling of uneasiness regarding yesterday's episode had not wholly disappeared, and he resolved to go by train to the neighbouring cathedral town, hunt up Cunningham, and learn from him what he had really seen that had prompted the remark about a wild beast in the woods. With this resolution taken, his usual cheerfulness partially returned, and he hummed a bright little melody as he sauntered to the morning-room for his customary cigarette. As he entered the room the melody made way abruptly for a pious invocation. Gracefully asprawl on the ottoman, in an attitude of almost exaggerated repose, was the boy of the woods. He was drier than when Van Cheele had last seen him, but no other alteration was noticeable in his toilet.

"How dare you come here?" asked Van Cheele furiously.

"You told me I was not to stay in the woods," said the boy calmly.

"But not to come here. Supposing my aunt should see you!"

And with a view to minimising that catastrophe, Van Cheele hastily obscured as much of his unwelcome guest as possible under the folds of a *Morning Post*. At that moment his aunt entered the room.

"This is a poor boy who has lost his way—and lost his memory. He doesn't know who he is or where he comes from," explained Van Cheele desperately, glancing apprehensively at the waif's face to see whether he was going to add inconvenient candour to his other savage propensities.

Miss Van Cheele was enormously interested.

"Perhaps his underlinen is marked," she suggested.

"He seems to have lost most of that, too," said Van Cheele, making frantic little grabs at the *Morning Post* to keep it in its place.

A naked homeless child appealed to Miss Van Cheele as warmly as

26

a stray kitten or derelict puppy would have done.

"We must do all we can for him," she decided, and in a very short time a messenger, dispatched to the rectory, where a page-boy was kept, had returned with a suit of pantry clothes, and the necessary accessories of shirt, shoes, collar, etc. Clothed, clean, and groomed, the boy lost none of his uncanniness in Van Cheele's eyes, but his aunt found him sweet.

"We must call him something till we know who he really is," she said. "Gabriel-Ernest, I think; those are nice suitable names."

Van Cheele agreed, but he privately doubted whether they were being grafted on to a nice suitable child. His misgivings were not diminished by the fact that his staid and elderly spaniel had bolted out of the house at the first incoming of the boy, and now obstinately remained shivering and yapping at the farther end of the orchard, while the canary, usually as vocally industrious as Van Cheele himself, had put itself on an allowance of frightened cheeps. More than ever, he was resolved to consult Cunningham without loss of time.

As he drove off to the station his aunt was arranging that Gabriel-Ernest should help her to entertain the infant members of her Sunday-school class at tea that afternoon.

Cunningham was not at first disposed to be communicative.

"My mother died of some brain trouble," he explained, "so you will understand why I am averse to dwelling on anything of an impossibly fantastic nature that I may see or think that I have seen."

"But what *did* you see?" persisted Van Cheele.

"What I thought I saw was something so extraordinary that no really sane man could dignify it with the credit of having actually happened. I was standing, the last evening I was with you, half-hidden in the hedge growth by the orchard gate, watching the dying glow of the sunset. Suddenly I became aware of a naked boy, a bather from some neighbouring pool, I took him to be, who was standing out on the bare hillside also watching the sunset. His pose was so suggestive of some wild faun of Pagan myth that I instantly wanted to engage him as a model, and in another moment, I think I should have hailed him. But just then the sun dipped out of view, and all the orange and pink slid out of the landscape, leaving it cold and grey. And at the same moment an astounding thing happened—the boy vanished too!"

"What! vanished away into nothing?" asked Van Cheele excitedly.

"No; that is the dreadful part of it," answered the artist; "on the open hillside where the boy had been standing a second ago, stood a large wolf, blackish in colour, with gleaming fangs and cruel, yellow eyes. You may think—"

But Van Cheele did not stop for anything as futile as thought. Already he was tearing at top speed towards the station. He dismissed the idea of a telegram. "Gabriel-Ernest is a werewolf" was a hopelessly inadequate effort at conveying the situation, and his aunt would think it was a code message to which he had omitted to give her the key. His one hope was that he might reach home before sundown. The cab which he chartered at the other end of the railway journey bore him with what seemed exasperating slowness along the country roads, which were pink and mauve with the flush of the sinking sun. His aunt was putting away some unfinished jams and cake when he arrived.

"Where is Gabriel-Ernest?" he almost screamed.

"He is taking the little Toop child home," said his aunt. "It was getting so late, I thought it wasn't safe to let it go back alone. What a lovely sunset, isn't it?"

But Van Cheele, although not oblivious of the glow in the western sky, did not stay to discuss its beauties. At a speed for which he was scarcely geared he raced along the narrow lane that led to the home of the Toops. On one side ran the swift current of the mill-stream, on the other rose the stretch of bare hillside. A dwindling rim of red sun showed still on the skyline, and the next turning must bring him in view of the ill-assorted couple he was pursuing. Then the colour went suddenly out of things, and a grey light settled itself with a quick shiver over the landscape. Van Cheele heard a shrill wail of fear, and stopped running.

Nothing was ever seen again of the Toop child or Gabriel-Ernest, but the latter's discarded garments were found lying in the road so it was assumed that the child had fallen into the water, and that the boy had stripped and jumped in, in a vain endeavour to save it. Van Cheele and some workmen who were nearby at the time testified to having heard a child scream loudly just near the spot where the clothes were found. Mrs. Toop, who had eleven other children, was decently resigned to her bereavement, but Miss Van Cheele sincerely mourned her lost foundling. It was on her initiative that a memorial brass was put up in the parish church to "Gabriel-Ernest, an unknown boy, who bravely sacrificed his life for another."

Van Cheele gave way to his aunt in most things, but he flatly refused to subscribe to the Gabriel-Ernest memorial.

Laura

"You are not really dying, are you?" asked Amanda.

"I have the doctor's permission to live till Tuesday," said Laura.

"But today is Saturday; this is serious!" gasped Amanda.

"I don't know about it being serious; it is certainly Saturday," said Laura.

"Death is always serious," said Amanda.

"I never said I was going to die. I am presumably going to leave off being Laura, but I shall go on being something. An animal of some kind, I suppose. You see, when one hasn't been very good in the life one has just lived, one reincarnates in some lower organism. And I haven't been very good, when one comes to think of it. I've been petty and mean and vindictive and all that sort of thing when circumstances have seemed to warrant it."

"Circumstances never warrant that sort of thing," said Amanda hastily.

"If you don't mind my saying so," observed Laura, "Egbert is a circumstance that would warrant any amount of that sort of thing. You're married to him—that's different; you've sworn to love, honour, and endure him: I haven't."

"I don't see what's wrong with Egbert," protested Amanda.

"Oh, I daresay the wrongness has been on my part," admitted Laura dispassionately; "he has merely been the extenuating circumstance. He made a thin, peevish kind of fuss, for instance, when I took the collie puppies from the farm out for a run the other day."

"They chased his young broods of speckled Sussex and drove two sitting hens off their nests, besides running all over the flower beds. You know how devoted he is to his poultry and garden."

"Anyhow, he needn't have gone on about it for the entire evening and then have said, 'Let's say no more about it' just when I was beginning to enjoy the discussion. That's where one of my petty vindictive revenges came in," added Laura with an unrepentant chuckle; "I turned the entire family of speckled Sussex into his seedling shed the day after the puppy episode."

"How could you?" exclaimed Amanda.

"It came quite easy," said Laura; "two of the hens pretended to be laying at the time, but I was firm."

"And we thought it was an accident!"

"You see," resumed Laura, "I really *have* some grounds for supposing that my next incarnation will be in a lower organism. I shall be an animal of some kind. On the other hand, I haven't been a bad sort in my way, so I think I may count on being a nice animal, something elegant and lively, with a love of fun. An otter, perhaps."

"I can't imagine you as an otter," said Amanda.

"Well, I don't suppose you can imagine me as an angel, if it comes to that," said Laura.

Amanda was silent. She couldn't.

"Personally, I think an otter life would be rather enjoyable," continued Laura; "salmon to eat all the year round, and the satisfaction of being able to fetch the trout in their own homes without having to wait for hours till they condescend to rise to the fly you've been dangling before them; and an elegant svelte figure—"

"Think of the otter hounds," interposed Amanda; "how dreadful to be hunted and harried and finally worried to death!"

"Rather fun with half the neighbourhood looking on, and anyhow not worse than this Saturday-to-Tuesday business of dying by inches; and then I should go on into something else. If I had been a moderately good otter, I suppose I should get back into human shape of some sort; probably something rather primitive—a little brown, unclothed Nubian boy, I should think."

"I wish you would be serious," sighed Amanda; "you really ought to be if you're only going to live till Tuesday."

As a matter of fact, Laura died on Monday.

"So dreadfully upsetting," Amanda complained to her uncle-in-law, Sir Lulworth Quayne. "I've asked quite a lot of people down for golf and fishing, and the rhododendrons are just looking their best."

"Laura always was inconsiderate," said Sir Lulworth; "she was born during Goodwood week, with an ambassador staying in the house who hated babies."

"She had the maddest kind of ideas," said Amanda; "do you know if there was any insanity in her family?"

"Insanity? No, I never heard of any. Her father lives in West Kensington, but I believe he's sane on all other subjects."

"She had an idea that she was going to be reincarnated as an otter," said Amanda.

"One meets with those ideas of reincarnation so frequently, even in the West," said Sir Lulworth, "that one can hardly set them down as being mad. And Laura was such an unaccountable person in this life that I should not like to lay down definite rules as to what she might be doing in an after state."

"You think she really might have passed into some animal form?" asked Amanda. She was one of those who shape their opinions rather readily from the standpoint of those around them.

Just then Egbert entered the breakfast-room, wearing an air of bereavement that Laura's demise would have been insufficient, in itself, to account for.

"Four of my speckled Sussex have been killed," he exclaimed; "the very four that were to go to the show on Friday. One of them was dragged away and eaten right in the middle of that new carnation bed that I've been to such trouble and expense over. My best flower bed and my best fowls singled out for destruction; it almost seems as if the brute that did the deed had special knowledge how to be as devastating as possible in a short space of time."

"Was it a fox, do you think?" asked Amanda.

"Sounds more like a polecat," said Sir Lulworth.

"No," said Egbert, "there were marks of webbed feet all over the place, and we followed the tracks down to the stream at the bottom of the garden; evidently an otter."

Amanda looked quickly and furtively across at Sir Lulworth.

Egbert was too agitated to eat any breakfast, and went out to superintend the strengthening of the poultry yard defences.

"I think she might at least have waited till the funeral was over," said Amanda in a scandalised voice.

"It's her own funeral, you know," said Sir Lulworth; "it's a nice point in etiquette how far one ought to show respect to one's own mortal remains."

Disregard for mortuary convention was carried to further lengths next day; during the absence of the family at the funeral ceremony the remaining survivors of the speckled Sussex were massacred. The marauder's line of retreat seemed to have embraced most of the flower beds on the lawn, but the strawberry beds in the lower garden had also suffered.

"I shall get the otter hounds to come here at the earliest possible moment," said Egbert savagely.

"On no account! You can't dream of such a thing!" exclaimed Amanda. "I mean, it wouldn't do, so soon after a funeral in the house."

"It's a case of necessity," said Egbert; "once an otter takes to that sort of thing it won't stop."

"Perhaps it will go elsewhere now there are no more fowls left," suggested Amanda.

"One would think you wanted to shield the beast," said Egbert.

"There's been so little water in the stream lately," objected Amanda; "it seems hardly sporting to hunt an animal when it has so little chance of taking refuge anywhere."

"Good gracious!" fumed Egbert, "I'm not thinking about sport. I want to have the animal killed as soon as possible."

Even Amanda's opposition weakened when, during church time on the following Sunday, the otter made its way into the house, raided half a salmon from the larder and worried it into scaly fragments on the Persian rug in Egbert's studio.

"We shall have it hiding under our beds and biting pieces out of our feet before long," said Egbert, and from what Amanda knew of this particular otter she felt that the possibility was not a remote one.

On the evening preceding the day fixed for the hunt Amanda spent a solitary hour walking by the banks of the stream, making what she imagined to be hound noises. It was charitably supposed by those who overheard her performance, that she was practising for farmyard imitations at the forthcoming village entertainment.

It was her friend and neighbour, Aurora Burret, who brought her news of the day's sport.

"Pity you weren't out; we had quite a good day. We found at once, in the pool just below your garden."

"Did you—kill?" asked Amanda.

"Rather. A fine she-otter. Your husband got rather badly bitten in trying to 'tail it.' Poor beast, I felt quite sorry for it, it had such a human look in its eyes when it was killed. You'll call me silly, but do you know who the look reminded me of? My dear woman, what is the matter?"

When Amanda had recovered to a certain extent from her attack of nervous prostration Egbert took her to the Nile Valley to recuperate. Change of scene speedily brought about the desired recovery of health and mental balance. The escapades of an adventurous otter in search of a variation of diet were viewed in their proper light. Amanda's normally placid temperament reasserted itself. Even a hurricane of shouted curses, coming from her husband's dressing-room, in her husband's voice, but hardly in his usual vocabulary, failed to disturb her serenity as she made a leisurely toilet one evening in a Cairo hotel.

"What is the matter? What has happened?" she asked in amused curiosity.

"The little beast has thrown all my clean shirts into the bath! Wait till I catch you, you little—"

"What little beast?" asked Amanda, suppressing a desire to laugh; Egbert's language was so hopelessly inadequate to express his outraged feelings.

"A little beast of a naked brown Nubian boy," spluttered Egbert.

And now Amanda is seriously ill.

Sredni Vashtar

Conradin was ten years old, and the doctor had pronounced his professional opinion that the boy would not live another five years. The doctor was silky and effete, and counted for little, but his opinion was endorsed by Mrs. De Ropp, who counted for nearly everything. Mrs. De Ropp was Conradin's cousin and guardian, and in his eyes, she represented those three-fifths of the world that are necessary and disagreeable and real; the other two-fifths, in perpetual antagonism to the foregoing, were summed up in himself and his imagination. One of these days Conradin supposed he would succumb to the mastering pressure of wearisome necessary things—such as illnesses and coddling restrictions and drawn-out dullness. Without his imagination, which was rampant under the spur of loneliness, he would have succumbed long ago.

Mrs. De Ropp would never, in her honestest moments, have confessed to herself that she disliked Conradin, though she might have been dimly aware that thwarting him 'for his good' was a duty which she did not find particularly irksome. Conradin hated her with a desperate sincerity which he was perfectly able to mask. Such few pleasures as he could contrive for himself gained an added relish from the likelihood that they would be displeasing to his guardian, and from the realm of his imagination she was locked out—an unclean thing, which should find no entrance.

In the dull, cheerless garden, overlooked by so many windows that were ready to open with a message not to do this or that, or a reminder that medicines were due, he found little attraction. The few fruit-trees that it contained were set jealously apart from his plucking, as though they were rare specimens of their kind blooming in an arid waste; it would probably have been difficult to find a market-gardener who would have offered ten shillings for their entire yearly produce.

In a forgotten corner, however, almost hidden behind a dismal shrub-bery, was a disused tool-shed of respectable proportions, and within its walls Conradin found a haven, something that took on the vary-ing aspects of a playroom and a cathedral. He had peopled it with a legion of familiar phantoms, evoked partly from fragments of history and partly from his own brain, but it also boasted two inmates of flesh and blood.

In one corner lived a ragged-plumaged Houdan hen, on which the boy lavished an affection that had scarcely another outlet. Fur-ther back in the gloom stood a large hutch, divided into two com-partments, one of which was fronted with close iron bars. This was the abode of a large polecat-ferret, which a friendly butcher-boy had once smuggled, cage and all, into its present quarters, in exchange for a long-secreted hoard of small silver. Conradin was dreadfully afraid of the lithe, sharp-fanged beast, but it was his most treasured possession. Its very presence in the tool-shed was a secret and fearful joy, to be kept scrupulously from the knowledge of the Woman, as he privately dubbed his cousin.

And one day, out of Heaven knows what material, he spun the beast a wonderful name, and from that moment it grew into a god and a religion. The Woman indulged in religion once a week at a church nearby, and took Conradin with her, but to him the church service was an alien rite in the House of Rimmon. Every Thursday, in the dim and musty silence of the tool-shed, he worshipped with mystic and elaborate ceremonial before the wooden hutch where dwelt Sredni Vashtar, the great ferret. Red flowers in their season and scarlet ber-ries in the winter-time were offered at his shrine, for he was a god who laid some special stress on the fierce impatient side of things, as opposed to the Woman's religion, which, as far as Conradin could observe, went to great lengths in the contrary direction.

And on great festivals powdered nutmeg was strewn in front of his hutch, an important feature of the offering being that the nutmeg had to be stolen. These festivals were of irregular occurrence, and were chiefly appointed to celebrate some passing event. On one occasion, when Mrs. De Ropp suffered from acute toothache for three days, Conradin kept up the festival during the entire three days, and almost succeeded in persuading himself that Sredni Vashtar was personally responsible for the toothache. If the malady had lasted for another day the supply of nutmeg would have given out.

The Houdan hen was never drawn into the cult of Sredni Vashtar.

Conradin had long ago settled that she was an Anabaptist. He did not pretend to have the remotest knowledge as to what an Anabaptist was, but he privately hoped that it was dashing and not very respectable. Mrs. De Ropp was the ground plan on which he based and detested all respectability.

After a while Conradin's absorption in the tool-shed began to attract the notice of his guardian. "It is not good for him to be pottering down there in all weathers," she promptly decided, and at breakfast one morning she announced that the Houdan hen had been sold and taken away overnight. With her short-sighted eyes she peered at Conradin, waiting for an outbreak of rage and sorrow, which she was ready to rebuke with a flow of excellent precepts and reasoning. But Conradin said nothing: there was nothing to be said. Something perhaps in his white set face gave her a momentary qualm, for at tea that afternoon there was toast on the table, a delicacy which she usually banned on the ground that it was bad for him; also, because the making of it "gave trouble," a deadly offence in the middle-class feminine eye.

"I thought you liked toast," she exclaimed, with an injured air, observing that he did not touch it.

"Sometimes," said Conradin.

In the shed that evening there was an innovation in the worship of the hutch-god. Conradin had been wont to chant his praises, tonight be asked a boon.

"Do one thing for me, Sredni Vashtar."

The thing was not specified. As Sredni Vashtar was a god he must be supposed to know. And choking back a sob as he looked at that other empty corner, Conradin went back to the world he so hated.

And every night, in the welcome darkness of his bedroom, and every evening in the dusk of the tool-shed, Conradin's bitter litany went up: "Do one thing for me, Sredni Vashtar."

Mrs. De Ropp noticed that the visits to the shed did not cease, and one day she made a further journey of inspection.

"What are you keeping in that locked hutch?" she asked. "I believe it's guinea-pigs. I'll have them all cleared away."

Conradin shut his lips tight, but the Woman ransacked his bedroom till she found the carefully hidden key, and forthwith marched down to the shed to complete her discovery. It was a cold afternoon, and Conradin had been bidden to keep to the house. From the furthest window of the dining-room the door of the shed could just be seen beyond the corner of the shrubbery, and there Conradin stationed himself. He saw the Woman enter, and then he imagined her opening the door of the sacred hutch and peering down with her short-sighted eyes into the thick straw bed where his god lay hidden. Perhaps she would prod at the straw in her clumsy impatience. And Conradin fervently breathed his prayer for the last time. But he knew as he prayed that he did not believe.

He knew that the Woman would come out presently with that pursed smile he loathed so well on her face, and that in an hour or two the gardener would carry away his wonderful god, a god no longer, but a simple brown ferret in a hutch. And he knew that the Woman would triumph always as she triumphed now, and that he would grow ever more sickly under her pestering and domineering and superior wisdom, till one day nothing would matter much more with him, and the doctor would be proved right. And in the sting and misery of his defeat, he began to chant loudly and defiantly the hymn of his threatened idol:

Sredni Vashtar went forth,
His thoughts were red thoughts and his teeth were white.
His enemies called for peace, but he brought them death.
Sredni Vashtar the Beautiful.

And then of a sudden he stopped his chanting and drew closer to the windowpane. The door of the shed still stood ajar as it had been left, and the minutes were slipping by. They were long minutes, but they slipped by nevertheless. He watched the starlings running and flying in little parties across the lawn; he counted them over and over again, with one eye always on that swinging door. A sour-faced maid came in to lay the table for tea, and still Conradin stood and waited and watched. Hope had crept by inches into his heart, and now a look of triumph began to blaze in his eyes that had only known the wistful patience of defeat. Under his breath, with a furtive exultation, he began once again the *paean* of victory and devastation.

And presently his eyes were rewarded: out through that doorway came a long, low, yellow-and-brown beast, with eyes a-blink at the waning daylight, and dark wet stains around the fur of jaws and throat. Conradin dropped on his knees. The great polecat-ferret made its way down to a small brook at the foot of the garden, drank for a moment, then crossed a little plank bridge and was lost to sight in the bushes. Such was the passing of Sredni Vashtar.

"Tea is ready," said the sour-faced maid; "where is the mistress?"

"She went down to the shed some time ago," said Conradin. And while the maid went to summon her mistress to tea, Conradin fished a toasting-fork out of the sideboard drawer and proceeded to toast himself a piece of bread. And during the toasting of it and the buttering of it with much butter and the slow enjoyment of eating it, Conradin listened to the noises and silences which fell in quick spasms beyond the dining-room door. The loud foolish screaming of the maid, the answering chorus of wondering ejaculations from the kitchen region, the scuttering footsteps and hurried embassies for outside help, and then, after a lull, the scared sobbings and the shuffling tread of those who bore a heavy burden into the house.

"Whoever will break it to the poor child? I couldn't for the life of me!" exclaimed a shrill voice. And while they debated the matter among themselves, Conradin made himself another piece of toast.

The Background

"That woman's art-jargon tires me," said Clovis to his journalist friend. "She's so fond of talking of certain pictures as 'growing on one,' as though they were a sort of fungus."

"That reminds me," said the journalist, "of the story of Henri Deplis. Have I ever told it you?"

Clovis shook his head.

"Henri Deplis was by birth a native of the Grand Duchy of Luxemburg. On maturer reflection he became a commercial traveller. His business activities frequently took him beyond the limits of the Grand Duchy, and he was stopping in a small town of Northern Italy when news reached him from home that a legacy from a distant and deceased relative had fallen to his share.

"It was not a large legacy, even from the modest standpoint of Henri Deplis, but it impelled him towards some seemingly harmless extravagances. In particular it led him to patronise local art as represented by the tattoo-needles of Signor Andreas Pincini. Signor Pincini was, perhaps, the most brilliant master of tattoo craft that Italy had ever known, but his circumstances were decidedly impoverished, and for the sum of six hundred *francs* he gladly undertook to cover his client's back, from the collar-bone down to the waist-line, with a glowing representation of the Fall of Icarus. The design, when finally developed, was a slight disappointment to Monsieur Deplis, who had suspected Icarus of being a fortress taken by Wallenstein in the Thirty Years' War, but he was more than satisfied with the execution of the work, which was acclaimed by all who had the privilege of seeing it as Pincini's masterpiece.

"It was his greatest effort, and his last. Without even waiting to be paid, the illustrious craftsman departed this life, and was buried under an ornate tombstone, whose winged cherubs would have afforded singularly little scope for the exercise of his favourite art. There remained, however, the widow Pincini, to whom the six hundred *francs* were due. And thereupon arose the great crisis in the life of Henri Deplis, traveller of commerce. The legacy, under the stress of numerous little calls on its substance, had dwindled to very insignificant proportions, and when a pressing wine bill and sundry other current accounts had been paid, there remained little more than 430 *francs* to offer to the widow.

"The lady was properly indignant, not wholly, as she volubly explained, on account of the suggested writing-off of 170 *francs*, but also at the attempt to depreciate the value of her late husband's acknowledged masterpiece. In a week's time Deplis was obliged to reduce his offer to 405 *francs*, which circumstance fanned the widow's indignation into a fury. She cancelled the sale of the work of art, and a few days later Deplis learned with a sense of consternation that she had presented it to the municipality of Bergamo, which had gratefully accepted it. He left the neighbourhood as unobtrusively as possible, and was genuinely relieved when his business commands took him to Rome, where he hoped his identity and that of the famous picture might be lost sight of.

"But he bore on his back the burden of the dead man's genius. On presenting himself one day in the steaming corridor of a vapour bath, he was at once hustled back into his clothes by the proprietor, who was a North Italian, and who emphatically refused to allow the celebrated Fall of Icarus to be publicly on view without the permission of the municipality of Bergamo. Public interest and official vigilance increased as the matter became more widely known, and Deplis was unable to take a simple dip in the sea or river on the hottest afternoon unless clothed up to the collar-bone in a substantial bathing garment.

Later on the authorities of Bergamo conceived the idea that salt water might be injurious to the masterpiece, and a perpetual injunction was obtained which debarred the muchly harassed commercial traveller from sea bathing under any circumstances. Altogether, he was fervently thankful when his firm of employers found him a new range of activities in the neighbourhood of Bordeaux. His thankfulness, however, ceased abruptly at the Franco-Italian frontier. An imposing array of official force barred his departure, and he was sternly reminded of the stringent law which forbids the exportation of Italian Works of art.

"A diplomatic parley ensued between the Luxemburgian and Italian Governments, and at one time the European situation became overcast with the possibilities of trouble. But the Italian Government stood firm; it declined to concern itself in the least with the fortunes or even the existence of Henri Deplis, commercial traveller, but was immovable in its decision that the Fall of Icarus (by the late Pincini, Andreas) at present the property of the municipality of Bergamo, should not leave the country.

"The excitement died down in time, but the unfortunate Deplis, who was of a constitutionally retiring disposition, found himself a few months later once more the storm-centre of a furious controversy. A certain German art expert, who had obtained from the municipality of Bergamo permission to inspect the famous masterpiece, declared it to be a spurious Pincini, probably the work of some pupil whom he had employed in his declining years. The evidence of Deplis on the subject was obviously worthless, as he had been under the influence of the customary narcotics during the long process of pricking in the design.

"The editor of an Italian art journal refuted the contentions of the German expert and undertook to prove that his private life did not conform to any modern standard of decency. The whole of Italy and Germany were drawn into the dispute, and the rest of Europe was soon involved in the quarrel. There were stormy scenes in the Spanish Parliament, and the University of Copenhagen bestowed a gold medal on the German expert (afterwards sending a commission to examine his proofs on the spot), while two Polish schoolboys in Paris committed suicide to show what *they* thought of the master.

"Meanwhile, the unhappy human background fared no better than before, and it was not surprising that he drifted into the ranks of Italian anarchists. Four times at least he was escorted to the frontier as a dangerous and undesirable foreigner, but he was always brought back as the Fall of Icarus (attributed to Pincini, Andreas, early Twentieth Century). And then one day, at an anarchist congress at Genoa, a fellow-worker, in the heat of debate, broke a phial full of corrosive liquid over his back. The red shirt that he was wearing mitigated the effects, but the Icarus was ruined beyond recognition. His assailant was severely reprimanded for assaulting a fellow-anarchist and received seven years' imprisonment for defacing a national art treasure. As soon as he was able to leave the hospital Henri Deplis was put across the frontier as an undesirable alien.

"In the quieter streets of Paris, especially in the neighbourhood of the Ministry of Fine Arts, you may sometimes meet a depressed, anxious-looking man, who, if you pass him the time of day, will answer you with a slight Luxemburgian accent. He nurses the illusion that he is one of the lost arms of the Venus de Milo, and hopes that the French Government may be persuaded to buy him. On all other subjects I believe he is tolerably sane."

The Blind Spot

"You've just come back from Adelaide's funeral, haven't you?" said Sir Lulworth to his nephew; "I suppose it was very like most other funerals?"

"I'll tell you all about it at lunch," said Egbert.

"You'll do nothing of the sort. It wouldn't be respectful either to your great-aunt's memory or to the lunch. We begin with Spanish olives, then a *borshch*, then more olives and a bird of some kind, and a rather enticing Rhenish wine, not at all expensive as wines go in this country, but still quite laudable in its way. Now there's absolutely nothing in that menu that harmonises in the least with the subject of your Great-Aunt Adelaide or her funeral. She was a charming woman, and quite as intelligent as she had any need to be, but somehow, she always reminded me of an English cook's idea of a Madras curry."

"She used to say you were frivolous," said Egbert. Something in his tone suggested that he rather endorsed the verdict.

"I believe I once considerably scandalised her by declaring that clear soup was a more important factor in life than a clear conscience. She had very little sense of proportion. By the way, she made you her principal heir, didn't she?"

"Yes," said Egbert, "and executor as well. It's in that connection that I particularly want to speak to you."

"Business is not my strong point at any time," said Sir Lulworth, "and certainly not when we're on the immediate threshold of lunch."

"It isn't exactly business," explained Egbert, as he followed his uncle into the dining-room.

"It's something rather serious. Very serious."

"Then we can't possibly speak about it now," said Sir Lulworth; "no one could talk seriously during a *borshch*. A beautifully constructed *borshch*, such as you are going to experience presently, ought not only to

45

banish conversation but almost to annihilate thought. Later on, when we arrive at the second stage of olives, I shall be quite ready to discuss that new book on Borrow, or, if you prefer it, the present situation in the Grand Duchy of Luxemburg. But I absolutely decline to talk anything approaching business till we have finished with the bird."

For the greater part of the meal Egbert sat in an abstracted silence, the silence of a man whose mind is focussed on one topic. When the coffee stage had been reached, he launched himself suddenly athwart his uncle's reminiscences of the Court of Luxemburg.

"I think I told you that Great-Aunt Adelaide had made me her executor. There wasn't very much to be done in the way of legal matters, but I had to go through her papers."

"That would be a fairly heavy task in itself. I should imagine there were reams of family letters."

"Stacks of them, and most of them highly uninteresting. There was one packet, however, which I thought might repay a careful perusal. It was a bundle of correspondence from her brother Peter."

"The Canon of tragic memory," said Lulworth.

"Exactly, of tragic memory, as you say; a tragedy that has never been fathomed."

"Probably the simplest explanation was the correct one," said Sir Lulworth; "he slipped on the stone staircase and fractured his skull in falling."

Egbert shook his head. "The medical evidence all went to prove that the blow on the head was struck by someone coming up behind him. A wound caused by violent contact with the steps could not possibly have been inflicted at that angle of the skull. They experimented with a dummy figure falling in every conceivable position."

"But the motive?" exclaimed Sir Lulworth; "no one had any interest in doing away with him, and the number of people who destroy Canons of the Established Church for the mere fun of killing must be extremely limited. Of course, there are individuals of weak mental balance who do that sort of thing, but they seldom conceal their handiwork; they are more generally inclined to parade it."

"His cook was under suspicion," said Egbert shortly.

"I know he was," said Sir Lulworth, "simply because he was about the only person on the premises at the time of the tragedy. But could anything be sillier than trying to fasten a charge of murder on to Sebastien? He had nothing to gain, in fact, a good deal to lose, from the death of his employer. The Canon was paying him quite as good wages as I was able to offer him when I took him over into my service. I have since raised them to something a little more in accordance with his real worth, but at the time he was glad to find a new place without troubling about an increase of wages. People were fighting rather shy of him, and he had no friends in this country. No; if anyone in the world was interested in the prolonged life and unimpaired digestion of the Canon it would certainly be Sebastien."

"People don't always weigh the consequences of their rash acts," said Egbert, "otherwise there would be very few murders committed. Sebastien is a man of hot temper."

"He is a southerner," admitted Sir Lulworth; "to be geographically exact I believe he hails from the French slopes of the Pyrenees. I took that into consideration when he nearly killed the gardener's boy the other day for bringing him a spurious substitute for sorrel. One must always make allowances for origin and locality and early environment; 'Tell me your longitude and I'll know what latitude to allow you,' is my motto."

"There, you see," said Egbert, "he nearly killed the gardener's boy."

"My dear Egbert, between nearly killing a gardener's boy and alto- gether killing a Canon there is a wide difference. No doubt you have often felt a temporary desire to kill a gardener's boy; you have never given way to it, and I respect you for your self-control. But I don't suppose you have ever wanted to kill an octogenarian Canon. Besides, as far as we know, there had never been any quarrel or disagreement between the two men. The evidence at the inquest brought that out very clearly."

"Ah!" said Egbert, with the air of a man coming at last into a deferred inheritance of conversational importance, "that is precisely what I want to speak to you about."

He pushed away his coffee cup and drew a pocket-book from his inner breast-pocket. From the depths of the pocket-book he pro- duced an envelope, and from the envelope he extracted a letter, closely written in a small, neat handwriting.

"One of the Canon's numerous letters to Aunt Adelaide," he ex- plained, "written a few days before his death. Her memory was already failing when she received it, and I daresay she forgot the contents as soon as she had read it; otherwise, in the light of what subsequently happened, we should have heard something of this letter before now. If it had been produced at the inquest, I fancy it would have made some difference in the course of affairs. The evidence, as you remarked just now, choked off suspicion against Sebastien by disclosing an utter absence of anything that could be considered a motive or provocation for the crime, if crime there was."

"Oh, read the letter," said Sir Lulworth impatiently.

"It's a long rambling affair, like most of his letters in his later years," said Egbert. "I'll read the part that bears immediately on the mystery.

"'I very much fear I shall have to get rid of Sebastien. He cooks divinely, but he has the temper of a fiend or an anthropoid ape, and I am really in bodily fear of him. We had a dispute the other day as to the correct sort of lunch to be served on Ash Wednesday, and I got so irritated and annoyed at his conceit and obstinacy that at last I threw a cupful of coffee in his face and called him at the same time an impudent jackanapes. Very little of the coffee went actually in his face, but I have never seen a human being show such deplorable lack of self-control. I laughed at the threat of killing me that he spluttered out in his rage, and thought the whole thing would blow over, but I have several times since caught him scowling and muttering in a highly unpleasant fashion, and lately I have fancied that he was dogging my footsteps about the grounds, particularly when I walk of an evening in the Italian Garden.'

"It was on the steps in the Italian Garden that the body was found," commented Egbert, and resumed reading.

"'I daresay the danger is imaginary; but I shall feel more at ease when he has quitted my service.'"

Egbert paused for a moment at the conclusion of the extract; then, as his uncle made no remark, he added: "If lack of motive was the only factor that saved Sebastien from prosecution, I fancy this letter will put a different complexion on matters."

"Have you shown it to anyone else?" asked Sir Lulworth, reaching out his hand for the incriminating piece of paper.

"No," said Egbert, handing it across the table, "I thought I would tell you about it first. Heavens, what are you doing?"

Egbert's voice rose almost to a scream. Sir Lulworth had flung the paper well and truly into the glowing centre of the grate. The small, neat handwriting shrivelled into black flaky nothingness.

"What on earth did you do that for?" gasped Egbert. "That letter was our one piece of evidence to connect Sebastien with the crime."

"That is why I destroyed it," said Sir Lulworth.

"But why should you want to shield him?" cried Egbert; "the man is a common murderer."

"A common murderer, possibly, but a very uncommon cook."

The Cobweb

The farmhouse kitchen probably stood where it did as a matter of accident or haphazard choice; yet its situation might have been planned by a master-strategist in farmhouse architecture. Dairy and poultry-yard, and herb garden, and all the busy places of the farm seemed to lead by easy access into its wide flagged haven, where there was room for everything and where muddy boots left traces that were easily swept away. And yet, for all that it stood so well in the centre of human bustle, its long, latticed window, with the wide window-seat, built into an embrasure beyond the huge fireplace, looked out on a wild spreading view of hill and heather and wooded combe.

The window nook made almost a little room in itself, quite the pleasantest room in the farm as far as situation and capabilities went. Young Mrs. Ladbruk, whose husband had just come into the farm by way of inheritance, cast covetous eyes on this snug corner, and her fingers itched to make it bright and cosy with chintz curtains and bowls of flowers, and a shelf or two of old china. The musty farm parlour, looking out on to a prim, cheerless garden imprisoned within high, blank walls, was not a room that lent itself readily either to comfort or decoration.

"When we are more settled, I shall work wonders in the way of making the kitchen habitable," said the young woman to her occasional visitors. There was an unspoken wish in those words, a wish which was unconfessed as well as unspoken. Emma Ladbruk was the mistress of the farm; jointly with her husband she might have her say, and to a certain extent her way, in ordering its affairs. But she was not mistress of the kitchen.

On one of the shelves of an old dresser, in company with chipped sauce-boats, pewter jugs, cheese-graters, and paid bills, rested a worn and ragged Bible, on whose front page was the record, in faded ink, of a baptism dated ninety-four years ago. "Martha Crale" was the name written on that yellow page. The yellow, wrinkled old dame who hobbled and muttered about the kitchen, looking like a dead autumn leaf which, the winter winds still pushed hither and thither, had once been Martha Crale; for seventy odd years she had been Martha Mountjoy. For longer than anyone could remember she had pattered to and fro between oven and wash-house and dairy, and out to chicken-run and garden, grumbling and muttering and scolding, but working unceasingly.

Emma Ladbruk, of whose coming she took as little notice as she would of a bee wandering in at a window on a summer's day, used at first to watch her with a kind of frightened curiosity. She was so old and so much a part of the place, it was difficult to think of her exactly as a living thing. Old Shep, the white-nozzled, stiff-limbed collie, waiting for his time to die, seemed almost more human than the withered, dried-up old woman. He had been a riotous, roistering puppy, mad with the joy of life, when she was already a tottering, hobbling dame; now he was just a blind, breathing carcase, nothing more, and she still worked with frail energy, still swept and baked and washed, fetched and carried. If there were something in these wise old dogs that did not perish utterly with death, Emma used to think to herself, what generations of ghost-dogs there must be out on those hills, that Martha had reared and fed and tended and spoken a last goodbye word to in that old kitchen.

And what memories she must have of human generations that had passed away in her time. It was difficult for anyone, let alone a stranger like Emma, to get her to talk of the days that had been; her shrill, quavering speech was of doors that had been left unfastened, pails that had got mislaid, calves whose feeding-time was overdue, and the various little faults and lapses that checker a farmhouse routine. Now and again, when election time came round, she would unstore her recollections of the old names round which the fight had waged in the days gone by. There had been a Palmerston, that had been a name down Tiverton way; Tiverton was not a far journey as the crow flies, but to Martha it was almost a foreign country.

Later there had been Northcotes and Aclands, and many other newer names that she had forgotten; the names changed, but it was always Libruls and Toories, Yellows and Blues. And they always quarrelled and shouted as to who was right and who was wrong. The one they quarrelled about most was a fine old gentleman with an angry face—she had seen his picture on the walls. She had seen it on the floor too, with a rotten apple squashed over it, for the farm had changed its politics from time to time. Martha had never been on one side or the other; none of "they" had ever done the farm a stroke of good. Such was her sweeping verdict, given with all a peasant's distrust of the outside world.

When the half-frightened curiosity had somewhat faded away, Emma Ladbruk was uncomfortably conscious of another feeling towards the old woman. She was a quaint old tradition, lingering about the place, she was part and parcel of the farm itself, she was something at once pathetic and picturesque—but she was dreadfully in the way. Emma had come to the farm full of plans for little reforms and improvements, in part the result of training in the newest ways and methods, in part the outcome of her own ideas and fancies. Reforms in the kitchen region, if those deaf old ears could have been induced to give them even a hearing, would have met with short shrift and scornful rejection, and the kitchen region spread over the zone of dairy and market business and half the work of the household.

Emma, with the latest science of dead-poultry dressing at her finger-tips, sat by, an unheeded watcher, while old Martha trussed the chickens for the market-stall as she had trussed them for nearly four-score years—all leg and no breast. And the hundred hints about effective cleaning and labour-lightening and the things that make for wholesomeness which the young woman was ready to impart or to put into action dropped away into nothingness before that wan, muttering, unheeding presence.

Above all, the coveted window corner, that was to be a dainty, cheerful oasis in the gaunt old kitchen, stood now choked and lumbered with a litter of odds and ends that Emma, for all her nominal authority, would not have dared or cared to displace; over them seemed to be spun the protection of something that was like a human cobweb. Decidedly Martha was in the way. It would have been an unworthy meanness to have wished to see the span of that brave old life shortened by a few paltry months, but as the days sped by Emma was conscious that the wish was there, disowned though it might be, lurking at the back of her mind.

She felt the meanness of the wish come over her with a qualm of self-reproach one day when she came into the kitchen and found an unaccustomed state of things in that usually busy quarter. Old Martha was not working. A basket of corn was on the floor by her side, and out in the yard the poultry were beginning to clamour a protest of overdue feeding-time. But Martha sat huddled in a shrunken bunch on the window seat, looking out with her dim old eyes as though she saw something stranger than the autumn landscape.

"Is anything the matter, Martha?" asked the young woman.

"'Tis death, 'tis death a-coming," answered the quavering voice; "I knew 'twere coming. I knew it. 'Tweren't for nothing that old Shep's been howling all morning. An' last night I heard the screech-owl give the death-cry, and there were something white as run across the yard yesterday; 'tweren't a cat nor a stoat, 'twere something. The fowls knew 'twere something; they all drew off to one side. Ay, there's been warnings. I knew it were a-coming."

The young woman's eyes clouded with pity. The old thing sitting there so white and shrunken had once been a merry, noisy child, playing about in lanes and hay-lofts and farmhouse garrets; that had been eighty odd years ago, and now she was just a frail old body cowering under the approaching chill of the death that was coming at last to take her. It was not probable that much could be done for her, but Emma hastened away to get assistance and counsel. Her husband, she knew, was down at a tree-felling some little distance off, but she might find some other intelligent soul who knew the old woman better than she did. The farm, she soon found out, had that faculty common to farmyards of swallowing up and losing its human population.

The poultry followed her in interested fashion, and swine grunted interrogations at her from behind the bars of their styes, but barnyard and rickyard, orchard and stables and dairy, gave no reward to her search. Then, as she retraced her steps towards the kitchen, she came suddenly on her cousin, young Mr. Jim, as everyone called him, who divided his time between amateur horse-dealing, rabbit-shooting, and flirting with the farm maids.

"I'm afraid old Martha is dying," said Emma. Jim was not the sort of person to whom one had to break news gently.

"Nonsense," he said; "Martha means to live to a hundred. She told me so, and she'll do it."

"She may be actually dying at this moment, or it may just be the beginning of the breakup," persisted Emma, with a feeling of contempt for the slowness and dullness of the young man.

A grin spread over his good-natured features.

"It don't look like it," he said, nodding towards the yard. Emma turned to catch the meaning of his remark. Old Martha stood in the middle of a mob of poultry scattering handfuls of grain around her. The turkey-cock, with the bronzed sheen of his feathers and the purple-red of his wattles, the gamecock, with the glowing metallic lustre of his Eastern plumage, the hens, with their ochres and buffs and umbers and their scarlet combs, and the drakes, with their bottle-green heads, made a medley of rich colour, in the centre of which the old woman looked like a withered stalk standing amid a riotous growth of gaily-hued flowers. But she threw the grain deftly amid the wilderness of beaks, and her quavering voice carried as far as the two people who were watching her. She was still harping on the theme of death coming to the farm.

"I knew 'twere a-coming. There's been signs an' warnings."

"Who's dead, then, old Mother?" called out the young man.

"'Tis young Mister Ladbruk," she shrilled back; "they've just a-carried his body in. Run out of the way of a tree that was coming down an' ran hisself on to an iron post. Dead when they picked un up. Aye, I knew 'twere coming."

And she turned to fling a handful of barley at a belated group of guinea-fowl that came racing toward her.

★★★★★★★★★★

The farm was a family property, and passed to the rabbit-shooting cousin as the next-of-kin. Emma Ladbruk drifted out of its history as a bee that had wandered in at an open window might flit its way out again. On a cold grey morning she stood waiting, with her boxes already stowed in the farm cart, till the last of the market produce should be ready, for the train she was to catch was of less importance than the chickens and butter and eggs that were to be offered for sale. From where she stood, she could see an angle of the long, latticed window that was to have been cosy with curtains and gay with bowls of flowers.

Into her mind came the thought that for months, perhaps for years, long after she had been utterly forgotten, a white, unheeding face would be seen peering out through those latticed panes, and a weak muttering voice would be heard quavering up and down those flagged passages. She made her way to a narrow, barred casement that opened into the farm larder. Old Martha was standing at a table trussing a pair of chickens for the market stall as she had trussed them for nearly fourscore years.

The East Wing

A Tragedy in the Manner of the Discursive Dramatists

It was early February and the hour was somewhere about two in the morning. Most of the house-party had retired to bed. Lucien Wattleskeat had merely retired to his bedroom, where he sat over the still vigorous old-age of a fire, balancing the entries in his bridge-book. They worked out at seventy-eight shillings on the right side as the result of two evenings' play, which was not so bad, considering that the stakes had been regrettably low.

Lucien was a young man who regarded himself with an un-demonstrative esteem, which the undiscerning were apt to mistake for indifference. Several women of his acquaintance were on the look-out for nice gills for him to marry, a vigil in which he took no share.

The atmosphere of the room was subtly tinged with an essence of tuberose, and more strongly impregnated with the odour of wood fire smoke. Lucien noticed this latter circumstance as he finished his bridge audit, and also noticed that the fire in the grate was not a wood one, neither was it smoking.

A stronger smell of smoke blew into the room a moment later as the door opened and Major Boventry, pyjama-clad and solemnly excited, stood in the doorway. "The house is on fire!" he exclaimed.

"Oh," said Lucien, "is that it? I thought perhaps you had come to talk to me. If you would shut the door the smoke wouldn't pour in so."

"We ought to do something," said the major with conviction.

"I hardly know the family," said Lucien, "but I suppose one will be expected to be present, even though the fire does not appear to be in this wing of the house."

"It may spread to here," said the major.

"Well, let's go and look at it," assented Lucien, "though it's against my principles to meet trouble half-way."

"Grasp your nettle, that's what I say," observed Boventry.

"In this case, major, it's not our nettle," retorted Lucien, carefully

55

shutting the bedroom door behind him.

In the passage they encountered Canon Clore, arrayed in a dressing-gown of Albanian embroidery which might have escaped remark in a *Te Deum* service in the Cathedral of the Assumption at Moscow, but which looked out of place in the corridor of an English country-house. But then, as Lucien observed to himself, at a fire one can wear anything.

"The house is on fire," said the canon, with the air of one who lends dignity to a tact by according it gracious recognition.

"It's in the East wing, I think," said the major.

"I suppose it is another case of suffragette militancy," said the canon; "I am in favour of women having the vote myself, even if, as some theologians assert, they have no souls. That, indeed, would furnish an additional argument for including them in the electorate, so tint all ejections of the community, the soulless and the souled, might be represented, and being in favour of the female vote I am naturally in favour of militant means to achieve it. Belonging as I do to a Church Militant I should be inconsistent if I professed to stand aghast at militant methods in vote-winning warfare. But at the same time 1 cannot resist pointing out that the women who are using violent means to wring the vote-right from a reluctant legislature are destroying the value of the very thing for which they are struggling.

"A vote is of no conceivable consequence to anybody unless it carries with it the implicit understanding that majority-rule is the settled order of the day, and the militants are actively engaged in demonstrating that any minority armed with a box of matches and a total disregard of consequences can force its opinions and its wishes on an indifferent or hostile community. It is not merely manor houses they are destroying, but the whole fabric of government by ballot box."

"Oughtn't we to be doing something about the fire?" said Major Boventry.

"I was going to suggest something of the sort myself," said the canon stiffly.

"Tomorrow may be too late, as the advertisements in the newspapers say," observed Lucien.

In the hall they met their hostess, Mrs. Gramplain.

"I'm so glad you have come," she said; "servants are so little help in an emergency of this kind. My husband has gone off in the car to summon the fire-brigade."

"Haven't you telephoned to them?" asked the major.

"The telephone unfortunately is in the East wing," said the hostess, "so is the telephone book. Both are being devoured by the flames at this moment. It makes one feel dreadfully isolated. Now if the fire had only broken out in the West wing instead, we could have used the telephone and had the fire-engines here by now."

"On the other hand," objected Lucien, "Canon Clore and Major Boventry and myself would probably have met with the fate that has overtaken the telephone book. I think I prefer the present arrangement."

"The butler and most of the other servants are in the dining-room, trying to save the Raeburns and the alleged Vandyke," continued Mrs. Gramplain, "and in that little room on the first landing, cut off from us by the cruel flames, is my poor darling Eva. Eva of the golden hair. Will none of you save her?"

"Who is Eva of the golden hair?" asked Lucien.

"My daughter," said Mrs. Gramplain.

"I didn't know you had a daughter," said Lucien, "and really I don't think I can risk my life to save someone I've never met or even heard about. You see, my life is not only wonderful and beautiful to myself, but if my life goes, nothing else really matters—to me. I don't suppose you can realise that, to me, the whole world as it exists today, the Ulster problem, the Albanian tangle, the Kikuvu controversy, the wide field of social reform and Antarctic exploration, the realms of finance, and research and international armaments, all this varied and crowded and complex world, all comes to a complete and absolute end, the moment my life is finished.

"Eva might be snatched from the flames and live to be the grandmother of brilliant and charming men and women, but as far as I should be concerned, she and they would no more exist than a vanished puff of cigarette smoke or a dissolved soda-water bubble. And if, in losing my life, I am to lose her life and theirs, as far as I personally am concerned with them, why on earth should I, personally, risk my life to save hers and theirs?"

"Major Boventry," exclaimed Mrs. Champlain, "you are not clever, but you are a man with honest human feelings. I have only known you for a few hours, but I am sure you are the man I take you for. You will not let my Eva perish."

"Lady," said the major stumblingly, "I would gladly give my life to rescue your Eva, or anybody's Eva for the matter of that, but my life is not mine to give. I am engaged to the sweetest little woman in the world. I am everything to her. What would my poor little Mildred say it they brought her news that I had cast away my life in an endeavour, perhaps fruitless, to save some unknown girl in a burning country house?"

"You are like all the rest of them," said Mrs. Gramplain bitterly; "I thought that you, at least, were stupid. It shows how rash it is to judge a man by his bridge play. It has been like this all my life," she continued in dull level tones; "I was married, when little more than a child, to my husband, and there has never been any real bond of affection between us. We have been polite and considerate to each other—nothing more. I sometimes think that if we had had a child, things might have been different."

"But—your daughter Eva?" queried the canon, and the two other men echoed his question.

"I have never had a daughter," said the woman quietly, yet amid the roar and crackle of the flames her voice carried, so that not a syllable was lost. "Eva is the outcome of my imagination. I so much wanted a little girl and at last I came to believe that she really existed. She grew up, year by year, in my mind, and when she was eighteen, I painted her portrait, a beautiful young girl with masses of golden hair. Since that moment the portrait has been Eva. I have altered it a little with the changing years—she is twenty-one now—and I have repainted her dress with every incoming fashion. On her last birthday I painted her a pair of beautiful diamond earrings. Every day I have sat with her for an hour or so, telling her my thoughts, or reading to her. And now she is there, above, with the flames and the smoke, unable to stir, waiting for the deliverance that does not come."

"It is beautiful," said Lucien, "it is the most beautiful thing I have ever heard."

"Where are you going?" asked his hostess, as the young man moved towards the blazing staircase of the East wing.

"I am going to try and save her," he answered; "as she has never existed my death cannot compromise her future existence. I shall go into nothingness, and she, as far as I am concerned, will go into nothingness too, but then she has never been anything else."

"But your life, your beautiful life?"

"Death in this case is more beautiful."

The major started forward.

"I am going too," he said simply.

"To save Eva?" cried the woman.

58

"Yes," he said; "my little Mildred will not grudge me to a woman who has never existed."

"How well he reads our sex," murmured Mrs. Gramplain, "and yet how badly he plays bridge."

The two men went side by side up the blazing staircase, the slender young figure in the well-fitting dinner-jacket and the thick-set military man in striped pyjamas of an obvious Swan and Edgar pattern. Down in the hall below them stood the woman in her pale wrapper and the canon in his wonderful-hued Albanian-work dressing-gown, looking like the arch-priests of some strange religion presiding at a human sacrifice.

As the rescue-party disappeared into the roaring cavern of smoke and flames the butler came into the hall, bearing with him one of the Raeburns.

"I think I hear the clanging of the fire-engines ma'am," he announced.

Mrs. Gramplain continued staring at the spot where the two men had disappeared.

"How stupid of me," she said presently to the canon, "I've just remembered I sent Eva to Exeter to be cleaned. Those two men have lost their lives for nothing."

"They have certainly lost their lives," said the canon.

"The irony of it all," said Mrs. Gramplain, "the tragic irony of it all"

"The real irony of the affair lies in the fact that it will be instrumental in working a social revolution of the utmost magnitude," said the canon; "when it becomes known through the length and breadth of the land that an army officer and a young ornament of the social world have lost their lives in a country-house fire, started by Suffragette incendiarism, the conscience of the country will be aroused, and people will cry out that the price is too heavy to pay. The militants will be in worse odour than ever, but, like the Importunate Widow, they will get their way.

"Over the charred bodies of Major Coventry and Lucien Wattleskeat the banners of progress and enfranchisement will be carried forward to victory, and the mothers of the nation will henceforth take their part in electing the mother of Parliaments. England will range herself with Finland and other enlightened countries which have already admitted women to the labours, honours and responsibilities of the polling-booth. In the early hours of this February morning a candle has been lighted—"

"The fire was caused by an over-heated flue, and not by Suffragettes, sir," interposed the butler.

At that moment a scurry of hoofs and a clanging of bells, together with the hoot of a motor-horn, was heard above the roaring of the flames.

"The fire-brigade!" exclaimed the canon.

"The fire-brigade and my husband," said Mrs. Gramplain in her dull level voice; "it will all begin over again now, the old life, the old unsatisfying weariness, the old monotony; nothing will be changed."

"Except the East wing," said the canon gently.

The Easter Egg

It was distinctly hard lines for Lady Barbara, who came of good fighting stock, and was one of the bravest women of her generation, that her son should be so undisguisedly a coward. Whatever good qualities Lester Slaggby may have possessed, and he was in some respects charming, courage could certainly never be imputed to him. As a child he had suffered from childish timidity, as a boy from unboyish funk, and as a youth he had exchanged unreasoning fears for others which were more formidable from the fact of having a carefully-thought-out basis. He was frankly afraid of animals, nervous with firearms, and never crossed the Channel without mentally comparing the numerical proportion of life belts to passengers.

On horseback he seemed to require as many hands as a Hindu god, at least four for clutching the reins, and two more for patting the horse soothingly on the neck. Lady Barbara no longer pretended not to see her son's prevailing weakness; with her usual courage she faced the knowledge of it squarely, and, mother-like, loved him none the less.

Continental travel, anywhere away from the great tourist tracks, was a favoured hobby with Lady Barbara, and Lester joined her as often as possible. Eastertide usually found her at Knobaltheim, an upland township in one of those small princedoms that make inconspicuous freckles on the map of Central Europe.

A long-standing acquaintanceship with the reigning family made her a personage of due importance in the eyes of her old friend the *burgomaster*, and she was anxiously consulted by that worthy on the momentous occasion when the prince made known his intention of coming in person to open a sanatorium outside the town. All the usual items in a programme of welcome, some of them fatuous and commonplace, others quaint and charming, had been arranged for, but the *burgomaster* hoped that the resourceful English lady might have something new and tasteful to suggest in the way of loyal greeting.

The prince was known to the outside world, if at all, as an old-fashioned reactionary, combating modern progress, as it were, with a wooden sword; to his own people he was known as a kindly old gentleman with a certain endearing stateliness which had nothing of standoffishness about it. Knobaltheim was anxious to do its best. Lady Barbara discussed the matter with Lester and one or two acquaintances in her little hotel, but ideas were difficult to come by.

"Might I suggest something to the *gnädige Frau?*" asked a sallow high-cheek-boned lady to whom the Englishwoman had spoken once or twice, and whom she had set down in her mind as probably a Southern Slav.

"Might I suggest something for the Reception *Fest?*" she went on, with a certain shy eagerness. "Our little child here, our baby, we will dress him in little white coat, with small wings, as an Easter angel, and he will carry a large white Easter egg, and inside shall be a basket of plover eggs, of which the prince is so fond, and he shall give it to His Highness as Easter offering. It is so pretty an idea; we have seen it done once in Styria."

Lady Barbara looked dubiously at the proposed Easter angel, a fair, wooden-faced child of about four years old. She had noticed it the day before in the hotel, and wondered rather how such a tow-headed child could belong to such a dark-visaged couple as the woman and her husband; probably, she thought, an adopted baby, especially as the couple were not young.

"Of course, *gnädige Frau* will escort the little child up to the prince," pursued the woman; "but he will be quite good, and do as he is told."

"We haf some pluffers' eggs shall come fresh from Wien," said the husband.

The small child and Lady Barbara seemed equally unenthusiastic about the pretty idea; Lester was openly discouraging, but when the *burgomaster* heard of it, he was enchanted. The combination of sentiment and plovers' eggs appealed strongly to his Teutonic mind.

On the eventful day the Easter angel, really quite prettily and quaintly dressed, was a centre of kindly interest to the gala crowd marshalled to receive His Highness. The mother was unobtrusive and less fussy than most parents would have been under the circumstances, merely stipulating that she should place the Easter egg herself in the arms that had been carefully schooled how to hold the precious burden. Then Lady Barbara moved forward, the child marching stolidly and with grim determination at her side. It had been promised cakes and sweeties galore if it gave the egg well and truly to the kind old gentleman who was waiting to receive it. Lester had tried to convey to it privately that horrible smackings would attend any failure in its share of the proceedings, but it is doubtful if his German caused more than an immediate distress.

Lady Barbara had thoughtfully provided herself with an emergency supply of chocolate sweetmeats; children may sometimes be timeservers, but they do not encourage long accounts. As they approached nearer to the princely dais Lady Barbara stood discreetly aside, and the stolid-faced infant walked forward alone, with staggering but steadfast gait. encouraged by a murmur of elderly approval. Lester, standing in the front row of the onlookers, turned to scan the crowd for the beaming faces of the happy parents. In a side-road which led to the railway station he saw a cab; entering the cab with every appearance of furtive haste were the dark-visaged couple who had been so plausibly eager for the "pretty idea." The sharpened instinct of cowardice lit up the situation to him in one swift flash.

The blood roared and surged to his head as though thousands of floodgates had been opened in his veins and arteries, and his brain was the common sluice in which all the torrents met. He saw nothing but a blur around him. Then the blood ebbed away in quick waves, till his very heart seemed drained and empty, and he stood nervelessly, helplessly, dumbly watching the child, bearing its accursed burden with slow, relentless steps nearer and nearer to the group that waited sheeplike to receive him. A fascinated curiosity compelled Lester to turn his head towards the fugitives; the cab had started at hot pace in the direction of the station.

The next moment Lester was running, running faster than any of those present had ever seen a man run, and—he was not running away. For that stray fraction of his life some unwonted impulse beset him, some hint of the stock he came from, and he ran unflinchingly towards danger. He stooped and clutched at the Easter egg as one tries to scoop up the ball in Rugby football. What he meant to do with it he had not considered, the thing was to get it. But the child had been promised cakes and sweetmeats if it safely gave the egg into the hands of the kindly old gentleman; it uttered no scream but it held to its charge with limpet grip. Lester sank to his knees, tugging savagely at the tightly clasped burden, and angry cries rose from the scandalized onlookers.

A questioning, threatening ring formed round him, then shrank back in recoil as he shrieked out one hideous word. Lady Barbara heard the word and saw the crowd race away like scattered sheep, saw the prince forcibly hustled away by his attendants; also, she saw her son lying prone in an agony of overmastering terror, his spasm of daring shattered by the child's unexpected resistance, still clutching frantically, as though for safety, at that white-satin *gewgaw*, unable to crawl even from its deadly neighbourhood, able only to scream and scream and scream. In her brain she was dimly conscious of balancing, or striving to balance, the abject shame which had him now in thrall against the one compelling act of courage which had flung him grandly and madly on to the point of danger.

It was only for the fraction of a minute that she stood watching the two entangled figures, the infant with its woodenly obstinate face and body tense with dogged resistance, and the boy limp and already nearly dead with a terror that almost stifled his screams; and over them the long gala streamers flapping gaily in the sunshine. She never forgot the scene; but then, it was the last she ever saw.

Lady Barbara carries her scarred face with its sightless eyes as bravely as ever in the world, but at Eastertide her friends are careful to keep from her ears any mention of the children's Easter symbol.

The Hedgehog

A "Mixed Double" of young people were contesting a game of lawn tennis at the rectory garden party; for the past five-and-twenty years at least mixed doubles of young people had done exactly the same thing on exactly the same spot at about the same time of year. The young people changed and made way for others in the course of time, but very little else seemed to alter. The present players were sufficiently conscious of the social nature of the occasion to be concerned about their clothes and appearance, and sufficiently sport-loving to be keen on the game. Both their efforts and their appearance came under the fourfold scrutiny of a quartet of ladies sitting as official spectators on a bench immediately commanding the court.

It was one of the accepted conditions of the rectory garden party that four ladies, who usually knew very little about tennis and a great deal about the players, should sit at that particular spot and watch the game. It had also come to be almost a tradition that two ladies should be amiable, and that the other two should be Mrs. Dole and Mrs. Hatch-Mallard.

"What a singularly unbecoming way Eva Jonelet has taken to doing her hair in," said Mrs. Hatch-Mallard; "it's ugly hair at the best of times, but she needn't make it look ridiculous as well. Someone ought to tell her."

Eva Jonelet's hair might have escaped Mrs. Hatch-Mallard's condemnation if she could have forgotten the more glaring fact that Eva was Mrs. Dole's favourite niece. It would, perhaps, have been a more comfortable arrangement if Mrs. Hatch-Mallard and Mrs. Dole could have been asked to the rectory on separate occasions, but there was only one garden party in the course of the year, and neither lady could have been omitted from the list of invitations without hopelessly wrecking the social peace of the parish.

"How pretty the yew trees look at this time of year," interposed a lady with a soft, silvery voice that suggested a chinchilla muff painted by Whistler.

"What do you mean by this time of year?" demanded Mrs. Hatch-Mallard. "Yew trees look beautiful at all times of the year. That is their great charm."

"Yew trees never look anything but hideous under any circumstances or at any time of year," said Mrs. Dole, with the slow, emphatic relish of one who contradicts for the pleasure of the thing. "They are only fit for graveyards and cemeteries."

Mrs. Hatch-Mallard gave a sardonic snort, which, being translated, meant that there were some people who were better fitted for cemeteries than for garden parties.

"What is the score, please?" asked the lady with the chinchilla voice.

The desired information was given her by a young gentleman in spotless white flannels, whose general toilet effect suggested solicitude rather than anxiety.

"What an odious young cub Bertie Dykson has become!" pronounced Mrs. Dole, remembering suddenly that Bertie was a favourite with Mrs. Hatch-Mallard. "The young men of today are not what they used to be twenty years ago."

"Of course not," said Mrs. Hatch-Mallard; "twenty years ago Bertie Dykson was just two years old, and you must expect some difference in appearance and manner and conversation between those two periods."

"Do you know," said Mrs. Dole, confidentially, "I shouldn't be surprised if that was intended to be clever."

"Have you anyone interesting coming to stay with you, Mrs. Norbury?" asked the chinchilla voice, hastily; "you generally have a house party at this time of year."

"I've got a most interesting woman coming," said Mrs. Norbury, who had been mutely struggling for some chance to turn the conversation into a safe channel; "an old acquaintance of mine, Ada Bleek—"

"What an ugly name," said Mrs. Hatch-Mallard.

"She's descended from the de la Bliques, an old Huguenot family of Touraine, you know."

"There weren't any Huguenots in Touraine," said Mrs. Hatch-Mallard, who thought she might safely dispute any fact that was three hundred years old.

"Well, anyhow, she's coming to stay with me," continued Mrs. Norbury, bringing her story quickly down to the present day, "she arrives this evening, and she's highly clairvoyant, a seventh daughter of a seventh daughter, you now, and all that sort of thing."

"How very interesting," said the chinchilla voice; "Exwood is just the right place for her to come to, isn't it? There are supposed to be several ghosts there."

"That is why she was so anxious to come," said Mrs. Norbury; "she put off another engagement in order to accept my invitation. She's had visions and dreams, and all those sort of things, that have come true in a most marvellous manner, but she's never actually seen a ghost, and she's longing to have that experience. She belongs to that Research Society, you know."

"I expect she'll see the unhappy Lady Cullumpton, the most famous of all the Exwood ghosts," said Mrs. Dole; "my ancestor, you know, Sir Gervase Cullumpton, murdered his young bride in a fit of jealousy while they were on a visit to Exwood. He strangled her in the stables with a stirrup leather, just after they had come in from riding, and she is seen sometimes at dusk going about the lawns and the stable yard, in a long green habit, moaning and trying to get the thong from round her throat. I shall be most interested to hear if your friend sees—"

"I don't know why she should be expected to see a trashy, traditional apparition like the so-called Cullumpton ghost, that is only vouched for by housemaids and tipsy stable-boys, when my uncle, who was the owner of Exwood, committed suicide there under the most tragical circumstances, and most certainly haunts the place."

"Mrs. Hatch-Mallard has evidently never read *Popple's County History*," said Mrs. Dole icily, "or she would know that the Cullumpton ghost has a wealth of evidence behind it—"

"Oh, Popple!" exclaimed Mrs. Hatch-Mallard scornfully; "any rubbishy old story is good enough for him. Popple, indeed! Now my uncle's ghost was seen by a Rural Dean, who was also a Justice of the Peace. I should think that would be good enough testimony for anyone. Mrs. Norbury, I shall take it as a deliberate personal affront if your clairvoyant friend sees any other ghost except that of my uncle."

"I daresay she won't see anything at all; she never has yet, you know," said Mrs. Norbury hopefully.

"It was a most unfortunate topic for me to have broached," she lamented afterwards to the owner of the chinchilla voice; "Exwood belongs to Mrs. Hatch-Mallard, and we've only got it on a short lease. A nephew of hers has been wanting to live there for some time, and if we offend her in any way, she'll refuse to renew the lease. I sometimes think these garden-parties are a mistake."

The Norburys played bridge for the next three nights till nearly one o'clock; they did not care for the game, but it reduced the time at their guest's disposal for undesirable ghostly visitations.

"Miss Bleek is not likely to be in a frame of mind to see ghosts," said Hugo Norbury, "if she goes to bed with her brain awhirl with royal spades and no trumps and grand slams."

"I've talked to her for hours about Mrs. Hatch-Mallard's uncle," said his wife, "and pointed out the exact spot where he killed himself, and invented all sorts of impressive details, and I've found an old portrait of Lord John Russell and put it in her room, and told her that it's supposed to be a picture of the uncle in middle age. If Ada does see a ghost at all it certainly ought to be old Hatch-Mallard's. At any rate, we've done our best."

The precautions were in vain. On the third morning of her stay Ada Bleek came down late to breakfast, her eyes looking very tired, but ablaze with excitement, her hair done anyhow, and a large brown volume hugged under her arm.

"At last, I've seen something supernatural!" she exclaimed, and gave Mrs. Norbury a fervent kiss, as though in gratitude for the opportunity afforded her.

"A ghost!" cried Mrs. Norbury, "not really!"

"Really and unmistakably!"

"Was it an oldish man in the dress of about fifty years ago?" asked Mrs. Norbury hopefully.

"Nothing of the sort," said Ada; "it was a white hedgehog."

"A white hedgehog!" exclaimed both the Norburys, in tones of disconcerted astonishment.

"A huge white hedgehog with baleful yellow eyes," said Ada; "I was lying half asleep in bed when suddenly I felt a sensation as of something sinister and unaccountable passing through the room. I sat up and looked round, and there, under the window, I saw an evil, creeping thing, a sort of monstrous hedgehog, of a dirty white colour, with black, loathsome claws that clicked and scraped along the floor, and narrow, yellow eyes of indescribable evil. It slithered along for a yard or two, always looking at me with its cruel, hideous eyes, then, when it reached the second window, which was open it clambered up the sill and vanished. I got up at once and went to the window; there wasn't a sign of it anywhere. Of course, I knew it must be something from another world, but it was not till I turned up Popple's chapter on local traditions that I realised what I had seen."

She turned eagerly to the large brown volume and read: "'Nicholas Herison, an old miser, was hung at Batchford in 1763 for the murder of a farm lad who had accidentally discovered his secret hoard. His ghost is supposed to traverse the countryside, appearing sometimes as a white owl, sometimes as a huge white hedgehog."

"I expect you read the Popple story overnight, and that made you *think* you saw a hedgehog when you were only half awake," said Mrs. Norbury, hazarding a conjecture that probably came very near the truth.

Ada scouted the possibility of such a solution of her apparition.

"This must be hushed up," said Mrs. Norbury quickly; "the servants—"

"Hushed up!" exclaimed Ada, indignantly; "I'm writing a long report on it for the Research Society."

It was then that Hugo Norbury, who is not naturally a man of brilliant resource, had one of the really useful inspirations of his life.

"It was very wicked of us, Miss Bleek," he said, "but it would be a shame to let it go further. That white hedgehog is an old joke of ours; stuffed albino hedgehog, you know, that my father brought home from Jamaica, where they grow to enormous size. We hide it in the room with a string on it, run one end of the string through the window; then we pull if from below and it comes scraping along the floor, just as you've described, and finally jerks out of the window. Taken in heaps of people; they all read up Popple and think it's old Harry Nicholson's ghost; we always stop them from writing to the papers about it, though. That would be carrying matters too far."

Mrs. Hatch-Mallard renewed the lease in due course, but Ada Bleek has never renewed her friendship.

The Image of the Lost Soul

There were a number of carved stone figures placed at intervals along the parapets of the old cathedral; some of them represented angels, others kings and bishops, and nearly all were in attitudes of pious exaltation and composure. But one figure, low down on the cold north side of the building, had neither crown, mitre, not nimbus, and its face was hard and bitter and downcast; it must be a demon, declared the fat blue pigeons that roosted and sunned themselves all day on the ledges of the parapet; but the old belfry jackdaw, who was an authority on ecclesiastical architecture, said it was a lost soul. And there the matter rested.

One autumn day there fluttered on to the cathedral roof a slender, sweet-voiced bird that had wandered away from the bare fields and thinning hedgerows in search of a winter roosting-place. It tried to rest its tired feet under the shade of a great angel-wing or to nestle in the sculptured folds of a kingly robe, but the fat pigeons hustled it away from wherever it settled, and the noisy sparrow-folk drove it off the ledges. No respectable bird sang with so much feeling, they cheeped one to another, and the wanderer had to move on.

Only the effigy of the Lost Soul offered a place of refuge. The pigeons did not consider it safe to perch on a projection that leaned so much out of the perpendicular, and was, besides, too much in the shadow. The figure did not cross its hands in the pious attitude of the other graven dignitaries, but its arms were folded as in defiance and their angle made a snug resting-place for the little bird. Every evening it crept trustfully into its corner against the stone breast of the image, and the darkling eyes seemed to keep watch over its slumbers. The lonely bird grew to love its lonely protector, and during the day it would sit from time to time on some rain-shoot or other abutment and trill forth its sweetest music in grateful thanks for its nightly shelter.

71

And, it may have been the work of wind and weather, or some other influence, but the wild drawn face seemed gradually to lose some of its hardness and unhappiness. Every day, through the long monotonous hours, the song of his little guest would come up in snatches to the lonely watcher, and at evening, when the vesper-bell was ringing and the great grey bats slid out of their hiding-places in the belfry roof, the bright-eyed bird would return, twitter a few sleepy notes, and nestle into the arms that were waiting for him. Those were happy days for the Dark Image. Only the great bell of the cathedral rang out daily its mocking message, "After joy . . . sorrow."

The folk in the verger's lodge noticed a little brown bird flitting about the cathedral precincts, and admired its beautiful singing. "But it is a pity," said they, "that all that warbling should be lost and wasted far out of hearing up on the parapet." They were poor, but they understood the principles of political economy. So, they caught the bird and put it in a little wicker cage outside the lodge door.

That night the little songster was missing from its accustomed haunt, and the Dark Image knew more than ever the bitterness of loneliness. Perhaps his little friend had been killed by a prowling cat or hurt by a stone. Perhaps . . . perhaps he had flown elsewhere. But when morning came there floated up to him, through the noise and bustle of the cathedral world, a faint heart-aching message from the prisoner in the wicker cage far below. And every day, at high noon, when the fat pigeons were stupefied into silence after their midday meal and the sparrows were washing themselves in the street-puddles, the song of the little bird came up to the parapets—a song of hunger and longing and hopelessness, a cry that could never be answered. The pigeons remarked, between mealtimes, that the figure leaned forward more than ever out of the perpendicular.

One day no song came up from the little wicker cage. It was the coldest day of the winter, and the pigeons and sparrows on the cathedral roof looked anxiously on all sides for the scraps of food which they were dependent on in hard weather.

"Have the lodge-folk thrown out anything on to the dust-heap?" inquired one pigeon of another which was peering over the edge of the north parapet.

"Only a little dead bird," was the answer.

There was a crackling sound in the night on the cathedral roof and a noise as of falling masonry. The belfry jackdaw said the frost was affecting the fabric, and as he had experienced many frosts it must have been so. In the morning it was seen that the Figure of the Lost Soul had toppled from its cornice and lay now in a broken mass on the dust-heap outside the verger's lodge.

"It is just as well," cooed the fat pigeons, after they had peered at the matter for some minutes; "now we shall have a nice angel put up there. Certainly, they will put an angel there."

"After joy . . . sorrow," rang out the great bell.

The Infernal Parliament

In an age when it has become increasingly difficult to accomplish anything new or original, Bavton Bidderdale interested his generation by dying of a new disease. 'We always knew he would do something remarkable one of these days,' observed his aunts; 'he has justified our belief in him.' But there is a section of humanity ever ready to refuse recognition to meritorious achievement, and a large and influential school of doctors asserted their belief that Bidderdale was not really dead. The funeral arrangements had to be held over until the matter was settled one way or the other, and the aunts went provisionally into half-mourning.

Meanwhile, Bidderdale remained in Hell as a guest pending his reception on a more regular footing. 'If you are not really supposed to be dead,' said the authorities of that region, 'we don't want to seem in an indecent hurry to grab you. The theory that Hell is in serious need of population is a thing of the past. Why, to take your family alone, there are any number of Bidderdales on our books, as you may discover later. It is part of our system that relations should be encouraged to live together down here. From observations made in another world we have abundant evidence that it promotes the ends we have in view. However, while you are a guest, we should like you to be treated with every consideration and be shown anything that specially interests you. Of course, you would like to see our Parliament?'

'Have you a Parliament in Hell?' asked Bidderdale in some surprise.

'Only quite recently. Of course, we've always had chaos, but not under parliamentary rules. Now, however, that Parliaments are becoming the fashion, in Turkey and Persia, and I suppose before long in Afghanistan and China, it seemed rather ostentatious to stand outside the movement. That young Fiend just going by is the member for East Brimstone; he'll delighted to show you over the institution.'

'You will just be in time to hear the opening of a debate,' said the member, as he led Bidderdale through a spacious outer lobby, decorated with frescoes representing the fall of man, the discovery of gold, the invention of playing cards, and other traditionally appropriate subjects. 'The member for Nether Furnace is proposing a motion "that this House do arrogantly protest to the legislatures of earthly countries against the wrongful and injurious misuse of the word 'fiendish,' in application to purely human misdemeanours, a misuse tending to create a false and detrimental impression concerning the Infernal Regions."'

A feature of the Parliament Chamber itself was its enormous size. The space allotted to members was small and very sparsely occupied, but the public galleries stretched away tier on tier as far as the eye could reach, and were packed to their utmost capacity.

'There seems to be a very great public interest in the debate,' exclaimed Bidderdale.

'Members are excused from attending the debates if they so desire,' the Fiend proceeded to explain; 'it is one of their most highly valued privileges. On the other hand, constituents are compelled to listen throughout to all the speeches. After all, you must remember, we are in Hell.'

Bidderdale repressed a shudder and turned his attention to the debate.

'Nothing,' the Fiend-Orator was observing, 'is more deplorable among the cultured races of the present day than the tendency to identify fiendhood, in the most sweeping fashion, with all manner of disreputable excesses, excesses which can only be alleged against us on the merest legendary evidence. Vices which are exclusively or predominatingly human are unblushingly described as inhuman, and, what is even more contemptible and ungenerous, as fiendish.

'If one investigates such statements as "inhuman treatment of pit ponies" or "fiendish cruelties in the Congo," so frequently to be heard in our brother Parliaments on earth, one finds accumulative and indisputable evidence that it is the human treatment of pit ponies and Congo natives that is really in question, and that no authenticated case of fiendish agency in these atrocities can be substantiated. It is, perhaps, a minor matter for complaint,' continued the orator, 'that the human race frequently pays us the doubtful compliment of describing as "devilish funny" jokes which are neither funny nor devilish.'

The orator paused, and an oppressive silence reigned over the vast chamber.

'What is happening?' whispered Bidderdale.

'Five minutes Hush,' explained his guide; 'it is a sign that the speaker was listened to in silent approval, which is the highest mark of appreciation that can be bestowed in Pandemonium. Let's come into the smoking-room.'

'Will the motion be carried?' asked Bidderdale, wondering inwardly how Sir Edward Grey would treat the protest if it reached the British Parliament, an *entente* with the Infernal Regions opened up a fascinating *vista*, in which the Foreign Secretary's imagination might hopelessly lose itself.

'Carried? Of course not,' said the Fiend; 'in the Infernal Parliament all motions are necessarily lost.'

'In earthly Parliaments nowadays nearly everything is found,' said Bidderdale, 'including salaries and travelling expenses.'

He felt that at any rate he was probably the first member of his family to make a joke in Hell.

'By the way,' he added, 'talking of earthly Parliaments, have you got the Party system down here?'

'In Hell? Impossible. You see we have no system of rewards. We have specialised so thoroughly on punishments that the other branch has been entirely neglected. And besides, government by delusion, as you practise it in your Parliament, would be unworkable here. I should be the last person to say anything against temptation, naturally, but we have a proverb down here "in baiting a mousetrap with cheese, always leave room for the mouse." Such a party-cry, for instance, as your "ninepence for fourpence" would be absolutely inoperative; it not only leaves no room for the mouse, it leaves no room for the imagination. You have a saying in your country, I believe, "there's no fool like a damned fool"; all the fools down here are, necessarily, damned, but—you wouldn't get them to nibble at ninepence for fourpence.'

'Couldn't they be scolded and lectured into believing it, as a sort of moral and intellectual duty?' asked Bidderdale.

'We haven't all your facilities,' said the Fiend; 'we've nothing down here that exactly corresponds to the Master of Elibank.'

At this moment Bidderdale's attention was caught by an item on a loose sheet of agenda paper: 'Vote on account of special Hells.'

'Ah,' he said, 'I've often heard the expression "there is a special Hell reserved for such-and-such a type of person." Do tell me about them.'

'I'll show you one in course of preparation,' said the Fiend, leading him down the corridor. 'This one is designed to accommodate one of the leading playwrights of your nation. You may observe scores of imps engaged in pasting notices of modern British plays into a huge press-cutting book, each under the name of the author, alphabetically arranged. The book will contain nearly half a million notices, I suppose, and it will form the sole literature supplied to this specially doomed individual.'

Bidderdale was not altogether impressed.

'Some dramatic authors wouldn't so very much mind spending eternity poring over a book of contemporary press-cuttings,' he observed.

The Fiend, laughing unpleasantly, lowered his voice.

'The letter "S" is missing.'

For the first time Bidderdale realised that he was in Hell.

The Interlopers

In a forest of mixed growth somewhere on the eastern spurs of the Carpathians, a man stood one winter night watching and listening, as though he waited for some beast of the woods to come within the range of his vision, and, later, of his rifle. But the game for whose presence he kept so keen an outlook was none that figured in the sportsman's calendar as lawful and proper for the chase; Ulrich von Gradwitz patrolled the dark forest in quest of a human enemy.

The forest lands of Gradwitz were of wide extent and well stocked with game; the narrow strip of precipitous woodland that lay on its outskirt was not remarkable for the game it harboured or the shooting it afforded, but it was the most jealously guarded of all its owner's territorial possessions. A famous law suit, in the days of his grandfather, had wrested it from the illegal possession of a neighbouring family of petty landowners; the dispossessed party had never acquiesced in the judgment of the Courts, and a long series of poaching affrays and similar scandals had embittered the relationships between the families for three generations. The neighbour feud had grown into a personal one since Ulrich had come to be head of his family; if there was a man in the world whom he detested and wished ill to it was Georg Znaeym, the inheritor of the quarrel and the tireless game-snatcher and raider of the disputed border-forest.

The feud might, perhaps, have died down or been compromised if the personal ill-will of the two men had not stood in the way; as boys they had thirsted for one another's blood, as men each prayed that misfortune might fall on the other, and this wind-scourged winter night Ulrich had banded together his foresters to watch the dark forest, not in quest of four-footed quarry, but to keep a look-out for the prowling thieves whom he suspected of being afoot from across the land boundary. The roebuck, which usually kept in the sheltered hollows during a storm-wind, were running like driven things tonight, and there was movement and unrest among the creatures that were wont to sleep through the dark hours. Assuredly there was a disturbing element in the forest, and Ulrich could guess the quarter from whence it came.

He strayed away by himself from the watchers whom he had placed in ambush on the crest of the hill, and wandered far down the steep slopes amid the wild tangle of undergrowth, peering through the tree trunks and listening through the whistling and skirling of the wind and the restless beating of the branches for sight and sound of the marauders. If only on this wild night, in this dark, lone spot, he might come across Georg Znaeym, man to man, with none to witness—that was the wish that was uppermost in his thoughts. And as he stepped round the trunk of a huge beech, he came face to face with the man he sought.

The two enemies stood glaring at one another for a long silent moment. Each had a rifle in his hand, each had hate in his heart and murder uppermost in his mind. The chance had come to give full play to the passions of a lifetime. But a man who has been brought up under the code of a restraining civilisation cannot easily nerve himself to shoot down his neighbour in cold blood and without word spoken, except for an offence against his hearth and honour. And before the moment of hesitation had given way to action a deed of Nature's own violence overwhelmed them both.

A fierce shriek of the storm had been answered by a splitting crash over their heads, and ere they could leap aside a mass of falling beech tree had thundered down on them. Ulrich von Gradwitz found himself stretched on the ground, one arm numb beneath him and the other held almost as helplessly in a tight tangle of forked branches, while both legs were pinned beneath the fallen mass. His heavy shooting-boots had saved his feet from being crushed to pieces, but if his fractures were not as serious as they might have been, at least it was evident that he could not move from his present position till someone came to release him.

The descending twig had slashed the skin of his face, and he had to wink away some drops of blood from his eyelashes before he could take in a general view of the disaster. At his side, so near that under ordinary circumstances he could almost have touched him, lay Georg Znaeym, alive and struggling, but obviously as helplessly pinioned down as himself. All round them lay a thick-strewn wreckage of splintered branches and broken twigs.

Relief at being alive and exasperation at his captive plight brought a strange medley of pious thank-offerings and sharp curses to Ulrich's lips. Georg, who was early blinded with the blood which trickled across his eyes, stopped his struggling for a moment to listen, and then gave a short, snarling laugh.

"So, you're not killed, as you ought to be, but you're caught, any-way," he cried; "caught fast. Ho, what a jest, Ulrich von Gradwitz snared in his stolen forest. There's real justice for you!"

And he laughed again, mockingly and savagely.

"I'm caught in my own forest-land," retorted Ulrich. "When my men come to release us you will wish, perhaps, that you were in a bet-ter plight than caught poaching on a neighbour's land, shame on you."

Georg was silent for a moment; then he answered quietly:

"Are you sure that your men will find much to release? I have men, too, in the forest tonight, close behind me, and *they* will be here first and do the releasing. When they drag me out from under these damned branches it won't need much clumsiness on their part to roll this mass of trunk right over on the top of you. Your men will find you dead under a fallen beech tree. For form's sake I shall send my condolences to your family."

"It is a useful hint," said Ulrich fiercely. "My men had orders to follow in ten minutes time, seven of which must have gone by already, and when they get me out—I will remember the hint. Only as you will have met your death poaching on my lands, I don't think I can decently send any message of condolence to your family."

"Good," snarled Georg, "good. We fight this quarrel out to the death, you and I and our foresters, with no cursed interlopers to come between us. Death and damnation to you, Ulrich von Gradwitz."

"The same to you, Georg Znaeym, forest-thief, game-snatcher."

Both men spoke with the bitterness of possible defeat before them, for each knew that it might be long before his men would seek him out or find him; it was a bare matter of chance which party would arrive first on the scene.

Both had now given up the useless struggle to free themselves from the mass of wood that held them down; Ulrich limited his en-deavours to an effort to bring his one partially free arm near enough to his outer coat-pocket to draw out his wine-flask. Even when he had accomplished that operation it was long before he could manage the unscrewing of the stopper or get any of the liquid down his throat.

But what a Heaven-sent draught it seemed! It was an open winter, and little snow had fallen as yet, hence the captives suffered less from the cold than might have been the case at that season of the year; nevertheless, the wine was warming and reviving to the wounded man, and he looked across with something like a throb of pity to where his enemy lay, just keeping the groans of pain and weariness from crossing his lips.

"Could you reach this flask if I threw it over to you?" asked Ulrich suddenly; "there is good wine in it, and one may as well be as comfortable as one can. Let us drink, even if tonight one of us dies."

"No, I can scarcely see anything; there is so much blood caked round my eyes," said Georg, "and in any case I don't drink wine with an enemy."

Ulrich was silent for a few minutes, and lay listening to the weary screeching of the wind. An idea was slowly forming and growing in his brain, an idea that gained strength every time that he looked across at the man who was fighting so grimly against pain and exhaustion. In the pain and languor that Ulrich himself was feeling the old fierce hatred seemed to be dying down.

"Neighbour," he said presently, "do as you please if your men come first. It was a fair compact. But as for me, I've changed my mind. If my men are the first to come you shall be the first to be helped, as though you were my guest. We have quarrelled like devils all our lives over this stupid strip of forest, where the trees can't even stand upright in a breath of wind. Lying here tonight thinking I've come to think we've been rather fools; there are better things in life than getting the better of a boundary dispute. Neighbour, if you will help me to bury the old quarrel I—I will ask you to be my friend."

Georg Znaeym was silent for so long that Ulrich thought, perhaps, he had fainted with the pain of his injuries. Then he spoke slowly and in jerks.

"How the whole region would stare and gabble if we rode into the market-square together. No one living can remember seeing a Znaeym and a von Gradwitz talking to one another in friendship. And what peace there would be among the forester folk if we ended our feud tonight. And if we choose to make peace among our people there is none other to interfere, no interlopers from outside . . . You would come and keep the Sylvester night beneath my roof, and I would come and feast on some high day at your castle . . . I would never fire a shot on your land, save when you invited me as a guest;

and you should come and shoot with me down in the marshes where the wildfowl are. In all the countryside there are none that could hinder if we willed to make peace. I never thought to have wanted to do other than hate you all my life, but I think I have changed my mind about things too, this last half-hour. And you offered me your wine-flask . . . Ulrich von Gradwitz, I will be your friend."

For a space both men were silent, turning over in their minds the wonderful changes that this dramatic reconciliation would bring about. In the cold, gloomy forest, with the wind tearing in fitful gusts through the naked branches and whistling round the tree-trunks, they lay and waited for the help that would now bring release and succour to both parties. And each prayed a private prayer that his men might be the first to arrive, so that he might be the first to show honourable attention to the enemy that had become a friend.

Presently, as the wind dropped for a moment, Ulrich broke silence.

"Let's shout for help," he said; he said; "in this lull our voices may carry a little way."

"They won't carry far through the trees and undergrowth," said Georg, "but we can try. Together, then."

The two raised their voices in a prolonged hunting call.

"Together again," said Ulrich a few minutes later, after listening in vain for an answering halloo.

"I heard nothing but the pestilential wind," said Georg hoarsely.

There was silence again for some minutes, and then Ulrich gave a joyful cry.

"I can see figures coming through the wood. They are following in the way I came down the hillside."

Both men raised their voices in as loud a shout as they could muster.

"They hear us! They've stopped. Now they see us. They're running down the hill towards us," cried Ulrich.

"How many of them are there?" asked Georg.

"I can't see distinctly," said Ulrich; "nine or ten,"

"Then they are yours," said Georg; "I had only seven out with me."

"They are making all the speed they can, brave lads," said Ulrich gladly.

"Are they your men?" asked Georg. "Are they your men?" he repeated impatiently as Ulrich did not answer.

"No," said Ulrich with a laugh, the idiotic chattering laugh of a man unstrung with hideous fear.

"Who are they?" asked Georg quickly, straining his eyes to see what the other would gladly not have seen.

"*Wolves.*"

The Lost Sanjak

The prison chaplain entered the condemned's cell for the last time, to give such consolation as he might.

"The only consolation I crave for," said the condemned, "is to tell my story in its entirety to someone who will at least give it a respectful hearing."

"We must not be too long over it," said the chaplain, looking at his watch.

The condemned repressed a shiver and commenced.

"Most people will be of opinion that I am paying the penalty of my own violent deeds. In reality I am a victim to a lack of specialisation in my education and character."

"Lack of specialisation!" said the chaplain.

"Yes. If I had been known as one of the few men in England familiar with the *fauna* of the Outer Hebrides, or able to repeat *stanzas* of Camoëns' poetry in, the original, I should have had no difficulty in proving my identity in the crisis when my identity became a matter of life and death for me. But my education was merely a moderately good one, and my temperament was of the general order that avoids specialization. I know a little in a general way about gardening and history and old masters, but I could never tell you off-hand whether 'Stella van der Loopen' was a chrysanthemum or a heroine of the American War of Independence, or something by Romney in the Louvre."

The chaplain shifted uneasily in his seat. Now that the alternatives had been suggested they all seemed dreadfully possible.

"I fell in love, or thought I did, with the local doctor's wife," continued the condemned. "Why I should have done so, I cannot say, for I do not remember that she possessed any particular attractions of mind or body. On looking back at past events, it seems to me that she must have been distinctly ordinary, but I suppose the doctor had fallen in love with her once, and what man has done man can do. She appeared to be pleased with the attentions which I paid her, and to that extent I suppose I might say she encouraged me, but I think she was honestly unaware that I meant anything more than a little neighbourly interest. When one is face to face with Death one wishes to be just."

The chaplain murmured approval. "At any rate, she was genuinely horrified when I took advantage of the doctor's absence one evening to declare what I believed to be my passion. She begged me to pass out of her life, and I could scarcely do otherwise than agree, though I hadn't the dimmest idea of how it was to be done. In novels and plays I knew it was a regular occurrence, and if you mistook a lady's sentiments or intentions you went off to India and did things on the frontier as a matter of course. As I stumbled along the doctor's carriage drive I had no very clear idea as to what my line of action was to be, but I had a vague feeling that I must look at the *Times* Atlas before going to bed. Then, on the dark and lonely highway, I came suddenly on a dead body."

The chaplain's interest in the story visibly quickened.

"Judging by the clothes it wore the corpse was that of a Salvation Army captain. Some shocking accident seemed to have struck him down, and the head was crushed and battered out of all human semblance. Probably, I thought, a motorcar fatality; and then, with a sudden overmastering insistence came another thought, that here was a remarkable opportunity for losing my identity and passing out of the life of the doctor's wife for ever. No tiresome and risky voyage to distant lands, but a mere exchange of clothes and identity with the unknown victim of an unwitnessed accident. With considerable difficulty I undressed the corpse, and clothed it anew in my own garments. Anyone who has valeted a dead Salvation Army captain in an uncertain light will appreciate the difficulty.

"With the idea, presumably, of inducing the doctor's wife to leave her husband's roof-tree for some habitation which would be run at my expense, I had crammed my pockets with a store of banknotes, which represented a good deal of my immediate worldly wealth. When, therefore, I stole away into the world in the guise of a nameless Salvationist, I was not without resources which would easily support so humble a role for a considerable period. I tramped to a neighbouring market-town, and, late as the hour was, the production of a few shillings procured me supper and a night's lodging in a cheap coffee-house. The next day I started forth on an aimless course of wandering from one small town to another. I was already somewhat disgusted with the upshot. of my sudden freak; in a few hours' time I was considerably more so.

"In the contents-bill of a local news sheet I read the announcement of my own murder at the hands of some person unknown; on buying a copy of the paper for a detailed account of the tragedy, which at first had aroused in me a certain grim amusement, I found that the deed was ascribed to a wandering Salvationist of doubtful antecedents, who had been seen lurking in the roadway near the scenes of the crime. I was no longer amused. The matter promised to be embarrassing. What I had mistaken for a motor accident was evidently a case of savage assault and murder, and, until the real culprit was found, I should have much difficulty in explaining my intrusion into the affair.

"Of course, I could establish my own identity; but how, without disagreeably involving the doctor's wife, could I give any adequate reason for changing clothes with the murdered man? While my brain worked feverishly at this problem, I subconsciously obeyed a secondary instinct—to get as far away as possible from the scene of the crime, and to get rid at all costs of my incriminating uniform. There I found a difficulty. I tried two or three obscure clothes shops, but my entrance invariably aroused an attitude of hostile suspicion in the proprietors, and on one excuse or another they avoided serving me with the now ardently desired change of clothing. The uniform that I had so thoughtlessly donned seemed as difficult to get out of as the fatal shirt of—You know, I forget the creature's name."

"Yes, yes," said the chaplain hurriedly. "Go on with your story."

"Somehow, until I could get out of those compromising garments, I felt It would not be safe to surrender myself to the police. The thing that puzzled me was why no attempt was made to arrest me, since there was no question as to the suspicion which followed me, like an inseparable shadow, wherever I went. Stares, nudgings, whisperings, and even loud-spoken remarks of 'that's 'im' greeted my every appearance, and the meanest and most deserted eating-house that I patronised soon became filled with a crowd of furtively watching customers. I began to sympathize with the feelings of Royal personages trying to do a little private shopping under the unsparing scrutiny of an irrepressible public. And still, with all this inarticulate shadowing, which weighed on my nerves almost worse than open hostility would have done, no attempt was made to interfere with my liberty.

"Later on, I discovered the reason. At the time of the murder on the lonely highway a series of important bloodhound trials had been taking place in the near neighbourhood, and some dozen and a half couples of trained animals had been put on the track of the supposed murderer on my track. One of our most public-spirited London dailies had offered a princely prize to the owner of the pair that should first track me down, end betting on the chances of the respective competitors became rife throughout the land. The dogs ranged far and wide over about thirteen counties, and though my own movements had become by this time perfectly well known to police and public alike, the sporting instincts of the nation stepped in to prevent my premature arrest. 'Give the dogs a chance,' was the prevailing sentiment, whenever some ambitious local constable wished to put an end to my drawn-out evasion of justice.

"My final capture by the winning pair was not a very dramatic episode, in fact, I'm not sure that they would have taken any notice of me if I hadn't spoken to them and patted them, but the event gave rise to an extraordinary amount of partisan excitement. The owner of the pair who were next nearest up at the finish was an American, and he lodged a protest on the ground that an otterhound had married into the family of the winning pair six generations ago, and that the prize had been offered to the first pair of bloodhounds to capture the murderer, and that a dog that had one sixty-fourth part of otterhound blood in it couldn't technically be considered a bloodhound. I forget how the matter was ultimately settled, but it aroused a tremendous amount of acrimonious discussion on both sides of the Atlantic.

"My own contribution to the controversy consisted in pointing out that the whole dispute was beside the mark, as the actual murderer had not yet been captured; but I soon discovered that on this point there was not the least, divergence of public or expert opinion. I had looked forward apprehensively to the proving of my identity and the establishment of my motives as a disagreeable necessity; I speedily found out that the most disagreeable part of the business was that it couldn't be done. When I saw in the glass the haggard and hunted expression which the experiences of the past few weeks had stamped on my erstwhile placid countenance, I could scarcely feel surprised that the few friends and relations I possessed refused to recognise me in my altered guise, and persisted in their obstinate but widely shared belief that it was I who had been done to death on the highway.

"To make matters worse, infinitely worse, an aunt of the really murdered man, an appalling female of an obviously low order of intelligence, identified me as her nephew, and gave the authorities a lurid account of my depraved youth and of her laudable but unavailing efforts to spank me into a better way. I believe it was even proposed to search me for fingerprints."

"But," said the chaplain, "surely your educational attainments—"

"That was just the crucial point," said the condemned; "that was where my lack of specialisation told so fatally against me. The dead Salvationist, whose identity I had so lightly and so disastrously adopted, had possessed a veneer of cheap modern education. It should have been easy to demonstrate that my learning was on altogether another plane to his, but in my nervousness, I bungled miserably over test after test that was put to me. The little French I had ever known deserted me; I could not render a simple phrase about the gooseberry of the gardener into that language, because I had forgotten the French for gooseberry."

The chaplain again wriggled uneasily in his seat.

"And then," resumed the condemned, "came the final discomfiture. In our village we had a modest little debating club, and I remembered having promised, chiefly, I suppose, to please and impress the doctor's wife, to give a sketchy kind of lecture on the Balkan Crisis. I had relied on being able to get up my facts from one or two standard works, and the back-numbers of certain periodicals. The prosecution had made a careful note of the circumstance that the man whom I claimed to be—and actually was—had posed locally as some sort of second-hand authority on Balkan affairs, and, in the midst of a string of questions on indifferent topics, the examining counsel asked me with a diabolical suddenness if I could tell the Court the whereabouts of Novibazar.

"I felt the question to be a crucial one; something told me that the answer was St. Petersburg or Baker Street. I hesitated, looked helplessly round at the sea of tensely expectant faces, pulled myself together, and chose Baker Street. And then I knew that everything was lost. The prosecution had no difficulty in demonstrating that an individual, even moderately versed in the affairs of the Near East, could never have so unceremoniously dislocated Novibazar from its accustomed corner of the map. It was an answer which the Salvation Army captain might conceivably have made—and I made it. The circumstantial evidence connecting the Salvationist with the crime was overwhelmingly convincing, and I had inextricably identified myself with the Salvationist. And thus, it comes to pass that in ten minutes' time I shall be hanged by the neck until I am dead in expiation of the murder of myself, which murder never took place, and of which, in any case, I am innocent."

★★★★★★★★★★

When the chaplain returned to his quarters some fifteen minutes later, the black flag was floating over the prison tower. Breakfast was waiting for him in the dining-room, but he first passed into his library, and, taking up the *Times* Atlas, consulted a map of the Balkan Peninsula.

"A thing like that," he observed, closing the volume with a snap, "might happen to anyone."

The Lumber-Room

The children were to be driven, as a special treat, to the sands at Jagborough. Nicholas was not to be of the party; he was in disgrace. Only that morning he had refused to eat his wholesome bread-and-milk on the seemingly frivolous ground that there was a frog in it. Older and wiser and better people had told him that there could not possibly be a frog in his bread-and-milk and that he was not to talk nonsense; he continued, nevertheless, to talk what seemed the veriest nonsense, and described with much detail the coloration and markings of the alleged frog.

The dramatic part of the incident was that there really was a frog in Nicholas's basin of bread-and-milk; he had put it there himself, so he felt entitled to know something about it. The sin of taking a frog from the garden and putting it into a bowl of wholesome bread-and-milk was enlarged on at great length, but the fact that stood out clearest in the whole affair, as it presented itself to the mind of Nicholas, was that the older, wiser, and better people had been proved to be profoundly in error in matters about which they had expressed the utmost assurance.

"You said there couldn't possibly be a frog in my bread-and-milk; there *was* a frog in my bread-and-milk," he repeated, with the insistence of a skilled tactician who does not intend to shift from favourable ground.

So, his boy-cousin and girl-cousin and his quite uninteresting younger brother were to be taken to Jagborough sands that afternoon and he was to stay at home. His cousins' aunt, who insisted, by an unwarranted stretch of imagination, in styling herself his aunt also, had hastily invented the Jagborough expedition in order to impress on Nicholas the delights that he had justly forfeited by his disgraceful conduct at the breakfast-table.

It was her habit, whenever one of the children fell from grace, to improvise something of a festival nature from which the offender would be rigorously debarred; if all the children sinned collectively, they were suddenly informed of a circus in a neighbouring town, a circus of unrivalled merit and uncounted elephants, to which, but for their depravity, they would have been taken that very day.

A few decent tears were looked for on the part of Nicholas when the moment for the departure of the expedition arrived. As a matter of fact, however, all the crying was done by his girl-cousin, who scraped her knee rather painfully against the step of the carriage as she was scrambling in. "How she did howl," said Nicholas cheerfully, as the party drove off without any of the elation of high spirits that should have characterized it.

"She'll soon get over that," said the *soi-disant* aunt; "it will be a glorious afternoon for racing about over those beautiful sands. How they will enjoy themselves!"

"Bobby won't enjoy himself much, and he won't race much either," said Nicholas with a grim chuckle; "his boots are hurting him. They're too tight."

"Why didn't he tell me they were hurting?" asked the aunt with some asperity.

"He told you twice, but you weren't listening. You often don't listen when we tell you important things."

"You are not to go into the gooseberry garden," said the aunt, changing the subject.

"Why not?" demanded Nicholas.

"Because you are in disgrace," said the aunt loftily.

Nicholas did not admit the flawlessness of the reasoning; he felt perfectly capable of being in disgrace and in a gooseberry garden at the same moment. His face took on an expression of considerable obstinacy. It was clear to his aunt that he was determined to get into the gooseberry garden, "only," as she remarked to herself, "because I have told him he is not to."

Now the gooseberry garden had two doors by which it might be entered, and once a small person like Nicholas could slip in there, he could effectually disappear from view amid the masking growth of artichokes, raspberry canes, and fruit bushes. The aunt had many other things to do that afternoon, but she spent an hour or two in trivial gardening operations among flower beds and shrubberies, whence she could watch the two doors that led to the forbidden paradise. She was a woman of few ideas, with immense powers of concentration.

Nicholas made one or two sorties into the front garden, wriggling his way with obvious stealth of purpose towards one or other of the doors, but never able for a moment to evade the aunt's watchful eye. As a matter of fact, he had no intention of trying to get into the gooseberry garden, but it was extremely convenient for him that his aunt should believe that he had; it was a belief that would keep her on self-imposed sentry-duty for the greater part of the afternoon. Having thoroughly confirmed and fortified her suspicions, Nicholas slipped back into the house and rapidly put into execution a plan of action that had long germinated in his brain.

By standing on a chair in the library one could reach a shelf on which reposed a fat, important-looking key. The key was as important as it looked; it was the instrument which kept the mysteries of the lumber-room secure from unauthorized intrusion, which opened a way only for aunts and such-like privileged persons. Nicholas had not had much experience of the art of fitting keys into keyholes and turning locks, but for some days past he had practised with the key of the schoolroom door; he did not believe in trusting too much to luck and accident. The key turned stiffly in the lock, but it turned. The door opened, and Nicholas was in an unknown land, compared with which the gooseberry garden was a stale delight, a mere material pleasure.

Often and often, Nicholas had pictured to himself what the lumber-room might be like, that region that was so carefully sealed from youthful eyes and concerning which no questions were ever answered. It came up to his expectations. In the first place it was large and dimly lit, one high window opening onto the forbidden garden being its only source of illumination. In the second place it was a storehouse of unimagined treasures. The aunt-by-assertion was one of those people who think that things spoil by use and consign them to dust and damp by way of preserving them. Such parts of the house as Nicholas knew best were rather bare and cheerless, but here there were wonderful things for the eye to feast on.

First and foremost, there was a piece of framed tapestry that was evidently meant to be a fire-screen. To Nicholas it was a living, breathing story; he sat down on a roll of Indian hangings, glowing in wonderful colours beneath a layer of dust, and took in all the details of the tapestry picture. A man, dressed in the hunting costume of some remote period, had just transfixed a stag with an arrow; it could not have been a difficult shot because the stag was only one or two paces away from him; in the thickly growing vegetation that the picture suggested it would not have been difficult to creep up to a feeding stag, and the two spotted dogs that were springing forward to join in the chase had evidently been trained to keep to heel till the arrow was discharged.

That part of the picture was simple, if interesting, but did the huntsman see, what Nicholas saw, that four galloping wolves were coming in his direction through the wood? There might be more than four of them hidden behind the trees, and in any case would the man and his dogs be able to cope with the four wolves if they made an attack? The man had only two arrows left in his quiver, and he might miss with one or both of them; all one knew about his skill in shooting was that he could hit a large stag at a ridiculously short range. Nicholas sat for many golden minutes revolving the possibilities of the scene; he was inclined to think that there were more than four wolves and that the man and his dogs were in a tight corner.

But there were other objects of delight and interest claiming his instant attention; there were quaint twisted candlesticks in the shape of snakes, and a teapot fashioned like a china duck, out of whose open beak the tea was supposed to come. How dull and shapeless the nursery teapot seemed in comparison! And there was a carved sandalwood box packed tight with aromatic cotton-wool, and between the layers of cotton-wool were little brass figures, hump-necked bulls, and peacocks and goblins, delightful to see and to handle. Less promising in appearance was a large square book with plain black covers; Nicholas peeped into it, and, behold, it was full of coloured pictures of birds.

And such birds! In the garden, and in the lanes when he went for a walk, Nicholas came across a few birds, of which the largest were an occasional magpie or wood-pigeons here were herons and bustards, kites, toucans, tiger-bitterns, brush turkeys, ibises, golden pheasants, a whole portrait gallery of undreamed-of creatures. And as he was admiring the colouring of the mandarin duck and assigning a life-history to it, the voice of his aunt in shrill vociferation of his name came from the gooseberry garden without. She had grown suspicious at his long disappearance, and had leapt to the conclusion that he had climbed over the wall behind the sheltering screen of the lilac bushes: she was now engaged in energetic and rather hopeless search for him among the artichokes and raspberry canes.

"Nicholas, Nicholas!" she screamed, "you are to come out of this at once. It's no use trying to hide there; I can see you all the time."

It was probably the first time for twenty years that anyone had smiled in that lumber-room.

Presently the angry repetitions of Nicholas's name gave way to a shriek, and a cry for somebody to come quickly. Nicholas shut the book, restored it carefully to its place in a corner, and shook some dust from a neighbouring pile of newspapers over it. Then he crept from the room, locked the door, and replaced the key exactly where he had found it. His aunt was still calling his name when he sauntered into the front garden.

"Who's calling?" he asked.

"Me," came the answer from the other side of the wall; "didn't you hear me? I've been looking for you in the gooseberry garden, and I've slipped into the rain-water tank. Luckily there's no water in it, but the sides are slippery and I can't get out. Fetch the little ladder from under the cherry tree—"

"I was told I wasn't to go into the gooseberry garden," said Nicholas promptly.

"I told you not to, and now I tell you that you may," came the voice from the rain-water tank, rather impatiently.

"Your voice doesn't sound like aunt's," objected Nicholas; "you may be the Evil One tempting me to be disobedient. Aunt often tells me that the Evil One tempts me and that I always yield. *This* time I'm not going to yield."

"Don't talk nonsense," said the prisoner in the tank; "go and fetch the ladder."

"Will there be strawberry jam for tea?" asked Nicholas innocently.

"Certainly, there will be," said the aunt, privately resolving that Nicholas should have none of it.

"Now I know that you are the Evil One and not aunt," shouted Nicholas gleefully; "when we asked aunt for strawberry jam yesterday, she said there wasn't any. I know there are four jars of it in the store cupboard, because I looked, and of course you know it's there, but she doesn't, because she said there wasn't any. Oh, Devil, you have sold yourself!"

There was an unusual sense of luxury in being able to talk to an aunt as though one was talking to the Evil One, but Nicholas knew, with childish discernment that such luxuries were not to be over-indulged in. He walked noisily away, and it was a kitchen-maid, in search of parsley, who eventually rescued the aunt from the rain-water tank. Tea that evening was partaken of in a fearsome silence.

The tide had been at its highest when the children had arrived at

Jagborough Cove, so there had been no sands to play on—a circumstance that the aunt had overlooked in the haste of organising her punitive expedition. The tightness of Bobby's boots had had a disastrous effect on his temper the whole of the afternoon, and altogether the children could not have been said to have enjoyed themselves. The aunt maintained the frozen muteness of one who has suffered undignified and unmerited detention in a rain-water tank for thirty-five minutes. As for Nicholas, he, too, was silent, in the absorption of one who has much to think about; it was just possible, he considered, that the huntsman would escape with his hounds while the wolves feasted on the stricken stag.

The Music on the Hill

Sylvia Seltoun ate her breakfast in the morning-room at Yessney with a pleasant sense of ultimate victory, such as a fervent Ironside might have permitted himself on the morrow of Worcester fight. She was scarcely pugnacious by temperament, but belonged to that more successful class of fighters who are pugnacious by circumstance. Fate had willed that her life should be occupied with a series of small struggles, usually with the odds slightly against her, and usually she had just managed to come through winning. And now she felt that she had brought her hardest and certainly her most important struggle to a successful issue.

To have married Mortimer Seltoun, "Dead Mortimer" as his more intimate enemies called him, in the teeth of the cold hostility of his family, and in spite of his unaffected indifference to women, was indeed an achievement that had needed some determination and adroitness to carry through; yesterday she had brought her victory to its concluding stage by wrenching her husband away from Town and its group of satellite watering-places and "settling him down," in the vocabulary of her kind, in this remote wood-girt manor farm which was his country house.

"You will never get Mortimer to go," his mother had said carpingly, "but if he once goes, he'll stay; Yessney throws almost as much a spell over him as Town does. One can understand what holds him to Town, but Yessney—" and the dowager had shrugged her shoulders.

There was a sombre almost savage wildness about Yessney that was certainly not likely to appeal to town-bred tastes, and Sylvia, notwithstanding her name, was accustomed to nothing much more sylvan than "leafy Kensington." She looked on the country as something excellent and wholesome in its way, which was apt to become troublesome if you encouraged it overmuch. Distrust of town life had been a new thing with her, born of her marriage with Mortimer, and she had watched with satisfaction the gradual fading of what she called "the Jermyn-Street-look" in his eyes as the woods and heather of Yessney had closed in on them yesternight. Her will-power and strategy had prevailed; Mortimer would stay.

Outside the morning-room windows was a triangular slope of turf, which the indulgent might call a lawn, and beyond its low hedge of neglected fuchsia bushes a steeper slope of heather and bracken dropped down into cavernous combes overgrown with oak and yew. In its wild open savagery, there seemed a stealthy linking of the joy of life with the terror of unseen things. Sylvia smiled complacently as she gazed with a School-of-Art appreciation at the landscape, and then of a sudden she almost shuddered.

"It is very wild," she said to Mortimer, who had joined her; "one could almost think that in such a place the worship of Pan had never quite died out."

"The worship of Pan never has died out," said Mortimer. "Other newer gods have drawn aside his votaries from time to time, but he is the Nature-God to whom all must come back at last. He has been called the Father of all the Gods, but most of his children have been stillborn."

Sylvia was religious in an honest, vaguely devotional kind of way, and did not like to hear her beliefs spoken of as mere aftergrowths, but it was at least something new and hopeful to hear Dead Mortimer speak with such energy and conviction on any subject.

"You don't really believe in Pan?" she asked incredulously.

"I've been a fool in most things," said Mortimer quietly, "but I'm not such a fool as not to believe in Pan when I'm down here. And if you're wise you won't disbelieve in him too boastfully while you're in his country."

It was not till a week later, when Sylvia had exhausted the attractions of the woodland walks round Yessney, that she ventured on a tour of inspection of the farm buildings. A farmyard suggested in her mind a scene of cheerful bustle, with churns and flails and smiling dairymaids, and teams of horses drinking knee-deep in duck-crowded ponds. As she wandered among the gaunt grey buildings of Yessney manor farm her first impression was one of crushing stillness and desolation, as though she had happened on some lone deserted homestead long given over to owls and cobwebs; then came a sense of furtive watchful hostility, the same shadow of unseen things that seemed to lurk in the wooded combes and coppices.

From behind heavy doors and shuttered windows came the restless stamp of hoof or rasp of chain halter, and at times a muffled bellow from some stalled beast. From a distant corner a shaggy dog watched her with intent unfriendly eyes; as she drew near it slipped quietly into its kennel, and slipped out again as noiselessly when she had passed by. A few hens, questing for food under a rick, stole away under a gate at her approach. Sylvia felt that if she had come across any human beings in this wilderness of barn and byre, they would have fled wraith-like from her gaze. At last, turning a corner quickly, she came upon a living thing that did not fly from her. Astretch in a pool of mud was an enormous sow, gigantic beyond the town-woman's wildest computation of swine-flesh, and speedily alert to resent and if necessary, repel the unwonted intrusion.

It was Sylvia's turn to make an unobtrusive retreat. As she threaded her way past rickyards and cowsheds and long blank walls, she started suddenly at a strange sound—the echo of a boy's laughter, golden and equivocal. Jan, the only boy employed on the farm, a tow-headed, wizen-faced yokel, was visibly at work on a potato clearing half-way up the nearest hillside, and Mortimer, when questioned, knew of no other probable or possible begetter of the hidden mockery that had ambushed Sylvia's retreat. The memory of that untraceable echo was added to her other impressions of a furtive sinister "something" that hung around Yessney.

Of Mortimer she saw very little; farm and woods and trout-streams seemed to swallow him up from dawn till dusk. Once, following the direction she had seen him take in the morning, she came to an open space in a nut copse, further shut in by huge yew trees, in the centre of which stood a stone pedestal surmounted by a small bronze figure of a youthful Pan. It was a beautiful piece of workmanship, but her attention was chiefly held by the fact that a newly cut bunch of grapes had been placed as an offering at its feet. Grapes were none too plentiful at the manor house, and Sylvia snatched the bunch angrily from the pedestal.

Contemptuous annoyance dominated her thoughts as she strolled slowly homeward, and then gave way to a sharp feeling of something that was very near fright; across a thick tangle of undergrowth a boy's face was scowling at her, brown and beautiful, with unutterably evil eyes. It was a lonely pathway, all pathways round Yessney were lonely for the matter of that, and she sped forward without waiting to give a closer scrutiny to this sudden apparition. It was not till she had reached the house that she discovered that she had dropped the bunch of grapes in her flight.

"I saw a youth in the wood today," she told Mortimer that evening, "brown-faced and rather handsome, but a scoundrel to look at. A gipsy lad, I suppose."

"A reasonable theory," said Mortimer, "only there aren't any gipsies in these parts at present."

"Then who was he?" asked Sylvia, and as Mortimer appeared to have no theory of his own, she passed on to recount her finding of the votive offering.

"I suppose it was your doing," she observed; "it's a harmless piece of lunacy, but people would think you dreadfully silly if they knew of it."

"Did you meddle with it in any way?" asked Mortimer.

"I—I threw the grapes away. It seemed so silly," said Sylvia, watching Mortimer's impassive face for a sign of annoyance.

"I don't think you were wise to do that," he said reflectively. "I've heard it said that the Wood Gods are rather horrible to those who molest them."

"Horrible perhaps to those that believe in them, but you see I don't," retorted Sylvia.

"All the same," said Mortimer in his even, dispassionate tone, "I should avoid the woods and orchards if I were you, and give a wide berth to the horned beasts on the farm."

It was all nonsense, of course, but in that lonely wood-girt spot nonsense seemed able to rear a bastard brood of uneasiness.

"Mortimer," said Sylvia suddenly, "I think we will go back to Town sometime soon."

Her victory had not been so complete as she had supposed; it had carried her on to ground that she was already anxious to quit.

"I don't think you will ever go back to Town," said Mortimer. He seemed to be paraphrasing his mother's prediction as to himself.

Sylvia noted with dissatisfaction and some self-contempt that the course of her next afternoon's ramble took her instinctively clear of the network of woods. As to the horned cattle, Mortimer's warning was scarcely needed, for she had always regarded them as of doubtful neutrality at the best: her imagination unsexed the most matronly dairy cows and turned them into bulls liable to "see red" at any moment. The ram who fed in the narrow paddock below the orchards

100

she had adjudged, after ample and cautious probation, to be of docile temper; today, however, she decided to leave his docility untested, for the usually tranquil beast was roaming with every sign of restlessness from corner to corner of his meadow. A low, fitful piping, as of some reedy flute, was coming from the depth of a neighbouring copse, and there seemed to be some subtle connection between the animal's restless pacing and the wild music from the wood. Sylvia turned her steps in an upward direction and climbed the heather-clad slopes that stretched in rolling shoulders high above Yessney.

She had left the piping notes behind her, but across the wooded combes at her feet the wind brought her another kind of music, the straining bay of hounds in full chase. Yessney was just on the outskirts of the Devon-and-Somerset country, and the hunted deer sometimes came that way. Sylvia could presently see a dark body, breasting hill after hill, and sinking again and again out of sight as he crossed the combes, while behind him steadily swelled that relentless chorus, and she grew tense with the excited sympathy that one feels for any hunted thing in whose capture one is not directly interested. And at last, he broke through the outermost line of oak scrub and fern and stood panting in the open, a fat September stag carrying a well-furnished head. His obvious course was to drop down to the brown pools of Undercombe, and thence make his way towards the red deer's favoured sanctuary, the sea.

To Sylvia's surprise, however, he turned his head to the upland slope and came lumbering resolutely onward over the heather. "It will be dreadful," she thought, "the hounds will pull him down under my very eyes." But the music of the pack seemed to have died away for a moment, and in its place, she heard again that wild piping, which rose now on this side, now on that, as though urging the failing stag to a final effort. Sylvia stood well aside from his path, half hidden in a thick growth of whortle bushes, and watched him swing stiffly upward, his flanks dark with sweat, the coarse hair on his neck showing light by contrast.

The pipe music shrilled suddenly around her, seeming to come from the bushes at her very feet, and at the same moment the great beast slewed round and bore directly down upon her. In an instant her pity for the hunted animal was changed to wild terror at her own danger; the thick heather roots mocked her scrambling efforts at flight, and she looked frantically downward for a glimpse of oncoming hounds. The huge antler spikes were within a few yards of her, and in a flash of numbing fear she remembered Mortimer's warning, to beware of horned beasts on the farm. And then with a quick throb of joy she saw that she was not alone; a human figure stood a few paces aside, knee-deep in the whortle bushes.

"Drive it off!" she shrieked. But the figure made no answering movement.

The antlers drove straight at her breast, the acrid smell of the hunted animal was in her nostrils, but her eyes were filled with the horror of something she saw other than her oncoming death. And in her ears rang the echo of a boy's laughter, golden and equivocal.

The Open Window

"My aunt will be down presently, Mr. Nuttel," said a very self-possessed young lady of fifteen; "in the meantime you must try and put up with me."

Framton Nuttel endeavoured to say the correct something which should duly flatter the niece of the moment without unduly discounting the aunt that was to come. Privately he doubted more than ever whether these formal visits on a succession of total strangers would do much towards helping the nerve cure which he was supposed to be undergoing.

"I know how it will be," his sister had said when he was preparing to migrate to this rural retreat; "you will bury yourself down there and not speak to a living soul, and your nerves will be worse than ever from moping. I shall just give you letters of introduction to all the people I know there. Some of them, as far as I can remember, were quite nice."

Framton wondered whether Mrs. Sappleton, the lady to whom he was presenting one of the letters of introduction came into the nice division.

"Do you know many of the people round here?" asked the niece, when she judged that they had had sufficient silent communion.

"Hardly a soul," said Framton. "My sister was staying here, at the rectory, you know, some four years ago, and she gave me letters of introduction to some of the people here."

He made the last statement in a tone of distinct regret.

"Then you know practically nothing about my aunt?" pursued the self-possessed young lady.

"Only her name and address," admitted the caller. He was wondering whether Mrs. Sappleton was in the married or widowed state. An undefinable something about the room seemed to suggest masculine habitation.

"Her great tragedy happened just three years ago," said the child; "that would be since your sister's time."

"Her tragedy?" asked Framton; somehow in this restful country spot tragedies seemed out of place.

"You may wonder why we keep that window wide open on an October afternoon," said the niece, indicating a large French window that opened on to a lawn.

"It is quite warm for the time of the year," said Framton; "but has that window got anything to do with the tragedy?"

"Out through that window, three years ago to a day, her husband and her two young brothers went off for their day's shooting. They never came back. In crossing the moor to their favourite snipe-shooting ground they were all three engulfed in a treacherous piece of bog. It had been that dreadful wet summer, you know, and places that were safe in other years gave way suddenly without warning. Their bodies were never recovered. That was the dreadful part of it." Here the child's voice lost its self-possessed note and became falteringly human. "Poor aunt always thinks that they will come back someday, they and the little brown spaniel that was lost with them, and walk in at that window just as they used to do.

"That is why the window is kept open every evening till it is quite dusk. Poor dear aunt, she has often told me how they went out, her husband with his white waterproof coat over his arm, and Ronnie, her youngest brother, singing 'Bertie, why do you bound?' as he always did to tease her, because she said it got on her nerves. Do you know, sometimes on still, quiet evenings like this, I almost get a creepy feeling that they will all walk in through that window—"

She broke off with a little shudder. It was a relief to Framton when the aunt bustled into the room with a whirl of apologies for being late in making her appearance.

"I hope Vera has been amusing you?" she said.

"She has been very interesting," said Framton.

"I hope you don't mind the open window," said Mrs. Sappleton briskly; "my husband and brothers will be home directly from shooting, and they always come in this way. They've been out for snipe in the marshes today, so they'll make a fine mess over my poor carpets. So, like you menfolk, isn't it?"

She rattled on cheerfully about the shooting and the scarcity of birds, and the prospects for duck in the winter. To Framton it was all purely horrible. He made a desperate but only partially successful effort to turn the talk on to a less ghastly topic, he was conscious that his hostess was giving him only a fragment of her attention, and her eyes were constantly straying past him to the open window and the lawn beyond. It was certainly an unfortunate coincidence that he should have paid his visit on this tragic anniversary.

"The doctors agree in ordering me complete rest, an absence of mental excitement, and avoidance of anything in the nature of violent physical exercise," announced Framton, who laboured under the tolerably widespread delusion that total strangers and chance acquaintances are hungry for the least detail of one's ailments and infirmities, their cause and cure. "On the matter of diet, they are not so much in agreement," he continued.

"No?" said Mrs. Sappleton, in a voice which only replaced a yawn at the last moment. Then she suddenly brightened into alert attention —but not to what Framton was saying.

"Here they are at last!" she cried. "Just in time for tea, and don't they look as if they were muddy up to the eyes!"

Framton shivered slightly and turned towards the niece with a look intended to convey sympathetic comprehension. The child was staring out through the open window with a dazed horror in her eyes. In a chill shock of nameless fear Framton swung round in his seat and looked in the same direction.

In the deepening twilight three figures were walking across the lawn towards the window, they all carried guns under their arms, and one of them was additionally burdened with a white coat hung over his shoulders. A tired brown spaniel kept close at their heels. Noiselessly they neared the house, and then a hoarse young voice chanted out of the dusk: "I said, Bertie, why do you bound?"

Framton grabbed wildly at his stick and hat; the hall door, the gravel drive, and the front gate were dimly noted stages in his headlong retreat. A cyclist coming along the road had to run into the hedge to avoid imminent collision.

"Here we are, my dear," said the bearer of the white mackintosh, coming in through the window, "fairly muddy, but most of it's dry. Who was that who bolted out as we came up?"

"A most extraordinary man, a Mr. Nuttel," said Mrs. Sappleton; "could only talk about his illnesses, and dashed off without a word of goodbye or apology when you arrived. One would think he had seen a ghost."

"I expect it was the spaniel," said the niece calmly; "he told me he had a horror of dogs. He was once hunted into a cemetery somewhere on the banks of the Ganges by a pack of pariah dogs, and had to spend the night in a newly dug grave with the creatures snarling and grinning and foaming just above him. Enough to make anyone lose their nerve."

Romance at short notice was her speciality.

The Peace of Mowsle Barton

Crefton Lockyer sat at his ease, an ease alike of body and soul, in the little patch of ground, half-orchard and half-garden, that abutted on the farmyard at Mowsle Barton. After the stress and noise of long years of city life, the repose and peace of the hill-begirt homestead struck on his senses with an almost dramatic intensity. Time and space seemed to lose their meaning and their abruptness; the minutes slid away into hours, and the meadows and fallows sloped away into middle distance, softly and imperceptibly. Wild weeds of the hedgerow straggled into the flower-garden, and wallflowers and garden bushes made counter-raids into farmyard and lane. Sleepy-looking hens and solemn preoccupied ducks were equally at home in yard, orchard, or roadway; nothing seemed to belong definitely to anywhere; even the gates were not necessarily to be found on their hinges.

And over the whole scene brooded the sense of a peace that had almost a quality of magic in it. In the afternoon you felt that it had always been afternoon, and must always remain afternoon; in the twilight you knew that it could never have been anything else but twilight. Crefton Lockyer sat at his ease in the rustic seat beneath an old medlar tree, and decided that here was the life-anchorage that his mind had so fondly pictured and that latterly his tired and jarred senses had so often pined for. He would make a permanent lodging-place among these simple friendly people, gradually increasing the modest comforts with which he would like to surround himself, but falling in as much as possible with their manner of living.

As he slowly matured this resolution in his mind an elderly woman came hobbling with uncertain gait through the orchard. He recognized her as a member of the farm household, the mother or possibly the mother-in-law of Mrs. Spurfield, his present landlady, and hastily formulated some pleasant remark to make to her. She forestalled him.

"There's a bit of writing chalked up on the door over yonder. What is it?"

She spoke in a dull impersonal manner, as though the question had been on her lips for years and has best be got rid of. Her eyes, however, looked impatiently over Crefton's head at the door of a small barn which formed the outpost of a straggling line of farm buildings.

"Martha Pillamon is an old witch" was the announcement that met Crefton's inquiring scrutiny, and he hesitated a moment before giving the statement wider publicity. For all he knew to the contrary, it might be Martha herself to whom he was speaking. It was possible that Mrs. Spurfield's maiden name had been Pillamon. And the gaunt, withered old dame at his side might certainly fulfil local conditions as to the outward aspect of a witch.

"It's something about someone called Martha Pillamon," he explained cautiously.

"What does it say?"

"It's very disrespectful," said Crefton; "it says she's a witch. Such things ought not to be written up."

"It's true, every word of it," said his listener with considerable satisfaction, adding as a special descriptive note of her own, "the old toad."

And as she hobbled away through the farmyard she shrilled out in her cracked voice, "Martha Pillamon is an old witch!"

"Did you hear what she said?" mumbled a weak, angry voice somewhere behind Crefton's shoulder. Turning hastily, he beheld another old crone, thin and yellow and wrinkled, and evidently in a high state of displeasure. Obviously, this was Martha Pillamon in person. The orchard seemed to be a favourite promenade for the aged women of the neighbourhood.

"'Tis lies, 'tis sinful lies," the weak voice went on. "'Tis Betsy Croot is the old witch. She an' her daughter, the dirty rat. I'll put a spell on 'em, the old nuisances."

As she limped slowly away her eye caught the chalk inscription on the barn door.

"What's written up there?" she demanded, wheeling round on Crefton.

"Vote for Soarker," he responded, with the craven boldness of the practised peacemaker.

The old woman grunted, and her mutterings and her faded red shawl lost themselves gradually among the tree-trunks. Crefton rose presently and made his way towards the farmhouse. Somehow a good deal of the peace seemed to have slipped out of the atmosphere.

The cheery bustle of tea-time in the old farm kitchen, which Crefton had found so agreeable on previous afternoons, seemed to have soured today into a certain uneasy melancholy. There was a dull, dragging silence around the board, and the tea itself, when Crefton came to taste it, was a flat, lukewarm concoction that would have driven the spirit of revelry out of a carnival.

"It's no use complaining of the tea," said Mrs. Spurfield hastily, as her guest stared with an air of polite inquiry at his cup. "The kettle won't boil, that's the truth of it."

Crefton turned to the hearth, where an unusually fierce fire was banked up under a big black kettle, which sent a thin wreath of steam from its spout, but seemed otherwise to ignore the action of the roaring blaze beneath it.

"It's been there more than an hour, an' boil it won't," said Mrs. Spurfield, adding, by way of complete explanation, "we're bewitched."

"It's Martha Pillamon as has done it," chimed in the old mother; "I'll be even with the old toad, I'll put a spell on her."

"It must boil in time," protested Crefton, ignoring the suggestions of foul influences. "Perhaps the coal is damp."

"It won't boil in time for supper, nor for breakfast tomorrow morning, not if you was to keep the fire agoing all night for it," said Mrs. Spurfield. And it didn't. The household subsisted on fried and baked dishes, and a neighbour obligingly brewed tea and sent it across in a moderately warm condition.

"I suppose you'll be leaving us now that things has turned up uncomfortable," Mrs. Spurfield observed at breakfast; "there are folks as deserts one as soon as trouble comes."

Crefton hurriedly disclaimed any immediate change of plans; he observed, however, to himself that the earlier heartiness of manner had in a large measure deserted the household. Suspicious looks, sulky silences, or sharp speeches had become the order of the day. As for the old mother, she sat about the kitchen or the garden all day, murmuring threats and spells against Martha Pillamon. There was something alike terrifying and piteous in the spectacle of these frail old morsels of humanity consecrating their last flickering energies to the task of making each other wretched. Hatred seemed to be the one faculty which had survived in undiminished vigour and intensity where all else was dropping into ordered and symmetrical decay.

And the uncanny part of it was that some horrid unwholesome

power seemed to be distilled from their spite and their cursings. No amount of sceptical explanation could remove the undoubted fact that neither kettle nor saucepan would come to boiling-point over the hottest fire. Crefton clung as long as possible to the theory of some defect in the coals, but a wood fire gave the same result, and when a small spirit-lamp kettle, which he ordered out by carrier, showed the same obstinate refusal to allow its contents to boil he felt that he had come suddenly into contact with some unguessed-at and very evil aspect of hidden forces. Miles away, down through an opening in the hills, he could catch glimpses of a road where motorcars sometimes passed, and yet here, so little removed from the arteries of the latest civilization, was a bat-haunted old homestead, where something un-mistakably like witchcraft seemed to hold a very practical sway.

Passing out through the farm garden on his way to the lanes beyond, where he hoped to recapture the comfortable sense of peaceful-ness that was so lacking around house and —especially hearth—Crefton came across the old mother, sitting mumbling to herself in the seat beneath the medlar tree. "Let un sink as swims, let un sink as swims," she was repeating over and over again, as a child repeats a half-learned lesson. And now and then she would break off into a shrill laugh, with a note of malice in it that was not pleasant to hear. Crefton was glad when he found himself out of earshot, in the quiet and seclusion of the deep overgrown lanes that seemed to lead away to nowhere; one, narrower and deeper than the rest, attracted his footsteps, and he was almost annoyed when he found that it really did act as a miniature roadway to a human dwelling.

A forlorn-looking cottage with a scrap of ill-tended cabbage gar-den and a few aged apple trees stood at an angle where a swift-flowing stream widened out for a space into a decent-sized pond before hur-rying away again trough the willows that had checked its course. Cref-ton leaned against a tree-trunk and looked across the swirling eddies of the pond at the humble little homestead opposite him; the only sign of life came from a small procession of dingy-looking ducks that marched in single file down to the water's edge. There is always some-thing rather taking in the way a duck changes itself in an instant from a slow, clumsy waddler of the earth to a graceful, buoyant swimmer of the waters, and Crefton waited with a certain arrested attention to watch the leader of the file launch itself on to the surface of the pond.

He was aware at the same time of a curious warning instinct that something strange and unpleasant was about to happen. The duck flung itself confidently forward into the water, and rolled immediately under the surface. Its head appeared for a moment and went under again, leaving a train of bubbles in its wake, while wings and legs churned the water in a helpless swirl of flapping and kicking. The bird was obviously drowning. Crefton thought at first that it had caught itself in some weeds, or was being attacked from below by a pike or water-rat. But no blood floated to the surface, and the wildly bobbing body made the circuit of the pond current without hindrance from any entanglement. A second duck had by this time launched itself into the pond, and a second struggling body rolled and twisted under the surface. There was something peculiarly piteous in the sight of the gasping beaks that showed now and again above the water, as though in terrified protest at this treachery of a trusted and familiar element.

Crefton gazed with something like horror as a third duck poised itself on the bank and splashed in, to share the fate of the other two. He felt almost relieved when the remainder of the flock, taking tardy alarm from the commotion of the slowly drowning bodies, drew themselves up with tense outstretched necks, and sidled away from the scene of danger, quacking a deep note of disquietude as they went. At the same moment Crefton became aware that he was not the only human witness of the scene; a bent and withered old woman, whom he recognized at once as Martha Pillamon, of sinister reputation, had limped down the cottage path to the water's edge, and was gazing fixedly at the gruesome whirligig of dying birds that went in horrible procession round the pool. Presently her voice rang out in a shrill note of quavering rage:

"'Tis Betsy Croot adone it, the old rat. I'll put a spell on her, see if I don't."

Crefton slipped quietly away, uncertain whether or no the old woman had noticed his presence. Even before she had proclaimed the guiltiness of Betsy Croot, the latter's muttered incantation "Let un sink as swims" had flashed uncomfortably across his mind. But it was the final threat of a retaliatory spell which crowded his mind with misgiving to the exclusion of all other thoughts or fancies. His reasoning powers could no longer afford to dismiss these old-wives' threats as empty bickerings. The household at Mowsle Barton lay under the displeasure of a vindictive old woman who seemed able to materialize her personal spites in a very practical fashion, and there was no saying what form her revenge for three drowned ducks might not take.

As a member of the household Crefton might find himself involved in some general and highly disagreeable visitation of Martha Pillamon's wrath. Of course, he knew that he was giving way to absurd fancies, but the behaviour of the spirit-lamp kettle and the subsequent scene at the pond had considerably unnerved him. And the vagueness of his alarm added to its terrors; when once you have taken the Impossible into your calculations its possibilities become practically limitless.

Crefton rose at his usual early hour the next morning, after one of the least restful nights he had spent at the farm. His sharpened senses quickly detected that subtle atmosphere of things-being-not-altogether well that hangs over a stricken household. The cows had been milked, but they stood huddled about in the yard, waiting impatiently to be driven out afield, and the poultry kept up an importunate querulous reminder of deferred feeding-time; the yard pump, which usually made discordant music at frequent intervals during the early morning, was today ominously silent. In the house itself there was a coming and going of scuttering footsteps, a rushing and dying away of hurried voices, and long, uneasy stillnesses. Crefton finished his dressing and made his way to the head of a narrow staircase. He could hear a dull, complaining voice, a voice into which an awed hush had crept, and recognised the speaker as Mrs. Spurfield.

"He'll go away, for sure," the voice was saying; "there are those as runs away from one as soon as real misfortune shows itself."

Crefton felt that he probably was one of "those," and that there were moments when it was advisable to be true to type.

He crept back to his room, collected and, packed his few belongings, placed the money due for his lodgings on a table, and made his way out by a back door into the yard. A mob of poultry surged expectantly towards him; shaking off their interested attentions he hurried along under cover of cowstall, piggery, and hayricks till he reached the lane at the back of the farm.

A few minutes' walk, which only the burden of his portmanteaux restrained from developing into an undisguised run, brought him to a main road, where the early carrier soon overtook him and sped him onward to the neighbouring town. At a bend of the road, he caught a last glimpse of the farm; the old gabled roofs and thatched barns, the straggling orchard, and the medlar tree, with its wooden seat, stood out with an almost spectral clearness in the early morning light, and over it all brooded that air of magic possession which Crefton had once mistaken for peace.

The bustle and roar of Paddington Station smote on his ears with a welcome protective greeting.

"Very bad for our nerves, all this rush and hurry," said a fellow-traveller; "give me the peace and quiet of the country."

Crefton mentally surrendered his share of the desired commodity. A crowded, brilliantly over-lighted music-hall, where an exuberant rendering of "1812" was being given by a strenuous orchestra, came nearest to his ideal of a nerve sedative.

The Penance

Octavian Ruttle was one of those lively cheerful individuals on whom amiability had set its unmistakable stamp, and, like most of his kind, his soul's peace depended in large measure on the unstinted approval of his fellows. In hunting to death, a small tabby cat, he had done a thing of which he scarcely approved himself, and he was glad when the gardener had hidden the body in its hastily dug grave under a lone oak-tree in the meadow, the same tree that the hunted quarry had climbed as a last effort towards safety. It had been a distasteful and seemingly ruthless deed, but circumstances had demanded the doing of it.

Octavian kept chickens; at least he kept some of them; others vanished from his keeping, leaving only a few bloodstained feathers to mark the manner of their going. The tabby cat from the large grey house that stood with its back to the meadow had been detected in many furtive visits to the hen-coups, and after due negotiation with those in authority at the grey house a sentence of death had been agreed on. "The children will mind, but they need not know," had been the last word on the matter.

The children in question were a standing puzzle to Octavian; in the course of a few months, he considered that he should have known their names, ages, the dates of their birthdays, and have been introduced to their favourite toys. They remained however, as non-committal as the long blank wall that shut them off from the meadow, a wall over which their three heads sometimes appeared at odd moments. They had parents in India—that much Octavian had learned in the neighbourhood; the children, beyond grouping themselves garment-wise into sexes, a girl and two boys, carried their life-story no further on his behoof. And now it seemed he was engaged in something which touched them closely, but must be hidden from their knowledge.

The poor helpless chickens had gone one by one to their doom, so it was meet that their destroyer should come to a violent end; yet Octavian felt some qualms when his share of the violence was ended. The little cat, headed off from its wonted tracks of safety, had raced unfriended from shelter to shelter, and its end had been rather piteous. Octavian walked through the long grass of the meadow with a step less jaunty than usual. And as he passed beneath the shadow of the high blank wall he glanced up and became aware that his hunting had had undesired witnesses. Three white set faces were looking down at him, and if ever an artist wanted a threefold study of cold human hate, impotent yet unyielding, raging yet masked in stillness, he would have found it in the triple gaze that met Octavian's eye.

"I'm sorry, but it had to be done," said Octavian, with genuine apology in his voice.

"Beast!"

The answer came from three throats with startling intensity.

Octavian felt that the blank wall would not be more impervious to his explanations than the bunch of human hostility that peered over its coping; he wisely decided to withhold his peace overtures till a more hopeful occasion.

Two days later he ransacked the best sweet shop in the neighbouring market town for a box of chocolates that by its size and contents should fitly atone for the dismal deed done under the oak tree in the meadow. The two first specimens that were shown him he hastily rejected; one had a group of chickens pictured on its lid, the other bore the portrait of a tabby kitten. A third sample was more simply bedecked with a spray of painted poppies, and Octavian hailed the flowers of forgetfulness as a happy omen. He felt distinctly more at ease with his surroundings when the imposing package had been sent across to the grey house, and a message returned to say that it had been duly given to the children.

The next morning, he sauntered with purposeful steps past the long blank wall on his way to the chicken-run and piggery that stood at the bottom of the meadow. The three children were perched at their accustomed look-out, and their range of sight did not seem to concern itself with Octavian's presence. As he became depressingly aware of the aloofness of their gaze, he also noted a strange variegation in the herbage at his feet; the greensward for a considerable space around was strewn and speckled with a chocolate-coloured hail, enlivened here and there with gay tinsel-like wrappings or the glistening mauve of crystallised violets. It was as though the fairy paradise of a greedy-minded child had taken shape and substance in the vegetation of the meadow. Octavian's blood-money had been flung back at him in scorn.

To increase his discomfiture the march of events tended to shift the blame of ravaged chicken-coops from the supposed culprit who had already paid full forfeit; the young chicks were still carried off, and it seemed highly probable that the cat had only haunted the chicken-run to prey on the rats which harboured there. Through the flowing channels of servant talk the children learned of this belated revision of verdict, and Octavian one day picked up a sheet of copy-book paper on which was painstakingly written: "Beast. Rats eated your chickens." More ardently than ever did he wish for an opportunity for sloughing off the disgrace that enwrapped him, and earning some happier nickname from his three unsparing judges.

And one day a chance inspiration came to him. Olivia, his two-year-old daughter, was accustomed to spend the hour from high noon till one o'clock with her father while the nursemaid gobbled and digested her dinner and novelette. About the same time the blank wall was usually enlivened by the presence of its three small wardens. Octavian, with seeming carelessness of purpose, brought Olivia well within hail of the watchers and noted with hidden delight the growing interest that dawned in that hitherto sternly hostile quarter.

His little Olivia, with her sleepy placid ways, was going to succeed where he, with his anxious well-meant overtures, had so signally failed. He brought her a large yellow dahlia, which she grasped tightly in one hand and regarded with a stare of benevolent boredom, such as one might bestow on amateur classical dancing performed in aid of a deserving charity.

Then he turned shyly to the group perched on the wall and asked with affected carelessness, "Do you like flowers?" Three solemn nods rewarded his venture.

"Which sorts do you like best?" he asked, this time with a distinct betrayal of eagerness in his voice.

"Those with all the colours, over there." Three chubby arms pointed to a distant tangle of sweetpea. Child-like, they had asked for what lay farthest from hand, but Octavian trotted off gleefully to obey their welcome behest. He pulled and plucked with unsparing hand, and brought every variety of tint that he could see into his bunch that was rapidly becoming a bundle. Then he turned to retrace his steps, and found the blank wall blanker and more deserted than ever, while the foreground was void of all trace of Olivia. Far down the meadow three children were pushing a go-cart at the utmost speed they could muster in the direction of the piggeries; it was Olivia's go-cart and Olivia sat in it, somewhat bumped and shaken by the pace at which she was being driven, but apparently retaining her wonted composure of mind.

Octavian stared for a moment at the rapidly moving group, and then started in hot pursuit, shedding as he ran sprays of blossom from the mass of sweet-pea that he still clutched in his hands. Fast as he ran the children had reached the piggery before he could overtake them, and he arrived just in time to see Olivia, wondering but unprotesting, hauled and pushed up to the roof of the nearest sty. They were old buildings in some need of repair, and the rickety roof would certainly not have borne Octavian's weight if he had attempted to follow his daughter and her captors on their new vantage ground.

"What are you going to do with her?" he panted. There was no mistaking the grim trend of mischief in those flushed by sternly composed young faces.

"Hang her in chains over a slow fire," said one of the boys. Evidently, they had been reading English history.

"Frow her down the pigs will d'vour her, every bit 'cept the palms of her hands," said the other boy. It was also evident that they had studied Biblical history.

The last proposal was the one which most alarmed Octavian, since it might be carried into effect at a moment's notice; there had been cases, he remembered, of pigs eating babies.

"You surely wouldn't treat my poor little Olivia in that way?" he pleaded.

"You killed our little cat," came in stern reminder from three throats.

"I'm sorry I did," said Octavian, and if there is a standard measurement in truths Octavian's statement was assuredly a large nine.

"We shall be very sorry when we've killed Olivia," said the girl, "but we can't be sorry till we've done it."

The inexorable child-logic rose like an unyielding rampart before Octavian's scared pleadings. Before he could think of any fresh line of appeal his energies were called out in another direction. Olivia had slid off the roof and fallen with a soft, unctuous splash into a morass of muck and decaying straw. Octavian scrambled hastily over the pigsty wall to her rescue, and at once found himself in a quagmire that engulfed his feet. Olivia, after the first shock of surprise at her sudden drop through the air, had been mildly pleased at finding herself in close and unstinted contact with the sticky element that oozed around her, but as she began to sink gently into the bed of slime a feeling dawned on her that she was not after all very happy, and she began to cry in the tentative fashion of the normally good child.

Octavian, battling with the quagmire, which seemed to have learned the rare art of giving way at all points without yielding an inch, saw his daughter slowly disappearing in the engulfing slush, her smeared face further distorted with the contortions of whimpering wonder, while from their perch on the pigsty roof the three children looked down with the cold unpitying detachment of the Parcae Sisters.

"I can't reach her in time," gasped Octavian, "she'll be choked in the muck. Won't you help her?"

"No one helped our cat," came the inevitable reminder.

"I'll do anything to show you how sorry I am about that," cried Octavian, with a further desperate flounder, which carried him scarcely two inches forward.

"Will you stand in a white sheet by the grave?"

"Yes," screamed Octavian.

"Holding a candle?"

"An' saying 'I'm a miserable Beast'?"

Octavian agreed to both suggestions.

"For a long, long time?"

"For half an hour," said Octavian. There was an anxious ring in his voice as he named the time-limit; was there not the precedent of a German king who did open-air penance for several days and nights at Christmas-time clad only in his shirt? Fortunately, the children did not appear to have read German history, and half an hour seemed long and goodly in their eyes.

"All right," came with threefold solemnity from the roof, and a moment later a short ladder had been laboriously pushed across to Octavian, who lost no time in propping it against the low pigsty wall. Scrambling gingerly along its rungs he was able to lean across the morass that separated him from his slowly foundering offspring and extract her like an unwilling cork from its slushy embrace. A few minutes later he was listening to the shrill and repeated assurances of the nursemaid that her previous experience of filthy spectacles had been

119

on a notably smaller scale.

That same evening when twilight was deepening into darkness Octavian took up his position as penitent under the lone oak-tree, having first carefully undressed the part. Clad in a zephyr shirt, which on this occasion thoroughly merited its name, he held in one hand a lighted candle and in the other a watch, into which the soul of a dead plumber seemed to have passed. A box of matches lay at his feet and was resorted to on the fairly frequent occasions when the candle succumbed to the night breezes. The house loomed inscrutable in the middle distance, but as Octavian conscientiously repeated the formula of his penance, he felt certain that three pairs of solemn eyes were watching his moth-shared vigil.

And the next morning his eyes were gladdened by a sheet of copy-book paper lying beside the blank wall, on which was written the message "Un-Beast."

The Purple of the Balkan Kings

Luitpold Wolkenstein, financier and diplomat on a small, obtru-
sive, self-important scale, sat in his favoured *café* in the world-wise
Habsburg capital, confronted with the *Neue Freie Presse* and the cup of
cream-topped coffee and attendant glass of water that a sleek-headed
piccolo had just brought him. For years longer than a dog's lifetime
sleek-headed *piccolos* had placed the *Neue Freie Presse* and a cup of
cream-topped coffee on his table; for years he had sat at the same
spot, under the dust-coated, stuffed eagle, that had once been a living,
soaring bird on the Styrian mountains, and was now made monstrous
and symbolical with a second head grafted on to its neck and a gilt
crown planted on either dusty skull. Today Luitpold Wolkenstein read
no more than the first article in his paper, but read it again and again.

"The Turkish fortress of Kirk Kilisseh has fallen . . . The Serbs, it is
officially announced, have taken Kumanovo . . . The fortress of Kirk
Kilisseh lost, Kumanovo taken by the Serbs, these are tiding for Con-
stantinople resembling something out of Shakespeare's tragedies of the
kings . . . The neighbourhood of Adrianople and the Eastern region,
where the great battle is now in progress, will not reveal merely the
future of Turkey, but also what position and what influence the Balkan
States are to have in the world."

For years longer than a dog's lifetime Luitpold Wolkenstein had
disposed of the pretensions and strivings of the Balkan States over the
cup of cream-topped coffee that sleek-headed *piccolos* had brought
him. Never travelling further eastward than the horse-fair at Temesvar,
never inviting personal risk in an encounter with anything more po-
tentially desperate than a hare or partridge, he had constituted himself
the critical appraiser and arbiter of the military and national prowess
of the small countries that fringed the Dual Monarchy on its Danube
border. And his judgment had been one of unsparing contempt for

121

small-scale efforts, of unquestioning respect for the big battalions and full purses. Over the whole scene of the Balkan territories and their troubled histories had loomed the commanding magic of the words "the Great Powers"—even more imposing in their Teutonic rendering, "*Die Grossmachte.*"

Worshipping power and force and money-mastery as an elderly nerve-ridden woman might worship youthful physical energy, the comfortable, plump-bodied *café*-oracle had jested and gibed at the ambitions of the Balkan kinglets and their peoples, had unloosed against them that battery of strange lip-sounds that a Viennese employs almost as an auxiliary language to express the thoughts when his thoughts are not complimentary. British travellers had visited the Balkan lands and reported high things of the Bulgarians and their future, Russian officers had taken peeps at their army and confessed "this is a thing to be reckoned with, and it is not we who have created it, they have done it by themselves."

But over his cups of coffee and his hour-long games of dominoes the oracle had laughed and wagged his head and distilled the worldly wisdom of his castle. The *Grossmachte* had not succeeded in stifling the roll of the war-drum, that was true; the big battalions of the Ottoman Empire would have to do some talking, and then the big purses and big threatenings of the Powers would speak and the last word would be with them.

In imagination Luitpold heard the onward tramp of the red-*fez*-*zed* bayonet bearers echoing through the Balkan passes, saw the little sheepskin-clad mannikins driven back to their villages, saw the augustly chiding spokesman of the Powers dictating, adjusting, restoring, settling things once again in their allotted places, sweeping up the dust of conflict, and now his ears had to listen to the war-drum rolling in quite another direction, had to listen to the tramp of battalions that were bigger and bolder and better skilled in war-craft than he had deemed possible in that quarter; his eyes had to read in the columns of his accustomed newspaper a warning to the *Grossmachte* that they had something new to learn, something new to reckon with, much that was time-honoured to relinquish.

"The Great Powers will have not little difficulty in persuading the Balkan States of the inviolability of the principle that Europe cannot permit any fresh partition of territory in the East without her approval. Even now, while the campaign is still undecided, there are rumours of a project of fiscal unity, extending over the entire Balkan lands, and further of a constitutional union in imitation of the German Empire. That is perhaps only a political straw blown by the storm, but it is not possible to dismiss the reflection that the Balkan States leagued together command a military strength with which the Great Powers will have to reckon . . .

The people who have poured out their blood on the battlefields and sacrificed the available armed men of an entire generation in order to encompass a union with their kinsfolk will not remain any longer in an attitude of dependence on the Great Powers or on Russia, but will go their own ways . . . The blood that has been poured forth today gives for the first time a genuine tone to the purple of the Balkan Kings. The Great Powers cannot overlook the fact that a people that has tasted victory will not let itself be driven back again within its former limits. Turkey has lost today not only Kirk Kilisseh and Kumanovo, but Macedonia also."

Luitpold Wolkenstein drank his coffee, but the flavour had somehow gone out of it. His world, his pompous, imposing, dictating world, had suddenly rolled up into narrower dimensions. The big purses and the big threats had been pushed unceremoniously on one side; a force that he could not fathom, could not comprehend, had made itself rudely felt. The august Caesars of Mammon and armament had looked down frowningly on the combat, and those about to die had *not* saluted, had no intention of saluting. A lesson was being imposed on unwilling learners, a lesson of respect for certain fundamental principles, and it was not the small struggling States who were being taught the lesson.

Luitpold Wolkenstein did not wait for the quorum of domino players to arrive. They would all have read the article in *the Freie Presse*. And there are moments when an oracle finds its greatest salvation in withdrawing itself from the area of human questioning.

The Remoulding of Groby Lington

A man is known by the company he keeps.

In the morning-room of his sister-in-law's house Groby Lington fidgeted away the passing minutes with the demure restlessness of advanced middle age. About a quarter of an hour would have to elapse before it would be time to say his goodbyes and make his way across the village green to the station, with a selected escort of nephews and nieces. He was a good-natured, kindly dispositioned man, and in theory he was delighted to pay periodical visits to the wife and children of his dead brother William; in practice, he infinitely preferred the comfort and seclusion of his own house and garden, and the companionship of his books and his parrot to these rather meaningless and tiresome incursions into a family circle with which he had little in common.

It was not so much the spur of his own conscience that drove him to make the occasional short journey by rail to visit his relatives, as an obedient concession to the more insistent but vicarious conscience of his brother, Colonel John, who was apt to accuse him of neglecting poor old William's family. Groby usually forgot or ignored the existence of his neighbour kinsfolk until such time as he was threatened with a visit from the colonel, when he would put matters straight by a burned pilgrimage across the few miles of intervening country to renew his acquaintance with the young people and assume a kindly if rather forced interest in the well-being of his sister-in-law.

On this occasion he had cut matters so fine between the timing of his exculpatory visit and the coming of Colonel John, that he would scarcely be home before the latter was due to arrive. Anyhow, Groby had got it over, and six or seven months might decently elapse before he need again sacrifice his comforts and inclinations on the altar of family sociability. He was inclined to be distinctly cheerful as he hopped about the room, picking up first one object, then another, and

125

subjecting each to a brief bird-like scrutiny.

Presently his cheerful listlessness changed sharply to an attitude of vexed attention. In a scrap-book of drawings and caricatures belonging to one of his nephews he had come across an unkindly clever sketch of himself and his parrot, solemnly confronting each other in postures of ridiculous gravity and repose, and bearing a likeness to one another that the artist had done his utmost to accentuate.

After the first flush of annoyance had passed away, Groby laughed good-naturedly and admitted to himself the cleverness of the drawing. Then the feeling of resentment repossessed him, resentment not against the caricaturist who had embodied the idea in pen and ink, but against the possible truth that the idea represented. Was it really the case that people grew in time to resemble the animals they kept as pets, and had he unconsciously become more and more like the comically solemn bird that was his constant companion?

Groby was unusually silent as he walked to the train with his escort of chattering nephews and nieces, and during the short railway journey his mind was more and more possessed with an introspective conviction that he had gradually settled down into a sort of parrot-like existence. What, after all, did his daily routine amount to but a sedate meandering and pecking and perching, in his garden, among his fruit trees, in his wicker chair on the lawn, or by the fireside in his library? And what was the sum total of his conversation with chance-encountered neighbours? "Quite a spring day, isn't it?" "It looks as though we should have some rain." "Glad to see you about again; you must take care of yourself." "How the young folk shoot up, don't they?"

Strings of stupid, inevitable perfunctory remarks came to his mind, remarks that were certainly not the mental exchange of human intelligences, but mere empty parrot-talk. One might really just as well salute one's acquaintances with "Pretty Polly. Puss, puss, miaow!" Groby began to fume against the picture of himself as a foolish feathered fowl which his nephews sketch had first suggested, and which his own accusing imagination was filling in with such unflattering detail.

"I'll give the beastly bird away," he said resentfully; though he knew at the same time that he would do no such thing. It would look so absurd after all the years that he had kept the parrot and made much of it suddenly to try and find it a new home.

"Has my brother arrived?" he asked of the stable-boy, who had come with the pony-carriage to meet him.

"Yessir, came down by the two-fifteen. Your parrot's dead." The boy made the latter announcement with the relish which his class finds in proclaiming a catastrophe.

"My parrot dead?" said Groby. "What caused its death?"

"The ipe," said the boy briefly.

"The ipe?" queried Groby. "Whatever's that?"

"The ipe what the colonel brought down with him," came the rather alarming answer.

"Do you mean to say my brother is ill?" asked Groby. "Is it something infectious?"

"Th' coloners so well as ever he was," said the boy; and as no further explanation was forthcoming Groby had to possess himself in mystified patience till he reached home. His brother was waiting for him at the hall door.

"Have you heard about the parrot?" he asked at once. "'Pon my soul I'm awfully sorry. The moment he saw the monkey I'd brought down as a surprise for you he squawked out, 'Rats to you, sir!' and the blessed monkey made one spring at him, got him by the neck and whirled him round like a rattle. He was as dead as mutton by the time I'd got him out of the little beggar's paws. Always been such a friendly little beast, the monkey has, should never have thought he'd got it in him to see red like that. Can't tell you how sorry I feel about it, and now of course you'll hate the sight of the monkey."

"Not at all," said Groby sincerely. A few hours earlier the tragic end which had befallen his parrot would have presented itself to him as a calamity; now it arrived almost as a polite attention on the part of the Fates.

"The bird was getting old, you know," he went on, in explanation of his obvious lack of decent regret at the loss of his pet. "I was really beginning to wonder if it was an unmixed kindness to let him go on living, till he succumbed to old age. What a charming little monkey!" he added, when he was introduced to the culprit.

The newcomer was a small, long-tailed monkey from the Western Hemisphere, with a gentle, half-shy, half-trusting manner that instantly captured Groby's confidence; a student of simian character might have seen in the fitful red light in its eyes some indication of the underlying temper which the parrot had so rashly put to the test with such dramatic consequences for itself. The servants, who had come to regard the defunct bird as a regular member of the household, and one who gave really very little trouble, were scandalized to find his bloodthirsty aggressor installed in his place as an honoured domestic pet.

"A nasty heathen ipe what don't never say nothing sensible and cheerful, same as pore Polly did," was the unfavourable verdict of the kitchen quarters.

One Sunday morning, some twelve or fourteen months after the visit of Colonel John and the parrot-tragedy, Miss Wepley sat decorously in her pew in the parish church, immediately in front of that occupied by Groby Lington. She was, comparatively speaking, a newcomer in the neighbourhood, and was not personally acquainted with her fellow-worshipper in the seat behind, but for the past two years the Sunday morning service had brought them regularly within each other's sphere of consciousness. Without having paid particular attention to the subject, she could probably have given a correct rendering of the way in which he pronounced certain words occurring in the responses, while he was well aware of the trivial fact that, in addition to her prayer book and handkerchief, a small paper packet of throat lozenges always reposed on the seat beside her.

Miss Wepley rarely had recourse to her lozenges, but in case she should be taken with a fit of coughing she wished to have the emergency duly provided for. On this particular Sunday the lozenges occasioned an unusual diversion in the even tenor of her devotions, far more disturbing to her personally than a prolonged attack of coughing would have been. As she rose to take part in the singing of the first hymn, she fancied that she saw the hand of her neighbour, who was alone in the pew behind her, make a furtive downward grab at the packet lying on the seat; on turning sharply round she found that the packet had certainly disappeared, but Mr. Lington was to all outward seeming serenely intent on his hymn-book. No amount of interrogatory glaring on the part of the despoiled lady could bring the least shade of conscious guilt to his face.

"Worse was to follow," as she remarked afterwards to a scandalized audience of friends and acquaintances. "I had scarcely knelt in prayer when a lozenge, one of *my* lozenges, came whizzing into the pew, just under my nose. I turned round and stared, but Mr. Lington had his eyes closed and his lips moving as though engaged in prayer. The moment I resumed my devotions another lozenge came rattling in, and then another. I took no notice for a while, and then turned round suddenly just as the dreadful man was about to flip another one at me. He hastily pretended to be turning over the leaves of his book but I was not to be taken in that time. He saw that he had been discovered and no more lozenges came. Of course, I have changed my pew."

"No gentleman would have acted in such a disgraceful manner," said one of her listeners; "and yet Mr. Lington used to be so respected by everybody. He seems to have behaved like a little ill-bred school-boy."

"He behaved like a monkey," said Miss Wepley.

Her unfavourable verdict was echoed in other quarters about the same time. Groby Lington had never been a hero in the eyes of his personal retainers, but he had shared the approval accorded to his defunct parrot as a cheerful well-dispositioned body, who gave no particular trouble. Of late months, however, this character would hardly have been endorsed by the members of his domestic establishment. The stolid stable-boy, who had first announced to him the tragic end of his feathered pet, was one of the first to give voice to the murmurs of disapproval which became rampant and general in the servants' quarters, and he had fairly substantial grounds for his disaffection.

In a burst of hot summer weather, he had obtained permission to bathe in a modest-sized pond in the orchard, and thither one afternoon Groby had bent his steps, attracted by loud imprecations of anger mingled with the shriller chattering of monkey-language. He beheld his plump diminutive servitor, clad only in a waistcoat and a pair of socks, storming ineffectually at the monkey which was seated on a low branch of an apple tree, abstractedly fingering the remainder of the boy's outfit, which he had removed just out of his reach.

"The ipe's been an' took my clothes," whined the boy, with the passion of his kind for explaining the obvious. His incomplete toilet effect rather embarrassed him, but he hailed the arrival of Groby with relief, as promising moral and material support in his efforts to get back his raided garments. The monkey had ceased its defiant jabbering, and doubtless with a little coaxing from its master it would hand back the plunder.

"If I lift you up," suggested Groby, "you will just be able to reach the clothes."

The boy agreed, and Groby clutched him firmly by the waistcoat, which was about all there was to catch hold of, and lifted him clear of the ground. Then, with a deft swing he sent him crashing into a clump of tag nettles, which closed receptively round him. The victim had not been brought up in a school which teaches one to repress one's emotions—if a fox had attempted to gnaw at his vitals, he would have flown to complain to the nearest hunt committee rather than have affected an attitude of stoical indifference. On this occasion the volume of sound which he produced under the stimulus of pain and rage and astonishment was generous and sustained, but above his bellowings he could distinctly hear the triumphant chattering of his enemy in the tree, and a peal of shrill laughter from Groby.

When the boy had finished an improvised St.Vitus caracole, which would have brought him fame on the boards of the Coliseum, and which indeed met with ready appreciation and applause from the retreating figure of Groby Lington, he found that the monkey had also discreetly retired, while his clothes were scattered on the grass at the foot of the tree.

"They'm two ipes, that's what they be," he muttered angrily, and if his judgment was severe, at least he spoke under the sting of considerable provocation.

It was a week or two later that the parlour-maid gave notice, having been terrified almost to tears by an outbreak of sudden temper on the part of the master anent some under done cutlets. "'E gnashed 'is teeth at me, 'e did reely," she informed a sympathetic kitchen audience.

"I'd like to see 'im talk like that to me, I would," said the cook defiantly, but her cooking from that moment showed a marked improvement.

It was seldom that Groby Lington so far detached himself from his accustomed habits as to go and form one of a house-party, and he was not a little piqued that Mrs. Glenduff should have stowed him away in the musty old Georgian wing of the house, in the next room, moreover, to Leonard Spabbink, the eminent pianist.

"He plays Liszt like an angel," had been the hostess's enthusiastic testimonial.

"He may play him like a trout for all I care," had been Groby's mental comment, "but I wouldn't mind betting that he snores. He's just the sort and shape that would. And if I hear him snoring through those ridiculous thin-panelled walls, there'll be trouble."

He did, and there was.

Groby stood it for about two and a quarter minutes, and then made his way through the corridor into Spabbink's room. Under Groby's vigorous measures the musicians flabby, redundant figure sat up in bewildered semi-consciousness like an icecream that has been taught to beg. Groby prodded him into complete wakefulness, and then the pettish self-satisfied pianist fairly lost his temper and slapped his domineering visitant on the hand. In another moment Spabbink was being nearly stifled and very effectually gagged by a pillow-case

130

tightly bound round his head, while his plump pyjama'd limbs were hauled out of bed and smacked, pinched, kicked, and bumped in a catch-as-catch-can progress across the floor, towards the flat shallow bath in whose utterly inadequate depths Groby perseveringly strove to drown him.

For a few moments the room was almost in darkness: Groby's candle had overturned in an early stage of the scuffle, and its flicker scarcely reached to the spot where splashings, smacks, muffled cries, and splutterings, and a chatter of ape-like rage told of the struggle that was being waged round the shores of the bath. A few instants later the one-sided combat was brightly lit up by the flare of blazing curtains and rapidly kindling panelling.

When the hastily aroused members of the house-party stampeded out on to the lawn, the Georgian wing was well alight and belching forth masses of smoke, but some moments elapsed before Groby appeared with the half-drowned pianist in his arms, having just bethought him of the superior drowning facilities offered by the pond at the bottom of the lawn. The cool night air sobered his rage, and when he found that he was innocently acclaimed as the heroic rescuer of poor Leonard Spabbink, and loudly commended for his presence of mind in tying a wet cloth round his head to protect him from smoke suffocation, he accepted the situation, and subsequently gave a graphic account of his finding the musician asleep with an overturned candle by his side and the conflagration well started.

Spabbink gave his version some days later, when he had partially recovered from the shock of his midnight castigation and immersion, but the gentle pitying smiles and evasive comments with which his story was greeted warned him that the public ear was not at his disposal. He refused, however, to attend the ceremonial presentation of the Royal Humane Society's life-saving medal.

It was about this time that Groby's pet monkey fell a victim to the disease which attacks so many of its kind when brought under the influence of a northern climate. Its master appeared to be profoundly affected by its loss, and never quite recovered the level of spirits that he had recently attained. In company with the tortoise, which Colonel John presented to him on his last visit, he potters about his lawn and kitchen garden, with none of his erstwhile sprightliness; and his nephews and nieces are fairly well justified in alluding to him as "Old Uncle Groby."

The Reticence of Lady Anne

Egbert came into the large, dimly lit drawing-room with the air of a man who is not certain whether he is entering a dovecote or a bomb factory, and is prepared for either eventuality. The little domestic quarrel over the luncheon-table had not been fought to a definite finish, and the question was how far Lady Anne was in a mood to renew or forgo hostilities. Her pose in the armchair by the tea-table was rather elaborately rigid; in the gloom of a December afternoon Egbert's *pince-nez* did not materially help him to discern the expression of her face.

By way of breaking whatever ice might be floating on the surface he made a remark about a dim religious light. He or Lady Anne were accustomed to make that remark between 4.30 and 6 on winter and late autumn evenings; it was a part of their married life. There was no recognised rejoinder to it, and Lady Anne made none.

Don Tarquinio lay astretch on the Persian rug, basking in the fire-light with superb indifference to the possible ill-humour of Lady Anne. His pedigree was as flawlessly Persian as the rug, and his ruff was coming into the glory of its second winter. The page-boy, who had Renaissance tendencies, had christened him Don Tarquinio. Left to themselves, Egbert and Lady Anne would unfailingly have called him Fluff, but they were not obstinate.

Egbert poured himself out some tea. As the silence gave no sign of breaking on Lady Anne's initiative, he braced himself for another Yermak effort.

"My remark at lunch had a purely academic application," he announced; "you seem to put an unnecessarily personal significance into it."

Lady Anne maintained her defensive barrier of silence. The bullfinch lazily filled in the interval with an air from *Iphigénie en Tauride*.

Egbert recognised it immediately, because it was the only air the bull-finch whistled, and he had come to them with the reputation for whistling it. Both Egbert and Lady Anne would have preferred something from *The Yeoman of the Guards* which was their favourite opera. In matters artistic they had a similarity of taste. They leaned towards the honest and explicit in art, a picture, for instance, that told its own story, with generous assistance from its title.

A riderless warhorse with harness in obvious disarray, staggering into a courtyard full of pale swooning women, and marginally noted "Bad News," suggested to their minds a distinct interpretation of some military catastrophe. They could see what it was meant to convey, and explain it to friends of duller intelligence.

The silence continued. As a rule, Lady Anise's displeasure became articulate and markedly voluble after four minutes of introductory muteness. Egbert seized the milk-jug and poured some of its contents into Don Tarquinio's saucer; as the saucer was already full to the brim an unsightly overflow was the result. Don Tarquinio looked on with a surprised interest that evanesced into elaborate unconsciousness when he was appealed to by Egbert to come and drink up some of the spilt matter. Don Tarquinio was prepared to play many roles in life, but a vacuum carpet-cleaner was not one of them.

"Don't you think we're being rather foolish?" said Egbert cheerfully.

If Lady Anne thought so she didn't say so.

"I daresay the fault has been partly on my side," continued Egbert, with evaporating cheerfulness. "After all, I'm only human, you know. You seem to forget that I'm only human."

He insisted on the point, as if there had been unfounded suggestions that he was built on Satyr lines, with goat continuations where the human left off.

The bullfinch recommenced its air from *Iphigénie en Tauride.* Egbert began to feel depressed. Lady Anne was not drinking her tea. Perhaps she was feeling unwell. But when Lady Anne felt unwell, she was not wont to be reticent on the subject. "No one knows what I suffer from indigestion" was one of her favourite statements; but the lack of knowledge can only have been caused by defective listening; the amount of information available on the subject would have supplied material for a monograph.

Evidently Lady Anne was not feeling unwell.

Egbert began to think he was being unreasonably dealt with; naturally he began to make concessions.

"I daresay," he observed, taking as central a position on the hearth-rug as Don Tarquinio could be persuaded to concede him, "I may have been to blame. I am willing, if I can thereby restore things to a happier standpoint, to undertake to lead a better life."

He wondered vaguely how it would be possible. Temptations came to him, in middle age, tentatively and without insistence, like a neglected butcher-boy who asks for a Christmas box in February for no more hopeful reason than that he didn't get one in December. He had no more idea of succumbing to them, than he had of purchasing the fish-knives and fur boas that ladies are impelled to sacrifice through the medium of advertisement columns during twelve months of the year. Still, there was something impressive in this unasked-for renunciation of possibly latent enormities.

Lady Anne showed no sign of being impressed.

Egbert looked at her nervously through his glasses. To get the worst of an argument with her was no new experience. To get the worst of a monologue was a humiliating novelty.

"I shall go and dress for dinner," he announced in a voice into which he intended some shade of sternness to creep.

At the door a final access of weakness impelled him to make a further appeal.

"Aren't we being very silly?"

"A fool," was Don Tarquinio's mental comment as the door closed on Egbert's retreat. Then he lifted his velvet forepaws in the air and leapt lightly on to a bookshelf immediately under the bullfinch's cage. It was the first time he had seemed to notice the bird's existence, but he was carrying out a long formed theory of action with the precision of nature deliberation. The bullfinch, who had fancied himself something of a despot, depressed himself of a sudden into a third of his normal displacement; then he fell to a helpless wing-beating and shrill cheeping. He had cost twenty-seven shillings without the cage, but Lady Anne made no sign of interfering. She had been dead for two hours.

The Saint and the Goblin

The little stone Saint occupied a retired niche in a side aisle of the old cathedral. No one quite remembered who he had been, but that in a way was a guarantee of respectability. At least so the Goblin said. The Goblin was a very fine specimen of quaint stone carving, and lived up in the corbel on the wall opposite the niche of the little Saint. He was connected with some of the best cathedral folk, such as the queer carvings in the choir stalls and chancel screen, and even the gargoyles high up on the roof. All the fantastic beasts and manikins that sprawled and twisted in wood or stone or lead overhead in the arches or away down in the crypt were in some way akin to him; consequently, he was a person of recognised importance in the cathedral world.

The little stone Saint and the Goblin got on very well together, though they looked at most things from different points of view. The Saint was a philanthropist in an old-fashioned way; he thought the world, as he saw it, was good, but might be improved. In particular he pitied the church mice, who were miserably poor. The Goblin, on the other hand, was of opinion that the world, as he knew it, was bad, but had better be let alone. It was the function of the church mice to be poor.

"All the same," said the Saint, "I feel very sorry for them."

"Of course, you do," said the Goblin; "it's *your* function to feel sorry for them. If they were to leave off being poor you couldn't fulfil your functions. You'd be a sinecure."

He rather hoped that the Saint would ask him what a sinecure meant, but the latter took refuge in a stony silence. The Goblin might be right, but still, he thought, he would like to do something for the church mice before winter came on; they were so very poor.

Whilst he was thinking the matter over, he was startled by something falling between his feet with a hard metallic clatter. It was a bright new *thaler*, one of the cathedral jackdaws, who collected such things, had flown in with it to a stone cornice just above his niche, and the banging of the sacristy door had startled him into dropping it. Since the invention of gunpowder, the family nerves were not what they had been.

"What have you got there?" asked the Goblin.

"A silver *thaler*," said the Saint. "Really," he continued, "it is most fortunate; now I can do something for the church mice."

"How will you manage it?" asked the Goblin.

The Saint considered.

"I will appear in a vision to the vergeress who sweeps the floors. I will tell her that she will find a silver *thaler* between my feet, and that she must take it and buy a measure of corn and put it on my shrine. When she finds the money, she will know that it was a true dream, and she will take care to follow my directions. Then the mice will have food all the winter."

"Of course, *you* can do that," observed the Goblin. "Now, I can only appear to people after they have had a heavy supper of indigestible things. My opportunities with the vergeress would be limited. There is some advantage in being a saint after all."

All this while the coin was lying at the Saint's feet. It was clean and glittering and had the Elector's arms beautifully stamped upon it. The Saint began to reflect that such an opportunity was too rare to be hastily disposed of. Perhaps indiscriminate charity might be harmful to the church mice. After all, it was their function to be poor; the Goblin had said so, and the Goblin was generally right.

"I've been thinking," he said to that personage, "that perhaps it would be really better if I ordered a *thaler's* worth of candles to be placed on my shrine instead of the corn."

He often wished, for the look of the thing, that people would sometimes burn candles at his shrine; but as they had forgotten who he was it was not considered a profitable speculation to pay him that attention.

"Candles would be more orthodox," said the Goblin.

"More orthodox, certainly," agreed the Saint, "and the mice could have the ends to eat; candle-ends are most fattening."

The Goblin was too well bred to wink; besides, being a stone goblin, it was out of the question.

★★★★★★★★★

"Well, if it ain't there, sure enough!" said the vergeress next morning. She took the shining coin down from the dusty niche and turned it over and over in her grimy hands. Then she put it to her mouth and bit it.

"She can't be going to eat it," thought the Saint, and fixed her with his stoniest stare.

"Well," said the woman, in a somewhat shriller key, "who'd have thought it! A saint, too!"

Then she did an unaccountable thing. She hunted an old piece of tape out of her pocket, and tied to crosswise, with a big loop, round the *thaler*, and hung it round the neck of the little Saint.

Then she went away.

"The only possible explanation," said the Goblin, "is that it's a bad one."

★★★★★★★★★★★

"What is that decoration your neighbour is wearing?" asked a wyvern that was wrought into the capital of an adjacent pillar.

The Saint was ready to cry with mortification, only, being of stone, he couldn't.

"It's a coin of—ahem!—fabulous value," replied the Goblin tactfully.

And the news went round the cathedral that the shrine of the little stone Saint had been enriched by a priceless offering.

"After all, it's something to have the conscience of a goblin," said the Saint to himself.

The church mice were as poor as ever. But that was their function.

The Secret Sin of Septimus Brope

"Who and what is Mr. Brope?" demanded the aunt of Clovis suddenly.

Mrs. Riversedge, who had been snipping off the heads of defunct roses, and thinking of nothing in particular, sprang hurriedly to mental attention. She was one of those old-fashioned hostesses who consider that one ought to know something about one's guests, and that the something ought to be to their credit.

"I believe he comes from Leighton Buzzard," she observed by way of preliminary explanation.

"In these days of rapid and convenient travel," said Clovis, who was dispersing a colony of green-fly with visitations of cigarette smoke, "to come from Leighton Buzzard does not necessarily denote any great strength of character. It might only mean mere restlessness. Now if he had left it under a cloud, or as a protest against the incurable and heartless frivolity of its inhabitants, that would tell us something about the man and his mission in life."

"What does he do?" pursued Mrs. Troyle magisterially.

"He edits the *Cathedral Monthly*," said her hostess, "and he's enormously learned about memorial brasses and transepts and the influence of Byzantine worship on modern liturgy, and all those sort of things. Perhaps he is just a little bit heavy and immersed in one range of subjects, but it takes all sorts to make a good house-party, you know. You don't find him *too* dull, do you?"

"Dullness I could overlook," said the aunt of Clovis: "what I cannot forgive is his making love to my maid."

"My dear Mrs. Troyle," gasped the hostess, "what an extraordinary idea! I assure you Mr. Brope would not dream of doing such a thing."

"His dreams are a matter of indifference to me; for all I care his slumbers may be one long indiscretion of unsuitable erotic advances, in which the entire servants' hall may be involved. But in his waking hours he shall not make love to my maid. It's no use arguing about it, I'm firm on the point."

"But you must be mistaken," persisted Mrs. Riversedge; "Mr. Brope would be the last person to do such a thing."

"He is the first person to do such a thing, as far as my information goes, and if I have any voice in the matter, he certainly shall be the last. Of course, I am not referring to respectably-intentioned lovers."

"I simply cannot think that a man who writes so charmingly and informingly about transepts and Byzantine influences would behave in such an unprincipled manner," said Mrs. Riversedge; "what evidence have you that he's doing anything of the sort? I don't want to doubt your word, of course, but we mustn't be too ready to condemn him unheard, must we?"

"Whether we condemn him or not, he has certainly not been unheard. He has the room next to my dressing-room, and on two occasions, when I dare say he thought I was absent, I have plainly heard him announcing through the wall, 'I love you, Florrie.' Those partition walls upstairs are very thin; one can almost hear a watch ticking in the next room."

"Is your maid called Florence?"

"Her name is Florinda."

"What an extraordinary name to give a maid!"

"I did not give it to her; she arrived in my service already christened."

"What I mean is," said Mrs. Riversedge, "that when I get maids with unsuitable names, I call them Jane; they soon get used to it."

"An excellent plan," said the aunt of Clovis coldly; "unfortunately I have got used to being called Jane myself. It happens to be my name."

She cut short Mrs. Riversedge's flood of apologies by abruptly remarking:

"The question is not whether I'm to call my maid Florinda, but whether Mr. Brope is to be permitted to call her Florrie. I am strongly of opinion that he shall not."

"He may have been repeating the words of some song," said Mrs. Riversedge hopefully; "there are lots of those sorts of silly refrains with girls' names," she continued, turning to Clovis as a possible authority on the subject. "'You mustn't call me Mary—'"

"I shouldn't think of doing so," Clovis assured her; "in the first place, I've always understood that your name was Henrietta; and then

I hardly know you well enough to take such a liberty."

"I mean there's a *song with* that refrain," hurriedly explained Mrs. Riversedge, "and there's 'Rhoda, Rhoda kept a *pagoda*,' and 'Maisie is a daisy,' and heaps of others. Certainly, it doesn't sound like Mr. Brope to be singing such songs, but I think we ought to give him the benefit of the doubt."

"I had already done so," said Mrs. Troyle, "until further evidence came my way.

She shut her lips with the resolute finality of one who enjoys the blessed certainty of being implored to open them again.

"Further evidence!" exclaimed her hostess; "do tell me!"

"As I was coming upstairs after breakfast Mr. Brope was just passing my room. In the most natural way in the world a piece of paper dropped out of a packet that he held in his hand and fluttered to the ground just at my door. I was going to call out to him 'You've dropped something,' and then for some reason I held back and didn't show myself till he was safely in his room. You see it occurred to me that I was very seldom in my room just at that hour, and that Florinda was almost always there tidying up things about that time. So, I picked up that innocent-looking piece of paper."

Mrs. Troyle paused again, with the self-applauding air of one who has detected an asp lurking in an apple-charlotte.

Mrs. Riversedge snipped vigorously at the nearest rose bush, incidentally decapitating a Viscountess Folkestone that was just coming into bloom.

"What was on the paper?" she asked.

"Just the words in pencil, 'I love you, Florrie,' and then underneath, crossed out with a faint line, but perfectly plain to read, 'Meet me in the garden by the yew.'"

"There *is* a yew tree at the bottom of the garden," admitted Mrs. Riversedge.

"At any rate he appears to be truthful," commented Clovis.

"To think that a scandal of this sort should be going on under my roof!" said Mrs. Riversedge indignantly.

"I wonder why it is that scandal seems so much worse under a roof," observed Clovis; "I've always regarded it as a proof of the superior delicacy of the cat tribe that it conducts most of its scandals above the slates."

"Now I come to think of it," resumed Mrs. Riversedge, "there are things about Mr. Brope that I've never been able to account for. His income, for instance: he only gets two hundred a year as editor of the *Cathedral Monthly*, and I know that his people are quite poor, and he hasn't any private means. Yet he manages to afford a flat somewhere in Westminster, and he goes abroad to Bruges and those sorts of places every year, and always dresses well, and gives quite nice luncheon-parties in the season. You can't do all that on two hundred a year, can you?"

"Does he write for any other papers?" queried Mrs. Troyle.

"No, you see he specializes so entirely on liturgy and ecclesiastical architecture that his field is rather restricted. He once tried the *Sporting and Dramatic* with an article on church edifices in famous fox-hunting centres, but it wasn't considered of sufficient general interest to be accepted. No, I don't see how he can support himself in his present style merely by what he writes."

"Perhaps he sells spurious transepts to American enthusiasts," suggested Clovis.

"How could you sell a transept?" said Mrs. Riversedge; "such a thing would be impossible."

"Whatever he may do to eke out his income," interrupted Mrs. Troyle, "he is certainly not going to fill in his leisure moments by making love to my maid."

"Of course not," agreed her hostess; "that must be put a stop to at once. But I don't quite know what we ought to do."

"You might put a barbed wire entanglement round the yew tree as a precautionary measure," said Clovis.

"I don't think that the disagreeable situation that has arisen is improved by flippancy," said Mrs. Riversedge; "a good maid is a treasure--"

"I am sure I don't know what I should do without Florinda," admitted Mrs. Troyle; "she understands my hair. I've long ago given up trying to do anything with it myself. I regard one's hair as I regard husbands: as long as one is seen together in public one's private divergences don't matter. Surely that was the luncheon gong."

Septimus Brope and Clovis had the smoking-room to themselves after lunch. The former seemed restless and preoccupied; the latter quietly observant.

"What is a lorry?" asked Septimus suddenly; "I don't mean the thing on wheels, of course I know what that is, but isn't there a bird with a name like that, the larger form of a lorikeet?"

"I fancy it's a lory, with one 'r,'" said Clovis lazily, "in which case it's no good to you."

Septimus Brope stared in some astonishment.

"How do you mean, no good to me?" he asked, with more than a trace of uneasiness in his voice.

"Won't rhyme with Florrie," explained Clovis briefly.

Septimus sat upright in his chair, with unmistakable alarm on his face.

"How did you find out? I mean how did you know I was trying to get a rhyme to Florrie?" he asked sharply.

"I didn't know," said Clovis, "I only guessed. When you wanted to turn the prosaic lorry of commerce into a feathered poem flitting through the verdure of a tropical forest, I knew you must be working up a sonnet, and Florrie was the only female name that suggested itself as rhyming with lorry."

Septimus still looked uneasy.

"I believe you know more," he said.

Clovis laughed quietly, but said nothing.

"How much do you know?" Septimus asked desperately.

"The yew tree in the garden," said Clovis.

"There! I felt certain I'd dropped it somewhere. But you must have guessed something before. Look here, you have surprised my secret. You won't give me away, will you? It is nothing to be ashamed of, but it wouldn't do for the editor of the *Cathedral Monthly* to go in openly for that sort of thing, would it?"

"Well, I suppose not," admitted Clovis.

"You see," continued Septimus, "I get quite a decent lot of money out of it. I could never live in the style I do on what I get as editor of the *Cathedral Monthly*."

Clovis was even more startled than Septimus had been earlier in the conversation, but he was better skilled in repressing surprise.

"Do you mean to say you get money out of—Florrie?" he asked.

"Not out of Florrie, as yet," said Septimus; "in fact, I don't mind saying that I'm having a good deal of trouble over Florrie. But there are a lot of others."

Clovis's cigarette went out.

"This is very interesting," he said slowly. And then, with Septimus Brope's next words, illumination dawned on him.

"There are heaps of others; for instance:

Cora with the lips of coral,
You and I will never quarrel.

145

"That was one of my earliest successes, and it still brings me in royalties. And then there is—'Esmeralda, when I first beheld her,' and 'Fair Teresa, how I love to please her,' both of those have been fairly popular. And there is one rather dreadful one," continued Septimus, flushing deep carmine, "which has brought me in more money than any of the others:

Lively little Lucie
With her naughty nez retrousee.

"Of course, I loathe the whole lot of them; in fact, I'm rapidly becoming something of a woman-hater under their influence, but I can't afford to disregard the financial aspect of the matter. And at the same time, you can understand that my position as an authority on ecclesiastical architecture and liturgical subjects would be weakened, if not altogether ruined, if it once got about that I was the author of 'Cora with the lips of coral' and all the rest of them."

Clovis had recovered sufficiently to ask in a sympathetic, if rather unsteady, voice what was the special trouble with "Florrie."

"I can't get her into lyric shape, try as I will," said Septimus mournfully. "You see, one has to work in a lot of sentimental, sugary compliment with a catchy rhyme, and a certain amount of personal biography or prophecy. They've all of them got to have a long string of past successes recorded about them, or else you've got to foretell blissful things about them and yourself in the future. For instance, there is:

Dainty little girlie Mavis,
She is such a rara avis.
All the money I can save is
All to be for Mavis mine.

"It goes to a sickening namby-pamby waltz tune, and for months nothing else was sung and hummed in Blackpool and other popular centres."

This time Clovis's self-control broke down badly.

"Please excuse me," he gurgled, "but I can't help it when I remember the awful solemnity of that article of yours that you so kindly read us last night, on the Coptic Church in its relation to early Christian worship."

Septimus groaned.

"You see how it would be," he said; "as soon as people knew me to be the author of that miserable sentimental twaddle, all respect for the serious labours of my life would be gone. I dare say I know more about memorial brasses than anyone living, in fact I hope one day to publish a monograph on the subject, but I should be pointed out everywhere as the man whose ditties were in the mouths of minstrels along the entire coast-line of our island home. Can you wonder that I positively hate Florrie all the time that I'm trying to grind out sugar-coated rhapsodies about her?"

"Why not give free play to your emotions, and be brutally abusive? An uncomplimentary refrain would have an instant success as a novelty if you were sufficiently outspoken."

"I've never thought of that," said Septimus, "and I'm afraid I couldn't break away from the habit of fulsome adulation and suddenly change my style."

"You needn't change your style in the least," said Clovis; "merely reverse the sentiment and keep to the inane phraseology of the thing. If you'll do the body of the song, I'll knock off the refrain, which is the thing that principally matters, I believe. I shall charge half-shares in the royalties, and throw in my silence as to your guilty secret. In the eyes of the world, you shall still be the man who has devoted his life to the study of transepts and Byzantine ritual; only sometimes, in the long winter evenings, when the wind howls drearily down the chimney and the rain beats against the windows, I shall think of you as the author of 'Cora with the lips of coral.' Of course, if in sheer gratitude at my silence you like to take me for a much-needed holiday to the Adriatic or somewhere equally interesting, paying all expenses, I shouldn't dream of refusing."

Later in the afternoon Clovis found his aunt and Mrs. Riversedge indulging in gentle exercise in the Jacobean garden.

"I've spoken to Mr. Brope about F.," he announced.

"How splendid of you! What did he say?" came in a quick chorus from the two ladies.

"He was quite frank and straightforward with me when he saw that I knew his secret," said Clovis, "and it seems that his intentions were quite serious, if slightly unsuitable. I tried to show him the impracticability of the course that he was following. He said he wanted to be understood, and he seemed to think that Florinda would excel in that requirement, but I pointed out that there were probably dozens of delicately nurtured, pure-hearted young English girls who would be capable of understanding him, while Florinda was the only person in the world who understood my aunt's hair.

"That rather weighed with him, for he's not really a selfish animal,

147

if you take him in the right way, and when I appealed to the memory of his happy childish days, spent amid the daisied fields of Leighton Buzzard (I suppose daisies do grow there), he was obviously affected. Anyhow, he gave me his word that he would put Florinda absolutely out of his mind, and he has agreed to go for a short trip abroad as the best distraction for his thoughts. I am going with him as far as Ragusa. If my aunt should wish to give me a really nice scarf-pin (to be chosen by myself), as a small recognition of the very considerable service I had done her, I shouldn't dream of refusing. I'm not one of those who think that because one is abroad one can go about dressed anyhow."

A few weeks later in Blackpool and places where they sing, the following refrain held undisputed sway:

How you bore me, Florrie,
With those eyes of vacant blue;
You'll be very sorry, Florrie,
If I marry you.
Though I'm easy-goin', Florrie,
This I swear is true,
I'll throw you down a quarry, Florrie,
If I marry you.

The Seventh Pullet

"It's not the daily grind that I complain of," said Blenkinthrope resentfully; "it's the dull grey sameness of my life outside of office hours. Nothing of interest comes my way, nothing remarkable or out of the common. Even the little things that I do try to find some interest in don't seem to interest other people. Things in my garden, for instance."

"The potato that weighed just over two pounds," said his friend Gorworth.

"Did I tell you about that?" said Blenkinthrope; "I was telling the others in the train this morning. I forgot if I'd told you."

"To be exact you told me that it weighed just under two pounds, but I took into account the fact that abnormal vegetables and freshwater fish have an after-life, in which growth is not arrested."

"You're just like the others," said Blenkinthrope sadly, "you only make fun of it."

"The fault is with the potato, not with us," said Gorworth; "we are not in the least interested in it because it is not in the least interesting. The men you go up in the train with every day are just in the same case as yourself; their lives are commonplace and not very interesting to themselves, and they certainly are not going to wax enthusiastic over the commonplace events in other men's lives.

"Tell them something startling, dramatic, piquant that has happened to yourself or to someone in your family, and you will capture their interest at once. They will talk about you with a certain personal pride to all their acquaintances. 'Man I know intimately, fellow called Blenkinthrope, lives down my way, had two of his fingers clawed clean off by a lobster he was carrying home to supper. Doctor says entire hand may have to come off.' Now that is conversation of a very high order. But imagine walking into a tennis club with the remark: 'I know a man who has grown a potato weighing two and a quarter pounds.'"

"But hang it all, my dear fellow," said Blenkinthrope impatiently, "haven't I just told you that nothing of a remarkable nature ever happens to me?"

"Invent something," said Gorworth. Since winning a prize for excellence in Scriptural knowledge at a preparatory school he had felt licensed to be a little more unscrupulous than the circle he moved in. Much might surely be excused to one who in early life could give a list of seventeen trees mentioned in the Old Testament.

"What sort of thing?" asked Blenkinthrope, somewhat snappishly.

"A snake got into your hen-run yesterday morning and killed six out of seven pullets, first mesmerising them with its eyes and then biting them as they stood helpless. The seventh pullet was one of that French sort, with feathers all over its eyes, so it escaped the mesmeric snare, and just flew at what it could see of the snake and pecked it to pieces."

"Thank you," said Blenkinthrope stiffly; "it's a very clever invention. If such a thing had really happened in my poultry-run I admit I should have been proud and interested to tell people about it. But I'd rather stick to fact, even if it is plain fact." All the same his mind dwelt wistfully on the story of the Seventh Pullet. He could picture himself telling it in the train amid the absorbed interest of his fellow-passengers. Unconsciously all sorts of little details and improvements began to suggest themselves.

Wistfulness was still his dominant mood when he took his seat in the railway carriage the next morning. Opposite him sat Stevenham, who had attained to a recognised brevet of importance through the fact of an uncle having dropped dead in the act of voting at a Parliamentary election. That had happened three years ago, but Stevenham was still deferred to on all questions of home and foreign politics.

"Hullo, how's the giant mushroom, or whatever it was?" was all the notice Blenkinthrope got from his fellow travellers.

Young Duckby, whom he mildly disliked, speedily monopolised the general attention by an account of a domestic bereavement.

"Had four young pigeons carried off last night by a whacking big rat. Oh, a monster he must have been; you could tell by the size of the hole he made breaking into the loft."

No moderate-sized rat ever seemed to carry out any predatory operations in these regions; they were all enormous in their enormity.

"Pretty hard lines that," continued Duckby, seeing that he had secured the attention and respect of the company; "four squeakers carried off at one swoop. You'd find it rather hard to match that in the way of unlooked-for bad luck."

"I had six pullets out of a pen of seven killed by a snake yesterday afternoon," said Blenkinthrope, in a voice which he hardly recognised as his own.

"By a snake?" came in excited chorus.

"It fascinated them with its deadly, glittering eyes, one after the other, and struck them down while they stood helpless. A bedridden neighbour, who wasn't able to call for assistance, witnessed it all from her bedroom window."

"Well, I never!" broke in the chorus, with variations.

"The interesting part of it is about the seventh pullet, the one that didn't get killed," resumed Blenkinthrope, slowly lighting a cigarette. His diffidence had left him, and he was beginning to realise how safe and easy depravity can seem once one has the courage to begin. "The six dead birds were Minorcas; the seventh was a Houdan with a mop of feathers all over its eyes. It could hardly see the snake at all, so of course it wasn't mesmerised like the others. It just could see something wriggling on the ground, and went for it and pecked it to death."

"Well, I'm blessed!" exclaimed the chorus.

In the course of the next few days Blenkinthrope discovered how little the loss of one's self-respect affects one when one has gained the esteem of the world. His story found its way into one of the poultry papers, and was copied thence into a daily news-sheet as a matter of general interest. A lady wrote from the North of Scotland recounting a similar episode which she had witnessed as occurring between a stoat and a blind grouse. Somehow a lie seems so much less reprehensible when one can call it a lee.

For a while the adapter of the Seventh Pullet story enjoyed to the full his altered standing as a person of consequence, one who had had some share in the strange events of his times. Then he was thrust once again into the cold grey background by the sudden blossoming into importance of Smith-Paddon, a daily fellow-traveller, whose little girl had been knocked down and nearly hurt by a car belonging to a musical-comedy actress.

The actress was not in the car at the time, but she was in numerous photographs which appeared in the illustrated papers of Zoto Do-breen inquiring after the well-being of Maisie, daughter of Edmund Smith-Paddon, Esq. With this new human interest to absorb them the travelling companions were almost rude when Blenkinthrope tried to explain his contrivance for keeping vipers and peregrine falcons out of his chicken-run.

Gorworth, to whom he unburdened himself in private, gave him the same counsel as heretofore.

"Invent something."

"Yes, but what?"

The ready affirmative coupled with the question betrayed a significant shifting of the ethical standpoint.

It was a few days later that Blenkinthrope revealed a chapter of family history to the customary gathering in the railway carriage.

"Curious thing happened to my aunt, the one who lives in Paris," he began. He had several aunts, but they were all geographically distributed over Greater London.

"She was sitting on a seat in the Bois the other afternoon, after lunching at the Roumanian Legation."

Whatever the story gained in picturesqueness from the dragging-in of diplomatic "atmosphere," it ceased from that moment to command any acceptance as a record of current events. Gorworth had warned his neophyte that this would be the case, but the traditional enthusiasm of the neophyte had triumphed over discretion.

"She was feeling rather drowsy, the effect probably of the champagne, which she's not in the habit of taking in the middle of the day."

A subdued murmur of admiration went round the company. Blenkinthrope's aunts were not used to taking champagne in the middle of the year, regarding it exclusively as a Christmas and New Year accessory.

"Presently a rather portly gentleman passed by her seat and paused an instant to light a cigar. At that moment a youngish man came up behind him, drew the blade from a swordstick, and stabbed him half a dozen times through and through. 'Scoundrel,' he cried to his victim, 'you do not know me. My name is Henri Leturc.' The elder man wiped away some of the blood that was spattering his clothes, turned to his assailant, and said: 'And since when has an attempted assassination been considered an introduction?' Then he finished lighting his cigar and walked away. My aunt had intended screaming for the police, but seeing the indifference with which the principal in the affair treated the matter she felt that it would be an impertinence on her part to interfere.

"Of course, I need hardly say she put the whole thing down to the effects of a warm, drowsy afternoon and the Legation champagne.

Now comes the astonishing part of my story. A fortnight later a bank manager was stabbed to death with a swordstick in that very part of the Bois. His assassin was the son of a charwoman formerly working at the bank, who had been dismissed from her job by the manager on account of chronic intemperance. His name was Henri Leturc."

From that moment Blenkinthrope was tacitly accepted as the Munchausen of the party. No effort was spared to draw him out from day to day in the exercise of testing their powers of credulity, and Blenkinthrope, in the false security of an assured and receptive audience, waxed industrious and ingenious in supplying the demand for marvels. Duckby's satirical story of a tame otter that had a tank in the garden to swim in, and whined restlessly whenever the water-rate was overdue, was scarcely an unfair parody of some of Blenkinthrope's wilder efforts. And then one day came Nemesis.

Returning to his villa one evening Blenkinthrope found his wife sitting in front of a pack of cards, which she was scrutinising with unusual concentration.

"The same old patience-game?" he asked carelessly.

"No, dear; this is the Death's Head patience, the most difficult of them all. I've never got it to work out, and somehow, I should be rather frightened if I did. Mother only got it out once in her life; she was afraid of it, too. Her great-aunt had done it once and fallen dead from excitement the next moment, and mother always had a feeling that she would die if she ever got it out. She died the same night that she did it. She was in bad health at the time, certainly, but it was a strange coincidence."

"Don't do it if it frightens you," was Blenkinthrope's practical comment as he left the room. A few minutes later his wife called to him.

"John, it gave me such a turn, I nearly got it out. Only the five of diamonds held me up at the end. I really thought I'd done it."

"Why, you can do it," said Blenkinthrope, who had come back to the room; "if you shift the eight of clubs on to that open nine the five can be moved on to the six."

His wife made the suggested move with hasty, trembling fingers, and piled the outstanding cards on to their respective packs. Then she followed the example of her mother and great-grand-aunt.

Blenkinthrope had been genuinely fond of his wife, but in the midst of his bereavement one dominant thought obtruded itself. Something sensational and real had at last come into his life; no longer was it a grey, colourless record. The headlines which might appropriately describe his domestic tragedy kept shaping themselves in his brain. "Inherited presentiment comes true." "The Death's Head patience: Card-game that justified its sinister name in three generations." He wrote out a full story of the fatal occurrence for the *Essex Vedette*, the editor of which was a friend of his, and to another friend he gave a condensed account, to be taken up to the office of one of the halfpenny dailies. But in both cases his reputation as a romancer stood fatally in the way of the fulfilment of his ambitions.

"Not the right thing to be Munchausening in a time of sorrow" agreed his friends among themselves, and a brief note of regret at the "sudden death of the wife of our respected neighbour, Mr. John Blenkinthrope, from heart failure," appearing in the news column of the local paper was the forlorn outcome of his visions of widespread publicity.

Blenkinthrope shrank from the society of his erstwhile travelling companions and took to travelling townwards by an earlier train. He sometimes tries to enlist the sympathy and attention of a chance acquaintance in details of the whistling prowess of his best canary or the dimensions of his largest beetroot; he scarcely recognises himself as the man who was once spoken about and pointed out as the owner of the Seventh Pullet.

The She-Wolf

Leonard Bilsiter was one of those people who have failed to find this world attractive or interesting, and who have sought compensation in an "unseen world" of their own experience or imagination— or invention. Children do that sort of thing successfully, but children are content to convince themselves, and do not vulgarise their beliefs by trying to convince other people. Leonard Bilsiter's beliefs were for "the few," that is to say, anyone who would listen to him.

His dabblings in the unseen might not have carried him beyond the customary platitudes of the drawing-room visionary if accident had not reinforced his stock-in-trade of mystical lore. In company with a friend, who was interested in a Ural mining concern, he had made a trip across Eastern Europe at a moment when the great Russian railway strike was developing from a threat to a reality; its outbreak caught him on the return journey, somewhere on the further side of Perm, and it was while waiting for a couple of days at a wayside station in a state of suspended locomotion that he made the acquaintance of a dealer in harness and metalware, who profitably whiled away the tedium of the long halt by initiating his English travelling companion in a fragmentary system of folk-lore that he had picked up from Trans-Baikal traders and natives.

Leonard returned to his home circle garrulous about his Russian strike experiences, but oppressively reticent about certain dark mysteries, which he alluded to under the resounding title of Siberian Magic. The reticence wore off in a week or two under the influence of an entire lack of general curiosity, and Leonard began to make more detailed allusions to the enormous powers which this new esoteric force, to use his own description of it, conferred on the initiated few who knew how to wield it. His aunt, Cecilia Hoops, who loved sensation perhaps rather better than she loved the truth, gave him as clamorous an advertisement as anyone could wish for by retailing an account of how he had turned a vegetable marrow into a wood pigeon before her very eyes. As a manifestation of the possession of supernatural powers, the story was discounted in some quarters by the respect accorded to Mrs. Hoops' powers of imagination.

However divided opinion might be on the question of Leonard's status as a wonderworker or a charlatan, he certainly arrived at Mary Hampton's house-party with a reputation for pre-eminence in one or other of those professions, and he was not disposed to shun such publicity as might fall to his share. Esoteric forces and unusual powers figured largely in whatever conversation he or his aunt had a share in, and his own performances, past and potential, were the subject of mysterious hints and dark avowals.

"I wish you would turn me into a wolf, Mr. Bilsiter," said his hostess at luncheon the day after his arrival.

"My dear Mary," said Colonel Hampton, "I never knew you had a craving in that direction."

"A she-wolf, of course," continued Mrs. Hampton; it would be too confusing to change one's sex as well as one's species at a moment's notice."

"I don't think one should jest on these subjects," said Leonard.

"I'm not jesting, I'm quite serious, I assure you. Only don't do it today; we have only eight available bridge players, and it would break up one of our tables. Tomorrow we shall be a larger party. Tomorrow night, after dinner—"

"In our present imperfect understanding of these hidden forces I think one should approach them with humbleness rather than mockery," observed Leonard, with such severity that the subject was forthwith dropped.

Clovis Sangrail had sat unusually silent during the discussion on the possibilities of Siberian Magic; after lunch he side-tracked Lord Pabham into the comparative seclusion of the billiard-room and delivered himself of a searching question.

"Have you such a thing as a she-wolf in your collection of wild animals? A she-wolf of moderately good temper?"

Lord Pabham considered. "There is Loiusa," he said, "a rather fine specimen of the timber-wolf. I got her two years ago in exchange for some Arctic foxes. Most of my animals get to be fairly tame before they've been with me very long; I think I can say Louisa has an angelic temper, as she-wolves go. Why do you ask?"

156

"I was wondering whether you would lend her to me for tomorrow night," said Clovis, with the careless solicitude of one who borrows a collar stud or a tennis racquet.

"Tomorrow night?"

"Yes, wolves are nocturnal animals, so the late hours won't hurt her," said Clovis, with the air of one who has taken everything into consideration; "one of your men could bring her over from Pabham Park after dusk, and with a little help he ought to be able to smuggle her into the conservatory at the same moment that Mary Hampton makes an unobtrusive exit."

Lord Pabham stared at Clovis for a moment in pardonable bewilderment; then his face broke into a wrinkled network of laughter.

"Oh, that's your game, is it? You are going to do a little Siberian Magic on your own account. And is Mrs. Hampton willing to be a fellow-conspirator?"

"Mary is pledged to see me through with it, if you will guarantee Louisa's temper."

"I'll answer for Louisa," said Lord Pabham.

By the following day the house-party had swollen to larger proportions, and Bilsiter's instinct for self-advertisement expanded duly under the stimulant of an increased audience. At dinner that evening he held forth at length on the subject of unseen forces and untested powers, and his flow of impressive eloquence continued unabated while coffee was being served in the drawing-room preparatory to a general migration to the card-room.

His aunt ensured a respectful hearing for his utterances, but her sensation-loving soul hankered after something more dramatic than mere vocal demonstration.

"Won't you do something to convince them of your powers, Leonard?" she pleaded; "change something into another shape. He can, you know, if he only chooses to," she informed the company.

"Oh, do," said Mavis Pellington earnestly, and her request was echoed by nearly everyone present. Even those who were not open to conviction were perfectly willing to be entertained by an exhibition of amateur conjuring.

Leonard felt that something tangible was expected of him.

"Has anyone present," he asked, "got a three-penny bit or some small object of no particular value?"

"You're surely not going to make coins disappear, or something primitive of that sort?" said Clovis contemptuously.

"I think it very unkind of you not to carry out my suggestion of turning me into a wolf," said Mary Hampton, as she crossed over to the conservatory to give her macaws their usual tribute from the dessert dishes.

"I have already warned you of the danger of treating these powers in a mocking spirit," said Leonard solemnly.

"I don't believe you can do it," laughed Mary provocatively from the conservatory; "I dare you to do it if you can. I defy you to turn me into a wolf."

As she said this she was lost to view behind a clump of azaleas.

"Mrs. Hampton—" began Leonard with increased solemnity, but he got no further. A breath of chill air seemed to rush across the room, and at the same time the macaws broke forth into ear-splitting screams.

"What on earth is the matter with those confounded birds, Mary?" exclaimed Colonel Hampton; at the same moment an even more piercing scream from Mavis Pellington stampeded the entire company from their seats. In various attitudes of helpless horror or instinctive defence they confronted the evil-looking grey beast that was peering at them from amid a setting of fern and azalea.

Mrs. Hoops was the first to recover from the general chaos of fright and bewilderment.

"Leonard!" she screamed shrilly to her nephew, "turn it back into Mrs. Hampton at once! It may fly at us at any moment. Turn it back!"

"I—I don't know how to," faltered Leonard, who looked more scared and horrified than anyone.

"What!" shouted Colonel Hampton, "you've taken the abominable liberty of turning my wife into a wolf, and now you stand there calmly and say you can't turn her back again!"

To do strict justice to Leonard, calmness was not a distinguishing feature of his attitude at the moment.

"I assure you I didn't turn Mrs. Hampton into a wolf; nothing was farther from my intentions," he protested.

"Then where is she, and how came that animal into the conservatory?" demanded the colonel.

"Of course, we must accept your assurance that you didn't turn Mrs. Hampton into a wolf," said Clovis politely, "but you will agree that appearances are against you."

"Are we to have all these recriminations with that beast standing there ready to tear us to pieces?" wailed Mavis indignantly.

"Lord Pabham, you know a good deal about wild beasts—" suggested Colonel Hampton.

"The wild beasts that I have been accustomed to," said Lord Pabham, "have come with proper credentials from well-known dealers, or have been bred in my own menagerie. I've never before been confronted with an animal that walks unconcernedly out of an azalea bush, leaving a charming and popular hostess unaccounted for. As far as one can judge from outward characteristics," he continued, "it has the appearance of a well-grown female of the North American timber-wolf, a variety of the common species *canis lupus*."

"Oh, never mind its Latin name," screamed Mavis, as the beast came a step or two further into the room; "can't you entice it away with food, and shut it up where it can't do any harm?"

"If it is really Mrs. Hampton, who has just had a very good dinner, I don't suppose food will appeal to it very strongly," said Clovis.

"Leonard," beseeched Mrs. Hoops tearfully, "even if this is none of your doing can't you use your great powers to turn this dreadful beast into something harmless before it bites us all—a rabbit or something?"

"I don't suppose Colonel Hampton would care to have his wife turned into a succession of fancy animals as though we were playing a round game with her," interposed Clovis.

"I absolutely forbid it," thundered the colonel.

"Most wolves that I've had anything to do with have been inordinately fond of sugar," said Lord Pabham; "if you like I'll try the effect on this one."

He took a piece of sugar from the saucer of his coffee cup and flung it to the expectant Louisa, who snapped it in mid-air. There was a sigh of relief from the company; a wolf that ate sugar when it might at the least have been employed in tearing macaws to pieces had already shed some of its terrors. The sigh deepened to a gasp of thanksgiving when Lord Pabham decoyed the animal out of the room by a pretended largesse of further sugar. There was an instant rush to the vacated conservatory. There was no trace of Mrs. Hampton except the plate containing the macaws' supper.

"The door is locked on the inside!" exclaimed Clovis, who had deftly turned the key as he affected to test it.

Everyone turned towards Bilsiter.

"If you haven't turned my wife into a wolf," said Colonel Hampton, "will you kindly explain where she has disappeared to, since she obviously could not have gone through a locked door? I will not press you for an explanation of how a North American timber-wolf suddenly appeared in the conservatory, but I think I have some right to inquire what has become of Mrs. Hampton."

Bilsiter's reiterated disclaimer was met with a general murmur of impatient disbelief.

"I refuse to stay another hour under this roof," declared Mavis Pellington.

"If our hostess has really vanished out of human form," said Mrs. Hoops, "none of the ladies of the party can very well remain. I absolutely decline to be chaperoned by a wolf!"

"It's a she-wolf," said Clovis soothingly.

The correct etiquette to be observed under the unusual circumstances received no further elucidation. The sudden entry of Mary Hampton deprived the discussion of its immediate interest.

"Someone has mesmerised me," she exclaimed crossly; "I found myself in the game larder, of all places, being fed with sugar by Lord Pabham. I hate being mesmerised, and the doctor has forbidden me to touch sugar."

The situation was explained to her, as far as it permitted of anything that could be called explanation.

"Then you really did turn me into a wolf, Mr. Bilsiter?" she exclaimed excitedly.

But Leonard had burned the boat in which he might now have embarked on a sea of glory. He could only shake his head feebly.

"It was I who took that liberty," said Clovis; "you see, I happen to have lived for a couple of years in North-Eastern Russia, and I have more than a tourist's acquaintance with the magic craft of that region. One does not care to speak about these strange powers, but once in a way, when one hears a lot of nonsense being talked about them, one is tempted to show what Siberian magic can accomplish in the hands of someone who really understands it. I yielded to that temptation. May I have some brandy? the effort has left me rather faint."

If Leonard Bilsiter could at that moment have transformed Clovis into a cockroach and then have stepped on him, he would gladly have performed both operations.

The Soul of Laploshka

Laploshka was one of the meanest men I have ever met, and quite one of the most entertaining. He said horrid things about other people in such a charming way that one forgave him for the equally horrid things he said about oneself behind one's back. Hating anything in the way of ill-natured gossip ourselves, we are always grateful to those who do it for us and do it well. And Laploshka did it really well.

Naturally Laploshka had a large circle of acquaintances, and as he exercised some care in their selection it followed that an appreciable proportion were men whose bank balances enabled them to acquiesce indulgently in his rather one-sided views on hospitality. Thus, although possessed of only moderate means, he was able to live comfortably within his income, and still more comfortably within those of various tolerantly disposed associates.

But towards the poor or to those of the same limited resources as himself his attitude was one of watchful anxiety; he seemed to be haunted by a besetting fear lest some fraction of a shilling or *franc*, or whatever the prevailing coinage might be, should be diverted from his pocket or service into that of a hard-up companion. A two-*franc* cigar would be cheerfully offered to a wealthy patron, on the principle of doing evil that good may come, but I have known him indulge in agonies of perjury rather than admit the incriminating possession of a copper coin when change was needed to tip a waiter. The coin would have been duly returned at the earliest opportunity—he would have taken means to insure against forgetfulness on the part of the borrower—but accidents might happen, and even the temporary estrangement from his penny or sou was a calamity to be avoided.

The knowledge of this amiable weakness offered a perpetual temptation to play upon Laploshka's fears of involuntary generosity. To offer him a lift in a cab and pretend not to have enough money to pay the fair, to fluster him with a request for a sixpence when his hand was full of silver just received in change, these were a few of the petty torments that ingenuity prompted as occasion afforded. To do justice to Laploshka's resourcefulness it must be admitted that he always emerged somehow or other from the most embarrassing dilemma without in any way compromising his reputation for saying "No."

But the gods send opportunities at some time to most men, and mine came one evening when Laploshka and I were supping together in a cheap boulevard restaurant. (Except when he was the bidden guest of someone with an irreproachable income, Laploshka was wont to curb his appetite for high living; on such fortunate occasions he let it go on an easy snaffle.) At the conclusion of the meal a somewhat urgent message called me away, and without heeding my companion's agitated protest, I called back cruelly, "Pay my share; I'll settle with you tomorrow." Early on the morrow Laploshka hunted me down by instinct as I walked along a side street that I hardly ever frequented. He had the air of a man who had not slept.

"You owe me two *francs* from last night," was his breathless greeting.

I spoke evasively of the situation in Portugal, where more trouble seemed brewing. But Laploshka listened with the abstraction of the deaf adder, and quickly returned to the subject of the two *francs*.

"I'm afraid I must owe it to you," I said lightly and brutally. "I haven't a *sou* in the world," and I added mendaciously, "I'm going away for six months or perhaps longer."

Laploshka said nothing, but his eyes bulged a little and his cheeks took on the mottled hues of an ethnographical map of the Balkan Peninsula. That same day, at sundown, he died. "Failure of the heart's action," was the doctor's verdict; but I, who knew better, knew that he died of grief.

There arose the problem of what to do with his two *francs*. To have killed Laploshka was one thing; to have kept his beloved money would have argued a callousness of feeling of which I am not capable. The ordinary solution, of giving it to the poor, would by no means fit the present situation, for nothing would have distressed the dead man more than such a misuse of his property. On the other hand, the bestowal of two *francs* on the rich was an operation which called for some tact.

An easy way out of the difficulty seemed, however, to present itself the following Sunday, as I was wedged into the cosmopolitan crowd which filled the side-aisle of one of the most popular Paris churches.

A collecting-bag, for "the poor of *Monsieur le Curé*," was buffeting its tortuous way across the seemingly impenetrable human sea, and a German in front of me, who evidently did not wish his appreciation of the magnificent music to be marred by a suggestion of payment, made audible criticisms to his companion on the claims of the said charity.

"They do not want money," he said; "they have too much money. They have no poor. They are all pampered."

If that were really the case my way seemed clear. I dropped Laploshka's two *francs* into the bag with a murmured blessing on the rich of *Monsieur le Curé*.

Some three weeks later chance had taken me to Vienna, and I sat one evening regaling myself in a humble but excellent little *gasthaus* up in the Wahringer quarter. The appointments were primitive, but the Schnitzel, the beer, and the cheese could not have been improved on. Good cheer brought good custom, and with the exception of one small table near the door every place was occupied. Half-way through my meal I happened to glance in the direction of that empty seat, and saw that it was no longer empty. Poring over the bill of fare with the absorbed scrutiny of one who seeks the cheapest among the cheap was Laploshka.

Once he looked across at me, with a comprehensive glance at my repast, as though to say, "It is my two *francs* you are eating," and then looked swiftly away. Evidently the poor of *Monsieur le Curé* had been genuine poor. The Schnitzel turned to leather in my mouth, the beer seemed tepid; I left the Emmenthaler untasted. My one idea was to get away from the room, away from the table where *that* was seated; and as I fled, I felt Laploshka's reproachful eyes watching the amount that I gave to the *piccolo*—out of his two *francs*.

I lunched next day at an expensive restaurant which I felt sure that the living Laploshka would never have entered on his own account, and I hoped that the dead Laploshka would observe the same barriers. I was not mistaken, but as I came out, I found him miserably studying the bill of fare stuck up on the portals. Then he slowly made his way over to a milk-hall. For the first time in my experience, I missed the charm and gaiety of Vienna life.

After that, in Paris or London or wherever I happened to be, I continued to see a good deal of Laploshka. If I had a seat in a box at a theatre, I was always conscious of his eyes furtively watching me from the dim recesses of the gallery. As I turned into my club on a rainy afternoon, I would see him taking inadequate shelter in a doorway opposite. Even if I indulged in the modest luxury of a penny chair in the park, he generally confronted me from one of the free benches, never staring at me, but always elaborately conscious of my presence. My friends began to comment on my changed looks, and advised me to leave off heaps of things. I should have liked to have left off Laploshka.

On a certain Sunday—it was probably Easter, for the crush was worse than ever—I was again wedged into the crowd listening to the music in the fashionable Paris church, and again the collection-bag was buffeting its way across the human sea. An English lady behind me was making ineffectual efforts to convey a coin into the still distant bag, so I took the money at her request and helped it forward to its destination. It was a two-*franc* piece. A swift inspiration came to me, and I merely dropped my own *sou* into the bag and slid the silver coin into my pocket. I had withdrawn Laploshka's two *francs* from the poor, who should never have had the legacy. As I backed away from the crowd, I heard a woman's voice say, "I don't believe he put my money in the bag. There are swarms of people in Paris like that!" But my mind was lighter that it had been for a long time.

The delicate mission of bestowing the retrieved sum on the deserving rich still confronted me. Again, I trusted to the inspiration of accident, and again fortune favoured me. A shower drove me, two days later, into one of the historic churches on the left bank of the Seine, and there I found, peering at the old wood-carvings, the Baron R., one of the wealthiest and most shabbily dressed men in Paris. It was now or never. Putting a strong American inflection into the French which I usually talked with an unmistakable British accent, I catechised the baron as to the date of the church's building, its dimensions, and other details which an American tourist would be certain to want to know.

Having acquired such information as the baron was able to impart on short notice, I solemnly placed the two-*franc* piece in his hand, with the hearty assurance that it was "*pour vous,*" and turned to go. The baron was slightly taken aback, but accepted the situation with a good grace. Walking over to a small box fixed in the wall, he dropped Laploshka's two *francs* into the slot. Over the box was the inscription, "*Pour les pauvres de M. le Curé.*"

That evening, at the crowded corner by the Café de la Paix, I caught a fleeting glimpse of Laploshka. He smiled, slightly raised his hat, and vanished. I never saw him again. After all, the money had been *given* to the deserving rich, and the soul of Laploshka was at peace.

The Story of St. Vespaluus

"Tell me a story," said the Baroness, staring out despairingly at the rain; it was that light, apologetic sort of rain that looks as if it was going to leave off every minute and goes on for the greater part of the afternoon.

"What sort of story?" asked Clovis, giving his croquet mallet a valedictory shove into retirement.

"One just true enough to be interesting and not true enough to be tiresome," said the Baroness.

Clovis rearranged several cushions to his personal solace and satisfaction; he knew that the Baroness liked her guests to be comfortable, and he thought it right to respect her wishes in that particular.

"Have I ever told you the story of St. Vespaluus?" he asked.

"You've told me stories about grand-dukes and lion-tamers and financiers' widows and a postmaster in Herzegovina," said the Baroness, "and about an Italian jockey and an amateur governess who went to Warsaw, and several about your mother, but certainly never anything about a saint."

"This story happened a long while ago," he said, "in those uncomfortable piebald times when a third of the people were Pagan, and a third Christian, and the biggest third of all just followed whichever religion the Court happened to profess. There was a certain king called Hkrikros, who had a fearful temper and no immediate successor in his own family; his married sister, however, had provided him with a large stock of nephews from which to select his heir. And the most eligible and royally-approved of all these nephews was the sixteen-year-old Vespaluus. He was the best looking, and the best horseman and javelin-thrower, and had that priceless princely gift of being able to walk past a supplicant with an air of not having seen him, but would certainly have given something if he had.

"My mother has that gift to a certain extent; she can go smilingly and financially unscathed through a charity bazaar, and meet the organizers next day with a solicitous 'had I but known you were in need of funds' air that is really rather a triumph in audacity. Now Hkrikros was a Pagan of the first water, and kept the worship of the sacred serpents, who lived in a hallowed grove on a hill near the royal palace, up to a high pitch of enthusiasm. The common people were allowed to please themselves, within certain discreet limits, in the matter of private religion, but any official in the service of the Court who went over to the new cult was looked down on, literally as well as metaphorically, the looking down being done from the gallery that ran round the royal bear-pit.

"Consequently, there was considerable scandal and consternation when the youthful Vespaluus appeared one day at a Court function with a rosary tucked into his belt, and announced in reply to angry questionings that he had decided to adopt Christianity, or at any rate to give it a trial. If it had been any of the other nephews the king would possibly have ordered something drastic in the way of scourging and banishment, but in the case of the favoured Vespaluus he determined to look on the whole thing much as a modern father might regard the announced intention of his son to adopt the stage as a profession. He sent accordingly for the Royal Librarian. The royal library in those days was not a very extensive affair, and the keeper of the king's books had a great deal of leisure on his hands. Consequently, he was in frequent demand for the settlement of other people's affairs when these strayed beyond normal limits and got temporarily unmanageable.

"'You must reason with Prince Vespaluus,' said the king, 'and impress on him the error of his ways. We cannot have the heir to the throne setting such a dangerous example.'

"'But where shall I find the necessary arguments?' asked the Librarian.

"'I give you free leave to pick and choose your arguments in the royal woods and coppices,' said the king; 'if you cannot get together some cutting observations and stinging retorts suitable to the occasion you are a person of very poor resource.'

"So, the Librarian went into the woods and gathered a goodly selection of highly argumentative rods and switches, and then proceeded to reason with Vespaluus on the folly and iniquity and above all the unseemliness of his conduct. His reasoning left a deep impression on the young prince, an impression which lasted for many weeks, during which time nothing more was heard about the unfortunate lapse into Christianity. Then a further scandal of the same nature agitated the Court. At a time when he should have been engaged in audibly invoking the gracious protection and patronage of the holy serpents, Vespaluus was heard singing a chant in honour of St. Odilo of Cluny.

"The king was furious at this new outbreak, and began to take a gloomy view of the situation; Vespaluus was evidently going to show a dangerous obstinacy in persisting in his heresy. And yet there was nothing in his appearance to justify such perverseness; he had not the pale eye of the fanatic or the mystic look of the dreamer. On the contrary, he was quite the best-looking boy at Court; he had an elegant, well-knit figure, a healthy complexion, eyes the colour of very ripe mulberries, and dark hair, smooth and very well cared for."

"It sounds like a description of what you imagine yourself to have been like at the age of sixteen," said the Baroness.

"My mother has probably been showing you some of my early photographs," said Clovis. Having turned the sarcasm into a compliment, he resumed his story.

"The king had Vespaluus shut up in a dark tower for three days, with nothing but bread and water to live on, the squealing and fluttering of bats to listen to, and drifting clouds to watch through one little window slit. The anti-Pagan section of the community began to talk portentously of the boy-martyr. The martyrdom was mitigated, as far as the food was concerned, by the carelessness of the tower warden, who once or twice left a portion of his own supper of broiled meat and fruit and wine by mistake in the prince's cell. After the punishment was over, Vespaluus was closely watched for any further symptom of religious perversity, for the king was determined to stand no more opposition on so important a matter, even from a favourite nephew. If there was any more of this nonsense, he said, the succession to the throne would have to be altered.

"For a time, all went well; the festival of summer sports was approaching, and the young Vespaluus was too engrossed in wrestling and foot-running and javelin-throwing competitions to bother himself with the strife of conflicting religious systems. Then, however, came the great culminating feature of the summer festival, the ceremonial dance round the grove of the sacred serpents, and Vespaluus, as we should say, 'sat it out.' The affront to the State religion was too public and ostentatious to be overlooked, even if the king had been so minded, and he was not in the least so minded. For a day and a half, he sat apart and brooded, and everyone thought he was debating within himself the question of the young prince's death or pardon; as a matter of fact, he was merely thinking out the manner of the boy's death. As the thing had to be done, and was bound to attract an enormous amount of public attention in any case, it was as well to make it as spectacular and impressive as possible.

"'Apart from his unfortunate taste in religions,' said the king, 'and his obstinacy in adhering to it, he is a sweet and pleasant youth, therefore it is meet and fitting that he should be done to death by the winged envoys of sweetness.'

"'Your Majesty means—?' said the Royal Librarian.

"'I mean,' said the king, 'that he shall be stung to death by bees. By the royal bees, of course.'

"'A most elegant death,' said the Librarian.

"'Elegant and spectacular, and decidedly painful,' said the king; 'it fulfils all the conditions that could be wished for.'

"The king himself thought out all the details of the execution ceremony. Vespaluus was to be stripped of his clothes, his hands were to be bound behind him, and he was then to be slung in a recumbent position immediately above three of the largest of the royal beehives, so that the least movement of his body would bring him in jarring contact with them. The rest could be safely left to the bees. The death throes, the king computed, might last anything from fifteen to forty minutes, though there was division of opinion and considerable wagering among the other nephews as to whether death might not be almost instantaneous, or, on the other hand, whether it might not be deferred for a couple of hours. Anyway, they all agreed, it was vastly preferable to being thrown down into an evil smelling bear-pit and being clawed and mauled to death by imperfectly carnivorous animals.

"It so happened, however, that the keeper of the royal hives had leanings towards Christianity himself, and moreover, like most of the Court officials, he was very much attached to Vespaluus. On the eve of the execution, therefore, he busied himself with removing the stings from all the royal bees; it was a long and delicate operation, but he was an expert bee-master, and by working hard nearly all night he succeeded in disarming all, or almost all, of the hive inmates."

"I didn't know you could take the sting from a live bee," said the Baroness incredulously.

"Every profession has its secrets," replied Clovis; "if it hadn't it wouldn't be a profession. Well, the moment for the execution arrived;

168

the king and Court took their places, and accommodation was found for as many of the populace as wished to witness the unusual spectacle. Fortunately, the royal bee-yard was of considerable dimensions, and was commanded, moreover, by the terraces that ran round the royal gardens; with a little squeezing and the erection of a few platforms room was found for everybody. Vespaluus was carried into the open space in front of the hives, blushing and slightly embarrassed, but not at all displeased at the attention which was being centred on him."

"He seems to have resembled you in more things than in appearance," said the Baroness.

"Don't interrupt at a critical point in the story," said Clovis. "As soon as he had been carefully adjusted in the prescribed position over the hives, and almost before the gaolers had time to retire to a safe distance, Vespaluus gave a lusty and well-aimed kick, which sent all three hives toppling one over another. The next moment he was wrapped from head to foot in bees; each individual insect nursed the dreadful and humiliating knowledge that in this supreme hour of catastrophe it could not sting, but each felt that it ought to pretend to. Vespaluus squealed and wriggled with laughter, for he was being tickled nearly to death, and now and again he gave a furious kick and used a bad word as one of the few bees that had escaped disarmament got its protest home.

"But the spectators saw with amazement that he showed no signs of approaching death agony, and as the bees dropped wearily away in clusters from his body his flesh was seen to be as white and smooth as before the ordeal, with a shiny glaze from the honey-smear of innumerable bee-feet, and here and there a small red spot where one of the rare stings had left its mark. It was obvious that a miracle had been performed in his favour, and one loud murmur, of astonishment or exultation, rose from the onlooking crowd. The king gave orders for Vespaluus to be taken down to await further orders, and stalked silently back to his midday meal, at which he was careful to eat heartily and drink copiously as though nothing unusual had happened. After dinner he sent for the Royal Librarian.

"'What is the meaning of this fiasco?' he demanded.

"'Your Majesty,' said that official, 'either there is something radically wrong with the bees—'

"'There is nothing wrong with my bees,' said the king haughtily, 'they are the best bees.'

"'Or else,' said the Librarian, 'there is something irremediably right about Prince Vespaluus.'

"'If Vespaluus is right I must be wrong,' said the king.

"The Librarian was silent for a moment. Hasty speech has been the downfall of many; ill-considered silence was the undoing of the luckless Court functionary.

"Forgetting the restraint due to his dignity, and the golden rule which imposes repose of mind and body after a heavy meal, the king rushed upon the keeper of the royal books and hit him repeatedly and promiscuously over the head with an ivory chess-board, a pewter wine-flagon, and a brass candlestick; he knocked him violently and often against an iron torch sconce, and kicked him thrice round the banqueting chamber with rapid, energetic kicks. Finally, he dragged him down a long passage by the hair of his head and flung him out of a window into the courtyard below."

"Was he much hurt?" asked the Baroness.

"More hurt than surprised," said Clovis. "You see, the king was notorious for his violent temper. However, this was the first time he had let himself go so unrestrainedly on the top of a heavy meal. The Librarian lingered for many days—in fact, for all I know, he may have ultimately recovered, but Hkrikros died that same evening. Vespaluus had hardly finished getting the honey stains off his body before a hurried deputation came to put the coronation oil on his head. And what with the publicly-witnessed miracle and the accession of a Christian sovereign, it was not surprising that there was a general scramble of converts to the new religion. A hastily consecrated bishop was overworked with a rush of baptisms in the hastily improvised Cathedral of St. Odilo.

"And the boy-martyr-that-might-have-been was transposed in the popular imagination into a royal boy-saint, whose fame attracted throngs of curious and devout sightseers to the capital. Vespaluus, who was busily engaged in organising the games and athletic contests that were to mark the commencement of his reign, had no time to give heed to the religious fervour which was effervescing round his personality; the first indication he had of the existing state of affairs was when the Court Chamberlain (a recent and very ardent addition to the Christian community) brought for his approval the outlines of a projected ceremonial cutting-down of the idolatrous serpent-grove.

"'Your Majesty will be graciously pleased to cut down the first tree with a specially consecrated axe,' said the obsequious official.

"'I'll cut off your head first, with any axe that comes handy,' said

Vespaluus indignantly; 'do you suppose that I'm going to begin my reign by mortally affronting the sacred serpents? It would be most unlucky.'

"'But Your Majesty's Christian principles?' exclaimed the bewildered Chamberlain.

"'I never had any,' said Vespaluus; 'I used to pretend to be a Christian convert just to annoy Hkrikros. He used to fly into such delicious tempers. And it was rather fun being whipped and scolded and shut up in a tower all for nothing. But as to turning Christian in real earnest, like you people seem to do, I couldn't think of such a thing. And the holy and esteemed serpents have always helped me when I've prayed to them for success in my running and wrestling and hunting, and it was through their distinguished intercession that the bees were not able to hurt me with their stings. It would be black ingratitude to turn against their worship at the very outset of my reign. I hate you for suggesting it.'

"The Chamberlain wrung his hands despairingly.

"'But, Your Majesty,' he wailed, 'the people are reverencing you as a saint, and the nobles are being Christianised in batches, and neighbouring potentates of that Faith are sending special envoys to welcome you as a brother. There is some talk of making you the patron saint of beehives, and a certain shade of honey-yellow has been christened Vespalussian gold at the Emperor's Court. You can't surely go back on all this.'

"'I don't mind being reverenced and greeted and honoured,' said Vespaluus; 'I don't even mind being sainted in moderation, as long as I'm not expected to be saintly as well. But I wish you clearly and finally to understand that I will not give up the worship of the august and auspicious serpents.'

"There was a world of unspoken bear-pit in the way he uttered those last words, and the mulberry-dark eyes flashed dangerously.

"'A new reign,' said the Chamberlain to himself, 'but the same old temper.'

"Finally, as a State necessity, the matter of the religions was compromised. At stated intervals the king appeared before his subjects in the national cathedral in the character of St. Vespaluus, and the idolatrous grove was gradually pruned and lopped away till nothing remained of it. But the sacred and esteemed serpents were removed to a private shrubbery in the royal gardens, where Vespaluus the Pagan and certain members of his household devoutly and decently worshipped them. That possibly is the reason why the boy-king's success in sports and hunting never deserted him to the end of his days, and that is also the reason why, in spite of the popular veneration for his sanctity, he never received official canonisation."

"It has stopped raining," said the Baroness.

The Story-Teller

It was a hot afternoon, and the railway carriage was correspondingly sultry, and the next stop was at Templecombe, nearly an hour ahead. The occupants of the carriage were a small girl, and a smaller girl, and a small boy. An aunt belonging to the children occupied one corner seat, and the further corner seat on the opposite side was occupied by a bachelor who was a stranger to their party, but the small girls and the small boy emphatically occupied the compartment. Both the aunt and the children were conversational in a limited, persistent way, reminding one of the attentions of a housefly that refused to be discouraged. Most of the aunt's remarks seemed to begin with "Don't," and nearly all of the children's remarks began with "Why?" The bachelor said nothing out loud.

"Don't, Cyril, don't," exclaimed the aunt, as the small boy began smacking the cushions of the seat, producing a cloud of dust at each blow.

"Come and look out of the window," she added.

The child moved reluctantly to the window. "Why are those sheep being driven out of that field?" he asked.

"I expect they are being driven to another field where there is more grass," said the aunt weakly.

"But there is lots of grass in that field," protested the boy, "there's nothing else but grass there. Aunt, there's lots of grass in that field."

"Perhaps the grass in the other field is better," suggested the aunt fatuously.

"Why is it better?" came the swift, inevitable question.

"Oh, look at those cows!" exclaimed the aunt? Nearly every field along the line had contained cows or bullocks, but she spoke as though she were drawing attention to a rarity.

"Why is the grass in the other field better?" persisted Cyril.

The frown on the bachelor's face was deepening to a scowl. He was a hard, unsympathetic man, the aunt decided in her mind. She was utterly unable to come to any satisfactory decision about the grass in the other field.

The smaller girl created a diversion by beginning to recite "*On the Road to Mandalay.*" She only knew the first line, but she put her limited knowledge to the fullest possible use. She repeated the line over and over again in a dreamy but resolute and very audible voice; it seemed to the bachelor as though some one had had a bet with her that she could not repeat the line aloud two thousand times without stopping. Whoever it was who had made the wager was likely to lose his bet.

"Come over here and listen to a story," said the aunt, when the bachelor had looked twice at her and once at the communication cord.

The children moved listlessly towards the aunt's end of the carriage. Evidently her reputation as a story-teller did not rank high in their estimation.

In a low, confidential voice, interrupted at frequent intervals by loud, petulant questions from her listeners, she began an unenterprising and deplorably uninteresting story about a little girl who was good, and made friends with everyone on account of her goodness, and was finally saved from a mad bull by a number of rescuers who admired her moral character.

"Wouldn't they have saved her if she hadn't been good?" demanded the bigger of the small girls. It was exactly the question that the bachelor had wanted to ask.

"Well, yes," admitted the aunt lamely, "but I don't think they would have run quite so fast to her help if they had not liked her so much."

"It's the stupidest story I've ever heard," said the bigger of the small girls, with immense conviction.

"I didn't listen after the first bit, it was so stupid," said Cyril.

The smaller girl made no actual comment on the story, but she had long ago recommenced a murmured repetition of her favourite line.

"You don't seem to be a success as a story-teller," said the bachelor suddenly from his corner.

The aunt bristled in instant defence at this unexpected attack.'

"It's a very difficult thing to tell stories that children can both understand and appreciate," she said stiffly.

"I don't agree with you," said the bachelor.

174

"Perhaps *you* would like to tell them a story," was the aunt's retort.

"Tell us a story," demanded the bigger of the small girls.

"Once upon a time," began the bachelor, "there was a little girl called Bertha, who was extraordinarily good."

The children's momentarily-aroused interest began at once to flicker; all stories seemed dreadfully alike, no matter who told them.

"She did all that she was told, she was always truthful, she kept her clothes clean, ate milk puddings as though they were jam tarts, learned her lessons perfectly, and was polite in her manners."

"Was she pretty?" asked the bigger of the small girls.

"Not as pretty as any of you," said the bachelor, "but she was horribly good."

There was a wave of reaction in favour of the story; the word horrible in connection with goodness was a novelty that commended itself. It seemed to introduce a ring of truth that was absent from the aunt's tales of infant life.

"She was so good," continued the bachelor, "that she won several medals for goodness, which she always wore, pinned on to her dress. There was a medal for obedience, another medal for punctuality, and a third for good behaviour. They were large metal medals and they clicked against one another as she walked. No other child in the town where she lived had as many as three medals, so everybody knew that she must be an extra good child."

"Horribly good," quoted Cyril.

"Everybody talked about her goodness, and the prince of the country got to hear about it, and he said that as she was so very good, she might be allowed once a week to walk in his park, which was just outside the town. It was a beautiful park, and no children were ever allowed in it, so it was a great honour for Bertha to be allowed to go there."

"Were there any sheep in the park?" demanded Cyril.

"No," said the bachelor, "there were no sheep."

"Why weren't there any sheep?" came the inevitable question arising out of that answer.

The aunt permitted herself a smile, which might almost have been described as a grin.

"There were no sheep in the park," said the bachelor, "because the prince's mother had once had a dream that her son would either be killed by a sheep or else by a clock falling on him. For that reason, the prince never kept a sheep in his park or a clock in his palace."

The aunt suppressed a gasp of admiration.

"Was the prince killed by a sheep or by a clock?" asked Cyril.

"He is still alive, so we can't tell whether the dream will come true," said the bachelor unconcernedly; "anyway, there were no sheep in the park, but there were lots of little pigs running all over the place."

"What colour were they?"

"Black with white faces, white with black spots, black all over, grey with white patchy, and some were white all over."

The story-teller paused to let a full idea of the park's treasures sink into the children's imaginations; then he resumed:

"Bertha was rather sorry to find that there were no flowers in the park. She had promised her aunts, with tears in her eyes, that she would not pick any of the kind prince's flowers, and she had meant to keep her promise, so of course it made her feel silly to find that there were no flowers to pick."

"Why weren't there any flowers?"

"Because the pigs had eaten them all," said the bachelor promptly. "The gardeners had told the prince that you couldn't have pigs and flowers, so he decided to have pigs and no flowers."

There was a murmur of approval at the excellence of the prince's decision; so many people would have decided the other way.

"There were lots of other delightful things in the park. There were ponds with gold and blue and green fish in them, and trees with beautiful parrots that said clever things at a moment's notice, and humming birds that hummed all the popular tunes of the day. Bertha walked up and down and enjoyed herself immensely, and thought to herself: 'If I were not so extraordinarily good, I should not have been allowed to come into this beautiful park and enjoy all that there is to be seen in it,' and her three medals clinked against one another as she walked and helped to remind her how very good, she really was. Just then an enormous wolf came prowling into the park to see if it could catch a fat little pig for its supper."

"What colour was it?" asked the children, amid an immediate quickening of interest.

"Mud-colour all over, with a black tongue and pale grey eyes that gleamed with unspeakable ferocity. The first thing that it saw in the park was Bertha; her pinafore was so spotlessly white and clean that it could be seen from a great distance. Bertha saw the wolf and saw that it was stealing towards her, and she began to wish that she had never been allowed to come into the park. She ran as hard as she could, and the wolf came after her with huge leaps and bounds. She managed to reach a shrubbery of myrtle bushes and she hid herself in one of the thickest of the bushes.

"The wolf came sniffing among the branches, its black tongue lolling out of its mouth and its pale grey eyes glaring with rage. Bertha was terribly frightened, and thought to herself: 'If I had not been so extraordinarily good, I should have been safe in the town at this moment.' However, the scent of the myrtle was so strong that the wolf could not sniff out where Bertha was hiding, and the bushes were so thick that he might have hunted about in them for a long time without catching sight of her, so he thought he might as well go off and catch a little pig instead. Bertha was trembling very much at having the wolf prowling and sniffing so near her, and as she trembled the medal for obedience clinked against the medals for good conduct and punctuality.

"The wolf was just moving away when he heard the sound of the medals clinking and stopped to listen; they clinked again in a bush quite near him. He dashed into the bush, his pale grey eyes gleaming with ferocity and triumph and dragged Bertha out and devoured her to the last morsel. All that was left of her were her shoes, bits of clothing, and the three medals for goodness."

"Were any of the little pigs killed?"

"No, they all escaped."

"The story began badly," said the smaller of the small girls, "but it had a beautiful ending."

"It is the most beautiful story that I ever heard," said the bigger of the small girls, with immense decision.

"It is the *only* beautiful story I have ever heard," said Cyril.

A dissentient opinion came from the aunt.

"A most improper story to tell to young children! You have undermined the effect of years of careful teaching."

"At any rate," said the bachelor, collecting his belongings preparatory to leaving the carriage, "I kept them quiet for ten minutes, which was more than you were able to do."

"Unhappy woman!" he observed to himself as he walked down the platform of Templecombe station; "for the next six months or so those children will assail her in public with demands for an improper story!"

The Toys of Peace

"Harvey," said Eleanor Bope, handing her brother a cutting from a London morning paper of the 19th of March, "just read this about children's toys, please; it exactly carries out some of our ideas about influence and upbringing."

The extract ran:

In the view of the National Peace Council, there are grave objections to presenting our boys with regiments of fighting men, batteries of guns, and squadrons of 'Dreadnoughts.' Boys, the Council admits, naturally love fighting and all the panoply of war . . . but that is no reason for encouraging, and perhaps giving permanent form to, their primitive instincts. At the Children's Welfare Exhibition, which opens at Olympia in three weeks' time, the Peace Council will make an alternative suggestion to parents in the shape of an exhibition of 'peace toys.' In front of a specially-painted representation of the Peace Palace at The Hague will be grouped, not miniature soldiers but miniature civilians, not guns but ploughs and the tools of industry . . . It is hoped that manufacturers may take a hint from the exhibit, which will bear fruit in the toy shops. (An actual extract from a London paper of March, 1914.)

"The idea is certainly an interesting and very well-meaning one," said Harvey; "whether it would succeed well in practice—"

"We must try," interrupted his sister; "you are coming down to us at Easter, and you always bring the boys some toys, so that will be an excellent opportunity for you to inaugurate the new experiment. Go about in the shops and buy any little toys and models that have special bearing on civilian life in its more peaceful aspects. Of course, you must explain the toys to the children and interest them in the new idea. I regret to say that the 'Siege of Adrianople' toy, that their Aunt Susan sent them, didn't need any explanation; they knew all the uniforms and flags, and even the names of the respective commanders, and when I heard them one day using what seemed to be the most objectionable language, they said it was Bulgarian words of command; of course, it *may* have been, but at any rate I took the toy away from them. Now I shall expect your Easter gifts to give quite a new impulse and direction to the children's minds; Eric is not eleven yet, and Bertie is only nine-and-a-half, so they are really at a most impressionable age."

"There is primitive instinct to be taken into consideration, you know," said Henry doubtfully, "and hereditary tendencies as well. One of their great-uncles fought in the most intolerant fashion at Inkerman—he was specially mentioned in dispatches, I believe—and their great-grandfather smashed all his Whig neighbours' hot houses when the great Reform Bill was passed. Still, as you say, they are at an impressionable age. I will do my best."

On Easter Saturday Harvey Bope unpacked a large, promising-looking red cardboard box under the expectant eyes of his nephews. "Your uncle has brought you the newest thing in toys," Eleanor had said impressively, and youthful anticipation had been anxiously divided between Albanian soldiery and a Somali camel-corps. Eric was hotly in favour of the latter contingency. "There would be Arabs on horseback," he whispered; "the Albanians have got jolly uniforms, and they fight all day long, and all night, too, when there's a moon, but the country's rocky, so they've got no cavalry."

A quantity of crinkly paper shavings was the first thing that met the view when the lid was removed; the most exiting toys always began like that. Harvey pushed back the top layer and drew forth a square, rather featureless building.

"It's a fort!" exclaimed Bertie.

"It isn't, it's the palace of the Mpret of Albania," said Eric, immensely proud of his knowledge of the exotic title; "it's got no windows, you see, so that passersby can't fire in at the Royal Family."

"It's a municipal dustbin," said Harvey hurriedly; "you see all the refuse and litter of a town is collected there, instead of lying about and injuring the health of the citizens."

In an awful silence he disinterred a little lead figure of a man in black clothes.

"That," he said, "is a distinguished civilian, John Stuart Mill. He

180

was an authority on political economy."

"Why?" asked Bertie.

"Well, he wanted to be; he thought it was a useful thing to be."

Bertie gave an expressive grunt, which conveyed his opinion that there was no accounting for tastes.

Another square building came out, this time with windows and chimneys.

"A model of the Manchester branch of the Young Women's Christian Association," said Harvey.

"Are there any lions?" asked Eric hopefully. He had been reading Roman history and thought that where you found Christians you might reasonably expect to find a few lions.

"There are no lions," said Harvey. "Here is another civilian, Robert Raikes, the founder of Sunday schools, and here is a model of a municipal wash-house. These little round things are loaves backed in a sanitary bakehouse. That lead figure is a sanitary inspector, this one is a district councillor, and this one is an official of the Local Government Board."

"What does he do?" asked Eric wearily.

"He sees to things connected with his Department," said Harvey. "This box with a slit in it is a ballot-box. Votes are put into it at election times."

"What is put into it at other times?" asked Bertie.

"Nothing. And here are some tools of industry, a wheelbarrow and a hoe, and I think these are meant for hop-poles. This is a model beehive, and that is a ventilator, for ventilating sewers. This seems to be another municipal dustbin—no, it is a model of a school of art and public library. This little lead figure is Mrs. Hemans, a poetess, and this is Rowland Hill, who introduced the system of penny postage. This is Sir John Herschel, the eminent astrologer."

"Are we to play with these civilian figures?" asked Eric.

"Of course," said Harvey, "these are toys; they are meant to be played with."

"But how?"

It was rather a poser. "You might make two of them contest a seat in Parliament," said Harvey, "and have an election—"

"With rotten eggs, and free fights, and ever so many broken heads!" exclaimed Eric.

"And noses all bleeding and everybody drunk as can be," echoed Bertie, who had carefully studied one of Hogarth's pictures.

181

"Nothing of the kind," said Harvey, "nothing in the least like that. Votes will be put in the ballot-box, and the Mayor will count them —and he will say which has received the most votes, and then the two candidates will thank him for presiding, and each will say that the contest has been conducted throughout in the pleasantest and most straightforward fashion, and they part with expressions of mutual esteem. There's a jolly game for you boys to play. I never had such toys when I was young."

"I don't think we'll play with them just now," said Eric, with an entire absence of the enthusiasm that his uncle had shown; "I think perhaps we ought to do a little of our holiday task. It's history this time; we've got to learn up something about the Bourbon period in France."

"The Bourbon period," said Harvey, with some disapproval in his voice.

"We've got to know something about Louis the Fourteenth," continued Eric; "I've learnt the names of all the principal battles already."

This would never do. "There were, of course, some battles fought during his reign," said Harvey, "but I fancy the accounts of them were much exaggerated; news was very unreliable in those days, and there were practically no war correspondents, so generals and commanders could magnify every little skirmish they engaged in till they reached the proportions of decisive battles. Louis was really famous, now, as a landscape gardener; the way he laid out Versailles was so much admired that it was copied all over Europe."

"Do you know anything about Madame Du Barry?" asked Eric; "didn't she have her head chopped off?"

"She was another great lover of gardening," said Harvey, evasively; "in fact, I believe the well-known rose Du Barry was named after her, and now I think you had better play for a little and leave your lessons till later."

Harvey retreated to the library and spent some thirty or forty minutes in wondering whether it would be possible to compile a history, for use in elementary schools, in which there should be no prominent mention of battles, massacres, murderous intrigues, and violent deaths. The York and Lancaster period and the Napoleonic era would, he admitted to himself, present considerable difficulties, and the Thirty Years' War would entail something of a gap if you left it out altogether. Still, it would be something gained if, at a highly impressionable age, children could be got to fix their attention on the invention of calico printing instead of the Spanish Armada or the Battle of Waterloo.

It was time, he thought, to go back to the boys' room, and see how they were getting on with their peace toys. As he stood outside the door, he could hear Eric's voice raised in command; Bertie chimed in now and again with a helpful suggestion.

"That is Louis the Fourteenth," Eric was saying, "that one in knee-breeches, that Uncle said invented Sunday schools. It isn't a bit like him, but it'll have to do."

"We'll give him a purple coat from my paintbox by and by," said Bertie.

"Yes, an' red heels. That is Madame de Maintenon, that one he called Mrs. Hemans. She begs Louis not to go on this expedition, but he turns a deaf ear. He takes Marshal Saxe with him, and we must pretend that they have thousands of men with them. The watchword is *Qui vive?* and the answer is *L'état c'est moi*—that was one of his favourite remarks, you know. They land at Manchester in the dead of the night, and a Jacobite conspirator gives them the keys of the fortress."

Peeping in through the doorway Harvey observed that the municipal dustbin had been pierced with holes to accommodate the muzzles of imaginary cannon, and now represented the principal fortified position in Manchester; John Stuart Mill had been dipped in red ink, and apparently stood for Marshal Saxe.

"Louis orders his troops to surround the Young Women's Christian Association and seize the lot of them. 'Once back at the Louvre and the girls are mine,' he exclaims. We must use Mrs. Hemans again for one of the girls; she says 'Never,' and stabs Marshal Saxe to the heart."

"He bleeds dreadfully," exclaimed Bertie, splashing red ink liberally over the facade of the Association building.

"The soldiers rush in and avenge his death with the utmost savagery. A hundred girls are killed"—here Bertie emptied the remainder of the red ink over the devoted building—"and the surviving five hundred are dragged off to the French ships. 'I have lost a Marshal,' says Louis, 'but I do not go back empty-handed.'"

Harvey stole away from the room, and sought out his sister.

"Eleanor," he said, "the experiment—"

"Yes?"

"Has failed. We have begun too late."

The Unrest-Cure

On the rack in the railway carriage immediately opposite Clovis was a solidly wrought travelling bag, with a carefully written label, on which was inscribed, "J. P. Huddle, The Warren, Tilfield, near Slowborough." Immediately below the rack sat the human embodiment of the label, a solid, sedate individual, sedately dressed, sedately conversational. Even without his conversation (which was addressed to a friend seated by his side, and touched chiefly on such topics as the backwardness of Roman hyacinths and the prevalence of measles at the rectory), one could have gauged fairly accurately the temperament and mental outlook of the travelling bag's owner. But he seemed unwilling to leave anything to the imagination of a casual observer, and his talk grew presently personal and introspective.

"I don't know how it is," he told his friend, "I'm not much over forty, but I seem to have settled down into a deep groove of elderly middle-age. My sister shows the same tendency. We like everything to be exactly in its accustomed place; we like things to happen exactly at their appointed times; we like everything to be usual, orderly, punctual, methodical, to a hair's breadth, to a minute. It distresses and upsets us if it is not so. For instance, to take a very trifling matter, a thrush has built its nest year after year in the catkin-tree on the lawn; this year, for no obvious reason, it is building in the ivy on the garden wall. We have said very little about it, but I think we both feel that the change is unnecessary, and just a little irritating."

"Perhaps," said the friend, "it is a different thrush."

"We have suspected that," said J. P. Huddle, "and I think it gives us even more cause for annoyance. We don't feel that we want a change of thrush at our time of life; and yet, as I have said, we have scarcely reached an age when these things should make themselves seriously felt."

"What you want," said the friend, "is an Unrest-cure."

"An Unrest-cure? I've never heard of such a thing."

"You've heard of Rest-cures for people who've broken down under stress of too much worry and strenuous living; well, you're suffering from overmuch repose and placidity, and you need the opposite kind of treatment."

"But where would one go for such a thing?"

"Well, you might stand as an Orange candidate for Kilkenny, or do a course of district visiting in one of the Apache quarters of Paris, or give lectures in Berlin to prove that most of Wagner's music was written by Gambetta; and there's always the interior of Morocco to travel in. But, to be really effective, the Unrest-cure ought to be tried in the home. How you would do it I haven't the faintest idea."

It was at this point in the conversation that Clovis became galvanised into alert attention. After all, his two days' visit to an elderly relative at Slowborough did not promise much excitement. Before the train had stopped, he had decorated his sinister shirt-cuff with the inscription, "J. P. Huddle, The Warren, Tilfield, near Slowborough."

★★★★★★★★★★

Two mornings later Mr. Huddle broke in on his sister's privacy as she sat reading *Country Life* in the morning room. It was her day and hour and place for reading *Country Life*, and the intrusion was absolutely irregular; but he bore in his hand a telegram, and in that household telegrams were recognised as happening by the hand of God. This particular telegram partook of the nature of a thunderbolt.

"Bishop examining confirmation class in neighbourhood unable stay rectory on account measles invokes your hospitality sending secretary arrange."

"I scarcely know the bishop; I've only spoken to him once," exclaimed J. P. Huddle, with the exculpating air of one who realises too late the indiscretion of speaking to strange bishops. Miss Huddle was the first to rally; she disliked thunderbolts as fervently as her brother did, but the womanly instinct in her told her that thunderbolts must be fed.

"We can curry the cold duck," she said. It was not the appointed day, for curry, but the little orange envelope involved a certain departure from rule and custom. Her brother said nothing, but his eyes thanked her for being brave.

"A young gentleman to see you," announced the parlourmaid.

"The secretary!" murmured the Huddles in unison; they instantly

186

stiffened into a demeanour which proclaimed that, though they held all strangers to be guilty, they were willing to hear anything they might have to say in their defence. The young gentleman, who came into the room with a certain elegant haughtiness, was not at all Huddle's idea of a bishop's secretary; he had not supposed that the episcopal establishment could have afforded such an expensively upholstered article when there were so many other claims on its resources. The face was fleetingly familiar; if he had bestowed more attention on the fellow-traveller sitting opposite him in the railway carriage two days before he might have recognised Clovis in his present visitor.

"You are the bishop's secretary?" asked Huddle, becoming consciously deferential.

"His confidential secretary," answered Clovis, "You may call me Stanislaus; my other name doesn't matter. The bishop and Colonel Alberti may be here to lunch. I shall be here in any case."

It sounded rather like the programme of a Royal visit.

"The bishop is examining a confirmation class in the neighbourhood, isn't he?" asked Miss Huddle.

"Ostensibly," was the dark reply, followed by a request for a large-scale map of the locality.

Clovis was still immersed in a seemingly profound study of the map when another telegram arrived It was addressed to "Prince Stanislaus, care of Huddle, The Warren, etc." Clovis glanced at the contents and announced: "The bishop and Alberti won't be here till late in the afternoon." Then he returned to his scrutiny of the map.

The luncheon was not a very festive function. The princely secretary ate and drank with fair appetite, but severely discouraged conversation. At the finish of the meal, he broke suddenly into a radiant smile, thanked his hostess for a charming repast, and kissed her hand with deferential rapture. Miss Huddle was unable to decide in her mind whether the action savoured of *Louis Quatorzian* courtliness or the reprehensible Roman attitude towards the Sabine women. It was not her day for having a headache, but she felt that the circumstances excused her, and retired to her room to have as much headache as was possible before the bishop's arrival. Clovis having asked the way to the nearest telegraph office, disappeared presently down the carriage drive. Mr. Huddle met him in the hall some two hours later, and asked when the bishop would arrive.

"He is in the library with Alberti," was the reply.

"But why wasn't I told? I never knew he had come!" exclaimed

Huddle.

"No one knows he is here," said Clovis; "the quieter we can keep matters the better. And on no account disturb him in the library. Those are his orders."

"But what is all this mystery about? And who is Alberti? And isn't the bishop going to have tea?"

"The bishop is out for blood, not tea."

"Blood!" gasped Huddle, who did not find that the thunderbolt improved on acquaintance.

"Tonight, is going to be a great night in the history of Christendom," said Clovis. "We are going to massacre every Jew in the neighbourhood."

"To massacre the Jews!" said Huddle indignantly. "Do you mean to tell me there's a general rising against them?"

"No, it's the bishop's own idea. He's in there arranging all the details now."

"But—the bishop is such a tolerant, humane man."

"That is precisely what will heighten the effect of his action. The sensation will be enormous."

That at least Huddle could believe.

"He will be hanged!" he exclaimed with conviction.

"A motor is waiting to carry him to the coast, where a steam yacht is in readiness."

"But there aren't thirty Jews in the whole neighbourhood," protested Huddle, whose brain, under the repeated shocks of the day, was operating with the uncertainty of a telegraph wire during earthquake disturbances.

"We have twenty-six on our list," said Clovis, referring to a bundle of notes. "We shall be able to deal with them all the more thoroughly."

"Do you mean to tell me that you are meditating violence against a man like Sir Leon Birberry," stammered Huddle; "he's one of the most respected men in the country."

"He's down on our list," said Clovis carelessly; "after all, we've got men we can trust to do our job, so we shan't have to rely on local assistance. And we've got some boy-scouts helping us as auxiliaries."

"Boy-scouts!"

"Yes; when they understood there was real killing to be done, they were even keener than the men."

"This thing will be a blot on the Twentieth Century!"

"And your house will be the blotting-pad. Have you realised that half the papers of Europe and the United States will publish pictures of it? By the way, I've sent some photographs of you and your sister, that I found in the library, to the *Matin* and *Die Woche*; I hope you don't mind. Also, a sketch of the staircase; most of the killing will probably be done on the staircase."

The emotions that were surging in J. P. Huddle's brain were almost too intense to be disclosed in speech, but he managed to gasp out: "There aren't any Jews in this house."

"Not at present," said Clovis.

"I shall go to the police," shouted Huddle with sudden energy.

"In the shrubbery," said Clovis, "are posted ten men, who have orders to fire on anyone who leaves the house without my signal of permission. Another armed picquet ambush near the front gate. The boy-scouts watch the back premises."

At this moment the cheerful hoot of a motor-horn was heard from the drive. Huddle rushed to the hall door with the feeling of a man half-awakened from a nightmare, and beheld Sir Leon Birberry, who had driven himself over in his car. "I got your telegram," he said; "what's up?"

Telegram? It seemed to be a day of telegrams.

"Come here at once. Urgent. James Huddle," was the purport of the message displayed before Huddle's bewildered eyes.

"I see it all!" he exclaimed suddenly in a voice shaken with agitation, and with a look of agony in the direction of the shrubbery he hauled the astonished Birberry into the house. Tea had just been laid in the hall, but the now thoroughly panic-stricken Huddle dragged his protesting guest upstairs, and in a few minutes' time the entire household had been summoned to that region of momentary safety. Clovis alone graced the tea-table with his presence; the fanatics in the library were evidently too immersed in their monstrous machinations to dally with the solace of teacup and hot toast.

Once the youth rose, in answer to the summons of the front-door bell, and admitted Mr. Paul Isaacs, shoemaker and parish councillor, who had also received a pressing invitation to The Warren. With an atrocious assumption of courtesy, which a Borgia could hardly have outdone, the secretary escorted this new captive of his net to the head of the stairway, where his involuntary host awaited him.

And then ensued a long ghastly vigil of watching and waiting. Once or twice Clovis left the house to stroll across to the shrubbery, returning always to the library, for the purpose evidently of making a brief report. Once he took in the letters from the evening postman, and brought them to the top of the stairs with punctilious politeness. After his next absence he came half-way up the stairs to make an announcement.

"The boy-scouts mistook my signal, and have killed the postman. I've had very little practice in this sort of thing, you see. Another time I shall do better."

The housemaid, who was engaged to be married to the evening postman, gave way to clamorous grief.

"Remember that your mistress has a headache," said J. P. Huddle. (Miss Huddle's headache was worse.)

Clovis hastened downstairs, and after a short visit to the library returned with another message:

"The bishop is sorry to hear that Miss Huddle has a headache. He is issuing orders that as far as possible no firearms shall be used near the house; any killing that is necessary on the premises will be done with cold steel. The bishop does not see why a man should not be a gentleman as well as a Christian."

That was the last they saw of Clovis; it was nearly seven o'clock, and his elderly relative liked him to dress for dinner. But though he had left them for ever, the lurking suggestion of his presence haunted the lower regions of the house during the long hours of the wakeful night, and every creak of the stairway, every rustle of wind through the shrubbery, was fraught with horrible meaning. At about seven next morning the gardener's boy and the early postman finally convinced the watchers that the Twentieth Century was still unblotted.

"I don't suppose," mused Clovis, as an early train bore him townwards, "that they will be in the least grateful for the Unrest-cure."

The Wolves of Cernogratz

"Are they any old legends attached to the castle?" asked Conrad of his sister. Conrad was a prosperous Hamburg merchant, but he was the one poetically-dispositioned member of an eminently practical family.

The Baroness Gruebel shrugged her plump shoulders.

"There are always legends hanging about these old places. They are not difficult to invent and they cost nothing. In this case there is a story that when anyone dies in the castle all the dogs in the village and the wild beasts in forest howl the night long. It would not be pleasant to listen to, would it?"

"It would be weird and romantic," said the Hamburg merchant.

"Anyhow, it isn't true," said the baroness complacently; "since we bought the place, we have had proof that nothing of the sort happens. When the old mother-in-law died last springtime, we all listened, but there was no howling. It is just a story that lends dignity to the place without costing anything."

"The story is not as you have told it," said Amalie, the grey old governess. Everyone turned and looked at her in astonishment. She was wont to sit silent and prim and faded in her place at table, never speaking unless someone spoke to her, and there were few who troubled themselves to make conversation with her. Today a sudden volubility had descended on her; she continued to talk, rapidly and nervously, looking straight in front of her and seeming to address no one in particular.

"It is not when *anyone* dies in the castle that the howling is heard. It was when one of the Cernogratz family died here that the wolves came from far and near and howled at the edge of the forest just before the death hour. There were only a few couple of wolves that had their lairs in this part of the forest, but at such a time the keepers say there would be scores of them, gliding about in the shadows and

191

howling in chorus, and the dogs of the castle and the village and all the farms round would bay and howl in fear and anger at the wolf chorus, and as the soul of the dying one left its body a tree would crash down in the park. That is what happened when a Cernogratz died in his family castle. But for a stranger dying here, of course no wolf would howl and no tree would fall. Oh, no."

There was a note of defiance, almost of contempt, in her voice as she said the last words. The well-fed, much-too-well-dressed baroness stared angrily at the dowdy old woman who had come forth from her usual and seemly position of effacement to speak so disrespectfully.

"You seem to know quite a lot about the von Cernogratz legends, Fraulein Schmidt," she said sharply; "I did not know that family histories were among the subjects you are supposed to be proficient in."

The answer to her taunt was even more unexpected and astonishing than the conversational outbreak which had provoked it.

"I am a von Cernogratz myself," said the old woman, "that is why I know the family history."

"You a von Cernogratz? You!" came in an incredulous chorus.

"When we became very poor," she explained, "and I had to go out and give teaching lessons, I took another name; I thought it would be more in keeping. But my grandfather spent much of his time as a boy in this castle, and my father used to tell me many stories about it, and, of course, I knew all the family legends and stories. When one has nothing left to one but memories, one guards and dusts them with especial care. I little thought when I took service with you that I should one day come with you to the old home of my family. I could wish it had been anywhere else."

There was silence when she finished speaking, and then the baroness turned the conversation to a less embarrassing topic than family histories. But afterwards, when the old governess had slipped away quietly to her duties, there arose a clamour of derision and disbelief.

"It was an impertinence," snapped out the baron, his protruding eyes taking on a scandalised expression; "fancy the woman talking like that at our table. She almost told us we were nobodies, and I don't believe a word of it. She is just Schmidt and nothing more. She has been talking to some of the peasants about the old Cernogratz family, and raked up their history and their stories."

"She wants to make herself out of some consequence," said the baroness; "she knows she will soon be past work and she wants to appeal to our sympathies. Her grandfather, indeed!"

The baroness had the usual number of grandfathers, but she never, never boasted about them.

"I dare say her grandfather was a pantry boy or something of the sort in the castle," sniggered the baron; "that part of the story may be true."

The merchant from Hamburg said nothing; he had seen tears in the old woman's eyes when she spoke of guarding her memories—or, being of an imaginative disposition, he thought he had.

"I shall give her notice to go as soon as the New Year festivities are over," said the baroness; "till then I shall be too busy to manage without her."

But she had to manage without her all the same, for in the cold biting weather after Christmas, the old governess fell ill and kept to her room.

"It is most provoking," said the baroness, as her guests sat round the fire on one of the last evenings of the dying year; "all the time that she has been with us I cannot remember that she was ever seriously ill, too ill to go about and do her work, I mean. And now, when I have the house full, and she could be useful in so many ways, she goes and breaks down. One is sorry for her, of course, she looks so withered and shrunken, but it is intensely annoying all the same."

"Most annoying," agreed the banker's wife, sympathetically; "it is the intense cold, I expect, it breaks the old people up. It has been unusually cold this year."

"The frost is the sharpest that has been known in December for many years," said the baron.

"And, of course, she is quite old," said the baroness; "I wish I had given her notice some weeks ago, then she would have left before this happened to her. Why, Wappi, what is the matter with you?"

The small, woolly lapdog had leapt suddenly down from its cushion and crept shivering under the sofa. At the same moment an outburst of angry barking came from the dogs in the castle-yard, and other dogs could be heard yapping and barking in the distance.

"What is disturbing the animals?" asked the baron.

And then the humans, listening intently, heard the sound that had roused the dogs to their demonstrations of fear and rage; heard a long-drawn whining howl, rising and falling, seeming at one moment leagues away, at others sweeping across the snow until it appeared to come from the foot of the castle walls. All the starved, cold misery of a frozen world, all the relentless hunger-fury of the wild, blended

193

with other forlorn and haunting melodies to which one could give no name, seemed concentrated in that wailing cry.

"Wolves!" cried the baron.

Their music broke forth in one raging burst, seeming to come from everywhere.

"Hundreds of wolves," said the Hamburg merchant, who was a man of strong imagination.

Moved by some impulse which she could not have explained, the baroness left her guests and made her way to the narrow, cheerless room where the old governess lay watching the hours of the dying year slip by. In spite of the biting cold of the winter night, the window stood open. With a scandalised exclamation on her lips, the baroness rushed forward to close it.

"Leave it open," said the old woman in a voice that for all its weakness carried an air of command such as the baroness had never heard before from her lips.

"But you will die of cold!" she expostulated.

"I am dying in any case," said the voice, "and I want to hear their music. They have come from far and wide to sing the death-music of my family. It is beautiful that they have come; I am the last von Cernogratz that will die in our old castle, and they have come to sing to me. Hark, how loud they are calling!"

The cry of the wolves rose on the still winter air and floated round the castle walls in long-drawn piercing wails; the old woman lay back on her couch with a look of long-delayed happiness on her face.

"Go away," she said to the baroness; "I am not lonely any more. I am one of a great old family . . . "

"I think she is dying," said the baroness when she had rejoined her guests; "I suppose we must send for a doctor. And that terrible howling! Not for much money would I have such death-music."

"That music is not to be bought for any amount of money," said Conrad.

"Hark! What is that other sound?" asked the baron, as a noise of splitting and crashing was heard.

It was a tree falling in the park.

There was a moment of constrained silence, and then the banker's wife spoke.

"It is the intense cold that is splitting the trees. It is also the cold that has brought the wolves out in such numbers. It is many years since we have had such a cold winter."

The baroness eagerly agreed that the cold was responsible for these things. It was the cold of the open window, too, which caused the heart failure that made the doctor's ministrations unnecessary for the old Fraulein. But the notice in the newspapers looked very well:—

On December 29th, at Schloss Cernogratz, Amalie von Cernogratz, for many years the valued friend of Baron and Baroness Gruebel.

Tobermory

It was a chill, rain-washed afternoon of a late August day, that indefinite season when partridges are still in security or cold storage, and there is nothing to hunt—unless one is bounded on the north by the Bristol Channel, in which case one may lawfully gallop after fat red stags. Lady Blemley's house-party was not bounded on the north by the Bristol Channel, hence there was a full (gathering of her guests round the tea-table on this particular afternoon. And, in spite of the blankness of the season and the triteness of the occasion, there was no trace in the company of that fatigued restlessness which means a dread of the pianola and a subdued hankering for auction bridge.

The undisguised open-mouthed attention of the entire party was fixed on the homely negative personality of Mr. Cornelius Appin. Of all her guests, he was the one who had come to Lady Blemley with the vaguest reputation. Someone had said he was "clever," and he had got his invitation in the moderate expectation, on the part of his hostess, that some portion at least of his cleverness would be contributed to the general entertainment.

Until teatime that day she had been unable to discover in what direction, if any, his cleverness lay. He was neither a wit nor a croquet, champion, a hypnotic force nor a begetter of amateur theatricals. Neither did his exterior suggest the sort of man in whom women are willing to pardon a generous measure of mental deficiency. He had subsided into mere Mr. Appin, and the Cornelius seemed a piece of transparent baptismal bluff. And now he was claiming to have launched on the world a discovery beside which the invention of gunpowder, of the printing-press, and of steam locomotion were inconsiderable trifles. Science had made bewildering strides in many directions during recent decades, but this thing seemed to belong to the domain of miracle rather than to scientific achievement.

"And do you really ask us to believe," Sir Wilfrid was saying, "that you have discovered a means for instructing animals in the art of human speech, and that dear old Tobermory has proved your first successful pupil?"

"It is a problem at which I have worked for the last seventeen years," said Mr. Appin, "but only during the last eight or nine months have I been rewarded with glimmerings of success. Of course, I have experimented with thousands of animals, but latterly only with cats, those wonderful creatures which have assimilated themselves so marvellously with our civilization while retaining all their highly developed feral instincts. Here and there among cats, one comes across an outstanding superior intellect, just as one does among the ruck of human beings, and when I made the acquaintance of Tobermory a week ago I saw at once that I was in contact with a 'Beyond-cat' of extraordinary intelligence. I had gone far along the road to success in recent experiments; with Tobermory, as you call him, I have reached the goal."

Mr. Appin concluded his remarkable statement in a voice which he strove to divest of a triumphant inflection. No one said "Rats," though Clovis's lips moved in a monosyllabic contortion, which probably invoked those rodents of disbelief.

"And do you mean to say," asked Miss Resker, after a slight pause, "that you have taught Tobermory to say and understand easy sentences of one syllable?"

"My dear Miss Resker," said the wonder-worker patiently, "one teaches little children and savages and backward adults in that piecemeal fashion; when one has once solved the problem of making a beginning with an animal of highly developed intelligence one has no need for those halting methods. Tobermory can speak our language with perfect correctness."

This time Clovis very distinctly said, "Beyond-rats!" Sir Wilfrid was more polite, but equally sceptical.

"Hadn't we better have the cat in and judge for ourselves?" suggested Lady Blemley.

Sir Wilfrid went in search of the animal, and the company settled themselves down to the languid expectation of witnessing some more or less adroit drawing-room ventriloquism.

In a minute Sir Wilfrid was back in the room, his face white beneath its tan and his eyes dilated with excitement.

"By Gad, it's true!"

His agitation was unmistakably genuine, and his hearers started forward in a thrill of awakened interest.

Collapsing into an armchair he continued breathlessly: "I found him dozing in the smoking-room, and called out to him to come for his tea. He blinked at me in his usual way, and I said, 'Come on, Toby; don't keep us waiting'; and, by Gad! he drawled out in a most horribly natural voice that he'd come when he dashed well pleased! I nearly jumped out of my skin!"

Appin had preached to absolutely incredulous hearers; Sir Wilfrid's statement carried instant conviction. A Babel like chorus of startled exclamation arose, amid which the scientist sat mutely enjoying the first fruit of his stupendous discovery.

In the midst of the clamour Tobermory entered the room and made his way with velvet tread and studied unconcern across to the group seated round the tea-table.

A sudden hush of awkwardness and constraint fell on the company. Somehow there seemed an element of embarrassment in addressing on equal terms a domestic cat of acknowledged dental ability.

"Will you have some milk, Tobermory?" asked Lady Blemley in a rather strained voice.

"I don't mind if I do," was the response, couched in a tone of even indifference. A shiver of suppressed excitement went through the listeners, and Lady Blemley might be excused for pouring out the saucerful of milk rather unsteadily.

"I'm afraid I've spilt a good deal of it," she said apologetically.

"After all, it's not my Axminster," was Tobermory's rejoinder.

Another silence fell on the group, and then Miss Resker, in her best district-visitor manner, asked if the human language had been difficult to learn. Tobermory looked squarely at her for a moment and then fixed his gaze serenely on the middle distance. It was obvious that boring questions lay outside his scheme of life.

"What do you think of human intelligence?" asked Mavis Pellington lamely.

"Of whose intelligence in particular?" asked Tobermory coldly.

"Oh, well, mine for instance," said Mavis, with a feeble laugh.

"You put me in an embarrassing position," said Tobermory, whose tone and attitude certainly did not suggest a shred of embarrassment. When your inclusion in this house-party was suggested Sir Wilfrid protested that you were the most brainless woman of his acquaintance, and that there was a wide distinction between hospitality and the care of the feeble-minded. Lady Blemley replied that your lack of brain-power was the precise quality which had earned you your invitation, as you were the only person, she could think of who might be idiotic enough to "buy their old car. You know, the one they call 'The Envy of Sisyphur,' because it goes quite nicely up-hill if you push it."

Lady Blemley's protestations would have had greater effect if she had not casually suggested to Mavis only that morning that the car in question would be just the thing for her down at her Devonshire home.

Major Barfield plunged in heavily to effect a diversion.

"How about your carryings-on with the tortoise-shell puss up at the stables, eh?"

The moment he had said it everyone realised the blunder.

"One does not usually discuss these matters in public," said Tobermory frigidly. "From a slight observation of your ways since you've been in this house, I should imagine you'd find it inconvenient if I were to shift the conversation on to your own little affairs."

The panic which ensued was not confined to the major.

"Would you like to go and see if cook has got your dinner ready?" suggested Lady Blemley hurriedly, affecting to ignore the fact that it wanted at least two hours to Tobermory's dinnertime.

"Thanks," said Tobermory, "not quite so soon after my tea. I don't want to die of indigestion."

"Cats have nine lives, you know," said Sir Wilfrid heartily.

"Possibly," answered Tobermory; "but only one liver."

"Adelaide!" said Mrs. Cornett, "do you mean to encourage that cat to go out and gossip about us in the servants' hall?"

The panic had indeed become general. A narrow ornamental balustrade ran in front of most of the bedroom windows at the Towers, and it was recalled with dismay that this had formed a favourite promenade for Tobermory at all hours, whence he could watch the pigeons—and heaven knew what else besides. If he intended to become reminiscent in his present outspoken strain the effect would be something more than disconcerting. Mrs. Cornett, who spent much time at her toilet table, and whose complexion was reputed to be of a nomadic though punctual disposition, looked as ill at ease as the major.

Miss Scrawen, who wrote fiercely sensuous poetry and led a blameless life, merely displayed irritation; if you are methodical and virtuous in private you don't necessarily want everyone to know it. Bertie van

Tahn, who was so depraved at seventeen that he had long ago given up trying to be any worse, turned a dull shade of gardenia white, but he did not commit the error of dashing out of the room like Odo Finsberry, a young gentleman who was understood to be reading for the Church and who was possibly disturbed at the thought of scandals he might hear concerning other people. Clovis had the presence of mind to maintain a composed exterior; privately he was calculating how long it would take to procured box of fancy mice through the agency of the *Exchange and Mart* as a species of hush-money.

Even in a delicate situation like the present, Agnes Resker could not endure to remain too long in the background.

"Why did I ever come down here?" she asked dramatically.

Tobermory immediately accepted the opening.

"Judging by what you said to Mrs. Cornett on the croquet-lawn yesterday, you were out for food. You described the Blemleys as the dullest people to stay with that you knew, but said they were clever enough to employ a first-rate cook; otherwise, they'd find it difficult to get anyone to come down a second time."

"There's not a word of truth in it! I appeal to Mrs. Cornett—" exclaimed the discomfited Agnes.

"Mrs. Cornett repeated your remark afterwards to Bertie van Tahn," continued Tobermory, "and said, 'That woman is a regular Hunger Marcher; she'd go anywhere for four square meals a day,' and Bertie van Tahn said—"

At this point the chronicle mercifully ceased. Tobermory had caught a glimpse of the big yellow Tom from the rectory working his way through the shrubbery towards the stable wing. In a flash he had vanished through the open French window.

With the disappearance of his too brilliant pupil Cornelius Appin found himself beset by a hurricane of bitter upbraiding, anxious inquiry, and frightened entreaty. The responsibility for the situation lay with him, and he must prevent matters from becoming worse. Could Tobermory impart his dangerous gift to other cats? was the first question he had to answer. It was possible, he replied, that he might have initiated his intimate friend the stable puss into his new accomplishment, but it was unlikely that his teaching could have taken a wider range as yet.

"Then," said Mrs. Cornett, "Tobermory may be a valuable cat and a great pet; but I'm sure you'll agree, Adelaide, that both he and the stable cat must be done away with without delay."

"You don't suppose I've enjoyed the last quarter of an hour, do you?" said Lady Blemley bitterly. "My husband and I are very fond of Tobermory—at least, we were before this horrible accomplishment was infused into him; but now, of course, the only thing is to have him destroyed as soon as possible."

"We can put some strychnine in the scraps he always gets at dinner-time," said Sir Wilfrid, "and I will go and drown the stable cat myself. The coachman will be very sore at losing his pet, but I'll say a very catching form of mange has broken out in both cats and we're afraid of it spreading to the kennels."

"But my great discovery!" expostulated Mr. Appin; "after all my years of research and experiment—"

"You can go and experiment on the short-horns at the farm, who are under proper control," said Mrs. Cornett, "or the elephants at the Zoological Gardens. They're said to be highly intelligent, and they have this recommendation, that they don't come creeping about our bedrooms and under chairs, and so forth."

An archangel ecstatically proclaiming the Millennium, and then finding that it clashed unpardonably with Henley and would have to be indefinitely postponed, could hardly have felt more crestfallen than Cornelius Appin at the reception of his wonderful achievement. Public opinion, however, was against him—in fact, had the general voice been consulted on the subject it is probable that a strong minority vote would have been in favour of including him in the strychnine diet.

Defective train arrangements and a nervous desire to see matters brought to a finish prevented an immediate dispersal of the party, but dinner that evening was not a social success. Sir Wilfrid had had rather a trying time with the stable cat and subsequently with the coachman. Agnes Resker ostentatiously limited her repast to a morsel of dry toast, which she bit as though it were a personal enemy; while Mavis Pellington maintained a vindictive silence throughout the meal. Lady Blemley kept up a flow of what she hoped was conversation, but her attention was fixed on the doorway. A plateful of carefully dosed fish scraps was in readiness on the sideboard, but sweets and savoury and dessert went their way, and no Tobermory appeared either in the dining-room or kitchen.

The sepulchral dinner was cheerful compared with the subsequent vigil in the smoking-room. Eating and drinking had at least supplied a distraction and cloak to the prevailing embarrassment. Bridge was out of the question in the general tension of nerves and tempers, and after Odo Finsberry had given a lugubrious rendering of "Mélisande in the Wood" to a frigid audience, music was tacitly avoided. At eleven the servants went to bed, announcing that the small window in the pantry had been left open as usual for Tobermory's private use. The guests read steadily through the current batch of magazines, and fell back gradually on the "Badminton Library" and bound volumes of *Punch*. Lady Blemley made periodic visits to the pantry, returning each time with an expression of listless depression which forestalled questioning.

At two o'clock Clovis broke the dominating silence.

"He won't turn up tonight. He's probably in the local newspaper office at the present moment, dictating the first instalment of his reminiscences. Lady What's-her-name's book won't be in it. It will be the event of the day."

Having made this contribution to the general cheerfulness, Clovis went to bed. At long intervals the various members of the house-party followed his example.

The servants taking round the early tea made a uniform announcement in reply to a uniform question. Tobermory had not returned.

Breakfast was, if anything, a more unpleasant function than dinner had been, but before its conclusion the situation was relieved. Tobermory's corpse was brought in from the shrubbery, where a gardener had just discovered it. From the bites on his throat, and the yellow fur which coated his claws it was evident that he had fallen in unequal combat with the big Tom from the rectory.

By midday most of the guests had quitted the Towers, and after lunch Lady Blemley had sufficiently recovered her spirits to write an extremely nasty letter to the rectory about the loss of her valuable pet.

Tobermory had been Appin's one successful pupil, and he was destined to have no successor. A few weeks later an elephant in the Dresden Zoological Garden, which had shown no previous signs of irritability, broke loose and killed an Englishman who had apparently been teasing it. The victim's name was variously reported in the papers as Oppin and Eppelin, but his front name was faithfully rendered Cornelius.

"If he was trying German irregular verbs on the poor beast," said Clovis, "he deserved all he got."

LEONAUR

ALSO FROM LEONAUR

AVAILABLE IN SOFTCOVER OR HARDCOVER WITH DUST JACKET

MR MUKERJI'S GHOSTS *by S. Mukerji*—Supernatural tales from the British Raj period by India's Ghost story collector.

KIPLINGS GHOSTS *by Rudyard Kipling*—Twelve stories of Ghosts, Hauntings, Curses, Werewolves & Magic.

THE COLLECTED SUPERNATURAL AND WEIRD FICTION OF WASHINGTON IRVING: VOLUME 1 *by Washington Irving*—Including one novel 'A History of New York', and nine short stories of the Strange and Unusual.

THE COLLECTED SUPERNATURAL AND WEIRD FICTION OF WASHINGTON IRVING: VOLUME 2 *by Washington Irving*—Including three novelettes 'The Legend of the Sleepy Hollow', 'Dolph Heyliger', 'The Adventure of the Black Fisherman' and thirty-two short stories of the Strange and Unusual.

THE COLLECTED SUPERNATURAL AND WEIRD FICTION OF JOHN KENDRICK BANGS: VOLUME 1 *by John Kendrick Bangs*—Including one novel 'Toppleton's Client or A Spirit in Exile', and ten short stories of the Strange and Unusual.

THE COLLECTED SUPERNATURAL AND WEIRD FICTION OF JOHN KENDRICK BANGS: VOLUME 2 *by John Kendrick Bangs*—Including four novellas 'A House-Boat on the Styx', 'The Pursuit of the House-Boat', 'The Enchanted Typewriter' and 'Mr. Munchausen' of the Strange and Unusual.

THE COLLECTED SUPERNATURAL AND WEIRD FICTION OF JOHN KENDRICK BANGS: VOLUME 3 *by John Kendrick Bangs*—Including twor novellas 'Olympian Nights', 'Roger Camerden: A Strange Story', and ten short stories of the Strange and Unusual.

THE COLLECTED SUPERNATURAL AND WEIRD FICTION OF MARY SHELLEY: VOLUME 1 *by Mary Shelley*—Including one novel 'Frankenstein or the Modern Prometheus', and fourteen short stories of the Strange and Unusual.

THE COLLECTED SUPERNATURAL AND WEIRD FICTION OF MARY SHELLEY: VOLUME 2 *by Mary Shelley*—Including one novel 'The Last Man', and three short stories of the Strange and Unusual.

THE COLLECTED SUPERNATURAL AND WEIRD FICTION OF AMELIA B. EDWARDS *by Amelia B. Edwards*—Contains two novelettes 'Monsieur Maurice', and 'The Discovery of the Treasure Isles', one ballad 'A Legend of Boisguilbert' and seventeen short stories to cill the blood.

LEONAUR

ALSO FROM LEONAUR

AVAILABLE IN SOFTCOVER OR HARDCOVER WITH DUST JACKET

THE COMPLETE FOUR JUST MEN: VOLUME 2 *by Edgar Wallace—The Law of the Four Just Men & The Three Just Men*—disillusioned with a world where the wicked and the abusers of power perpetually go unpunished, the Just Men set about to rectify matters according to their own standards, and retribution is dispensed on swift and deadly wings.

THE COMPLETE RAFFLES: 1 *by E. W. Hornung—The Amateur Cracksman & The Black Mask*—By turns urbane gentleman about town and accomplished cricketer, life is just too ordinary for Raffles and that sets him on a series of adventures that have long been treasured as a real antidote to the 'white knights' who are the usual heroes of the crime fiction of this period.

THE COMPLETE RAFFLES: 2 *by E. W. Hornung—A Thief in the Night & Mr Justice Raffles*—By turns urbane gentleman about town and accomplished cricketer, life is just too ordinary for Raffles and that sets him on a series of adventures that have long been treasured as a real antidote to the 'white knights' who are the usual heroes of the crime fiction of this period.

THE COLLECTED SUPERNATURAL AND WEIRD FICTION OF WILKIE COLLINS: VOLUME 1 *by Wilkie Collins*—Contains one novel 'The Haunted Hotel', one novella 'Mad Monkton', three novelettes 'Mr Percy and the Prophet', 'The Biter Bit' and 'The Dead Alive' and eight short stories to chill the blood.

THE COLLECTED SUPERNATURAL AND WEIRD FICTION OF WILKIE COLLINS: VOLUME 2 *by Wilkie Collins*—Contains one novel 'The Two Destinies', three novellas 'The Frozen deep', 'Sister Rose' and 'The Yellow Mask' and two short stories to chill the blood.

THE COLLECTED SUPERNATURAL AND WEIRD FICTION OF WILKIE COLLINS: VOLUME 3 *by Wilkie Collins*—Contains one novel 'Dead Secret,' two novelettes 'Mrs Zant and the Ghost' and 'The Nun's Story of Gabriel's Marriage' and five short stories to chill the blood.

FUNNY BONES *selected by Dorothy Scarborough*—An Anthology of Humorous Ghost Stories.

MONTEZUMA'S CASTLE AND OTHER WEIRD TALES *by Charles B. Cory*—Cory has written a superb collection of eighteen ghostly and weird stories to chill and thrill the avid enthusiast of supernatural fiction.

SUPERNATURAL BUCHAN *by John Buchan*—Stories of Ancient Spirits, Uncanny Places & Strange Creatures.

www.ingramcontent.com/pod-product-compliance
Lightning Source LLC
Chambersburg PA
CBHW032146020726
47496CB00003B/737